FIRST PRESSINGS
The History of Rhythm & Blues
Volume 3: 1953

Compiled and edited by
GALEN GART

BIG NICKEL PUBLICATIONS
P.O. Box 157, Milford, New Hampshire 03055 U.S.A.

ISBN 0-936433-03-5. First printing August 1989. Printed in the U.S.A.

INTRODUCTION

Those familiar with the *First Pressings* series will doubtless remember that our publication of the first two volumes in 1986 was intended to begin to bring to light many of the key articles and news stories of the music industry pertaining to the evolution of postwar Rhythm & Blues music beginning with the year 1948. Now, Volume 3 of the series picks up where the first two volumes left off, or more specifically, with the year 1953, during the era of R&B music's most auspicious pre-rock popularity.

Readers will note, too, that there have been a number of substantive as well as stylistic changes since publication of the first two books in the series. Gone is the reliance on a single source of primary information, as was the case previously, in favor of a method designed to provide the reader with significantly wider coverage of R&B developments than was heretofore possible. The inclusion of numerous record company advertisements, also lacking from the previous books, is another entirely new feature which we hope will meet with reader approval. Furthermore, an up-to-date typeset format has allowed us to condense more information on a single page and thus significantly lower the cost of the end product to both individuals and institutions.

Despite the changes, our aim is still to satisfy those music scholars, historians and record collectors who desire a month-by-month chronicle of R&B's history in the 1950s era, as told from the viewpoint of those who witnessed these developments and reported on them as they occurred. We have endeavored to keep the language and perspective true to the times, and hope this book will succeed as much as its predecessors have in doing so.

A few words should be said concerning the subject of record reviews. Copyright considerations have precluded our use of the original reviewer quotes, as was possible previously; however, the "dot" rating system used in this book's "Record Roundup" section is designed to provide a relative scale to a given release's commercial potential, as seen through the eyes of contemporary observers. In addition, the organization of the new R&B releases in a weekly (rather than monthly) format should enable readers with access to the primary material to locate the original reviews more quickly and easily, if so desired. Lastly, Gospel Music enthusiasts will note the inclusion of considerably more news stories and record listings pertaining to this important and long-neglected field in black music.

We hope in the not-too-distant future to be bringing you additional volumes covering Rhythm & Blues' continuing story in the 1950s. As always, reader comments, criticisms and suggestions are welcome.

Nashua, New Hampshire
July 1989

FIRST PRESSINGS
The History of Rhythm & Blues
Volume 3: 1953

MABON HOT WITH 'I DON'T KNOW'

NEW YORK, Jan. 10—Stretching its huge tentacles across the nation like a hundred-legged octopus, "I Don't Know," the Willie Mabon release on the Chess label, has shot into the top slot in almost every rhythm and blues city on the charts.

The tune has caught on like wild-fire and has provided the market with a much-needed shot in the arm. On the strength of the commotion, Buddy Morrow did the tune for RCA Victor in the pop field and Tennessee Ernie waxed it in the c.&w. market. Tune was also acquired by Republic Music, Sammy Kaye firm, a few weeks ago. Mabon wrote the smash hit, which is now leading all regional and national r.&b. charts.

Mabon, the hottest thing in r.&b. showbiz at the moment, had several top booking agencies up in a dither about his personal appearance contracts before Gale Agency's Tim Gale flew out to Chicago last week to get the boy's name on the dotted line.

The artist's upcoming stand at the Apollo Theater in Harlem promises to be one of the most successful for the house in a long time. After his New York stint, Mabon will leave on a tour of the South, beginning on February 7 with a week's engagement at the Riviera Club in St. Louis with chirp Bette McLaurin.

Thrush Answers Mabon Hit

Lovely thrush Linda Hayes has a new disking out to answer Willie Mabon's smash hit "I Don't Know" on the Chess label. Titled "Yes I Know (What You're Putting Down)," tune was recently cut for Recorded in Hollywood waxery and rushed to distribs this week. Chick tells her man the score in this sock answer to the Mabon tune, which is currently cleaning up in both the pop and r.&b. markets.

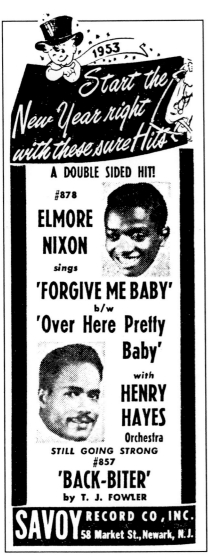
MOON DOG R.&B. UNIT SKEDS ROAD DATES

CANTON, O., Jan. 24—Cleveland spinner Alan (Moon Dog) Freed and his manager, Lew Platt, of Canton, are planning a package of blues and rhythm artists to play auditoriums and ballrooms in the midwest and southern Canada.

Freed is known for his "Moon Dog" programs on radio and TV and in recent months has been staging "Moon Dog" dances in Akron, Youngstown, Lorain and Canton to big crowds. At Cleveland Arena a year ago, a "Moon Dog" dance drew to a police-estimated crowd of 25,000.

Freed and Platt are dickering with an agent in New York to produce and book the show. Dates in Ontario were included in the plans because over a third of all mail at WJW, "Moon Dog's" home station, comes from Canada, it was claimed.

Okeh Skeds Pop Launch for Feb.

NEW YORK, Dec. 27—Okeh Records will begin shipment of pop releases on a regular schedule sometime next month. Recent talent pacted by the label includes Frank Assunto's Dukes of Dixieland crew from New Orleans, a regular feature at the Famous Door for the past season. Also signed to a term pact was singer Frank Murphy from Philadelphia.

According to label execs, since Okeh has switched half of its line to indie distributors, the firm has made sensational strides in the r.&b. field. "My Story" with Chuck Willis and "Gabbin' Blues" with Big Maybelle are both on the juke box charts, and the Willis disk is also a retail bestseller this week. This is the first time the diskery has had two r.&b. sides on the chart since it started to release disks for this market a few years back.

Treniers Can't Ride on 'Silver'

NEW YORK, Jan. 17—The Lone Ranger may utter his stirring cry of "Hi-Yo, Silver" over the radio, but the Treniers, Okeh wax artists, cannot use the copyrighted slogan as the title of a song. This was the information the label received this week from Lone Ranger, Inc. and they have thus withdrawn the Treniers' waxing of the ditty from the market.

The disking will be released with another ditty, "Moon Dog," written by Fletcher Peck, with the original coupling of "Poon Tang."

Mesners Reactivate Score Subsid

HOLLYWOOD, Dec. 27—Leo and Eddie Mesner, heads of Aladdin Records, are reactivating their Score label, which has been dormant the past year, in a new drive for gospel and sacred business. Eddie Mesner leaves January 10 for a Southern sweep to select new artists for the religious waxery. Mesner has inked Papa Lightfoot, New Orleans harmonica and vocal artist, and the Flasher Brothers, harmony group, to Aladdin.

Other r.&b. talent signings this week included Specialty's signing of Robert Anderson, Chicago choral director, to their sacred roster. Anderson was last with Premium and Miracle labels. Lew Chudd of Imperial added Gene Gilmore, Chicago chirper to the r.&b. roster of that company.

Mercury Enjoined on Mel Walker

NEWARK, N.J., Dec. 27—Savoy Records was granted a preliminary injunction enjoining Mercury Records from manufacturing, producing or selling disks cut by Mel Walker, r.&b. artist, by Judge E. Modarelli in Federal District Court here yesterday.

Walker, whose real name is Melvin Lightsey, had filed a petition of bankruptcy, which was granted. The issue at law was whether this bankruptcy dissolved Walker's obligations to Herman Lubinsky's Savoy diskery, which held Walker under contract. Walker felt it did, for he went to Mercury under a new agreement and waxed sides for that company.

The court, in its decision, stated that it could reasonably be inferred that the petition for bankruptcy was filed "for the sole purpose of evading Lightsey's (Walker's) obligations under his contract with Savoy. Such a purpose violates the spirit and purpose of the Bankruptcy Act."

Lubinsky, Savoy chief, noted that Walker's contract with the diskery had three years to run and said he would expect Walker to fulfill the contract.

GILLESPIE TUNE BOUGHT BY LUDLOW FIRM

NEW YORK, Jan. 10—"Oo-Shoo-Be-Do-Be," the tune waxed by Dizzy Gillespie on his Dee Gee label, was bought this week by Ludlow Music, one of the Howie Richmond publishing firms. Tune, authored by Joe Carroll and Bill Graham, has been stirring action in Philadelphia, where jock Bob Horn started it rolling. Disk has moved in two fields, pop and r.&b.

Gillespie's Dee Gee firm, headquartered in Detroit, is a partnership managed by the bebop maestro and recording exec Dave Usher.

CHARLES BROWN TO REFORM ORCH.

NEW YORK, Jan. 3—Rhythm and blues chanter Charles Brown will disband his trio immediately and reorganize his full band, it was learned this week.

Presently in Tucson, Ariz., where he ended his six-month tour packaged with his trio, along with blues warblers Billy Ford and Mr. Sad Head, Brown stated he would immediately begin auditioning for additional sidemen and female vocalists.

Fats Clarke, manager of the Charles Brown road attraction, declared that the newly formed band will begin a ten-month tour as soon as the unit is organized and rehearsals are completed.

BIHARIS' FLAIR LABEL DEBUTS FOR C.&W.

HOLLYWOOD, Dec. 27—Another indie label here expanded from rhythm and blues into the country field when the Bihari brothers, of Modern and RPM, kicked off Flair Records.

Joe Bihari, who will function as a.&r. chief for the new diskery, has inked Roy Harris of WJXN, Jackson, Miss.; the Magnolia Boys, and the Carroll County Boys, another Jackson crew. Bihari and his brother Saul will embark on a three week tour of the South, seeking talent to make up a 10-artist roster, starting in mid-January.

Modern distributors will handle Flair. Meteor Records, which has been started by Les Bihari, Memphis, has worked out a similar deal whereby all Modern distribs will handle his new r.&b. label.

Fletcher Henderson, Swing Giant, Dead at 55

NEW YORK, Jan. 3—Fletcher Henderson, one of the best known names of the jazz and swing eras, died here Monday night (29) in Harlem Hospital, after a long illness. Henderson achieved lasting fame as an arranger, composer, bandleader and pianist from 1920 to 1950. He was 55 years old.

Born in Cuthbert, Ga., Henderson received his degree from Atlanta University. He toured the country with his first orchestra with Ethel Waters. Later he led the way to the great era of swing in the 1930s, and thru his sparkling arrangements for the Benny Goodman band from 1934 to 1950. Many of the sidemen who played in his orchestra became notable jazz figures in their own right, including Cootie Williams, Roy Eldridge, Henry (Red) Allen, John Kirby, Benny Carter, Don Redman and Coleman Hawkins.

PAUL E.X. BROWN NAMED MARCH OF DIMES CHAIRMAN

ATLANTA, Dec. 27—Paul E.X. Brown, pioneer of Negro sports casting in Georgia radio, has been appointed Chairman of the 1953 March of Dimes Campaign-Negro Division. The appointment was announced here recently by Gen. Alvan C. Gillem, State Director.

In addition to sports broadcasting at WERD-Atlanta, Brown conducts two daily musical programs, "The Swing Club," featuring pops, and "The Gospel Train," a full hour of gospel recordings. Brown, who started in radio in Chicago in 1942, has had news programs on stations WSBC, Chicago, Ill.; WJOB, Hammond, Ind., and WEDR-Birmingham, Ala.

Notes from the R.&B. Beat

JACK'S NEW FLACK: Jack Walker, that irrepressible promotion and publicity man for Atlantic Records and the Shaw Agency, started a deejay show over station WOV, New York, last week. Walker is on every evening with his r.&b. show.... The Griffin Brothers, famous brother-bandleader team who record for the Dot label, recently announced that they were seeking a sister-singing act to put with the brother leaders. Applications for up to 22 pairs of sisters were received at last count. Nearly 15 pairs have been auditioned already, and all contestants will be heard before a choice is made. The Griffin band has just finished a week at Pep's, Philadelphia, and on January 16 will start a Southern tour under Ralph Weinberg. They will open in Miami and work their way back up the East Coast.

The long-awaited Johnny Ace follow-up to "My Song" will be out in a week or so. Duke Records' prexy Don Robey, who made the announcement, said he refused to be rushed into a session until he had the "right material." Title of the new disk is "Cross My Heart".... Fats Domino and the Clovers open their two-week one-nighter trek on January 15 at Roanoke, and finish up at Virginia Beach on February 1.... New talent signed by Joe Davis of Beacon Music for the M-G-M r.&b. department includes Millie Bosman, Teddy Williams, the Crickets, Boote Green, Al King, Paula Watson and Beulah Bryant.... Ivory Joe Hunter goes out on a one-nighter tour thru Texas on January 31..... It's reported that Rev. Gatemouth Moore, Coral artist, will start a lawsuit against Aladdin Records and Helen Humes for using his copyrighted tune "Did You Ever Love a Woman" without giving him writer's credit. Charles Brown did the vocal on the waxing.... Ralph Bass, Federal Records, in from the West Coast to do some New York waxings. Ralph's flipping these days for the way "The Bells" by Billy Ward and his Dominoes has been breaking.... Amos Milburn, originally skedded to open an Eastern swing in Philadelphia, has been held over on the Coast for three more months. Milburn is booked by the Shaw Agency.... Down Texas way, Peacock chief Don Robey has inked Ben DeCosta's Arthur Prysock package for 19 dates beginning February 9. Marie Adams, Peacock thrush will join Prysock (Decca Records) for a one-nighter tour beginning February 13. A special thanks goes to Don for sending out those huge boxes of real Texas pecans to all his friends and associates in the biz.

MARIE ADAMS

PHILLY FLASHES: George Woods, former r.&b. deejay with WWRL, Woodside, N.Y., has joined WHAT in Philadelphia.... Vi Burnside back in Philadelphia next week at Butler Cafe.... In the same city, Big Maybelle follows her Earle Theater date with a pitch at Emerson's Grille, newest of the town's musical spots.... Johnny Sparrow returns to the Red Rooster with Curtis Harmon's Top Notes to follow... Saxophonist Morris Lane and warbler Lee Richardson usher in the new entertainment policy at Christy's, another new Philadelphia musical spot.... Arthur Davey, who had been with Plink, Plank and Plunk, has rejoined his old unit, Steve Gibson and the Red Caps.... Bull Moose Jackson opens at the Showboat on January 26.

JAZZ JOTS: The closeness of the jazz and r.&b. fields is being demonstrated again with the reaction to the new Illinois Jacquet Mercury waxing of "Lean Baby" and "The Cool Rage," which is already showing action on territorial r.&b. charts. Jacquet's cutting of "Port of Rico" has passed the 100,000 mark.... Illinois Jacquet, Willie Mabon and Bette McLaurin will be on the same bill at the Regal Theater, Chicago, show opening January 30.... Ruth Brown has been set for the Billy Eckstine-Count Basie tour this spring. unit will start out on February 27 in Roanoke, Va., and will play thru the South to Texas. Package will tour for about seven weeks.... Rosita Davis, a former singer with the Duke Ellington ork, has

(Continued on next page)

ROOST AND FOX ARE COOL ON "WHALIN'"

NEW YORK, Dec. 27—Roost Records, r.&b. diskery, has turned over the master and stampers of "Cool Whalin'" by Babs Gonzales to pubber rep Harry Fox. Fox charged that waxed ditty made unauthorized use in its lyrics of portions of copyrighted pop standards such as "Blue Moon," "Dinah," "Ol' Man River" and "Honeysuckle Rose."

The agreement also calls for diskery to turn in an accounting of manufacturing activity on the platter. Record had begun to catch favor until further activity was stopped by Fox. The etching was originally produced by Babs Records, which subsequently sold the master to Roost. Fox's office contended that permission would never have been granted to use quotes from standard tunes for a ditty termed "suggestive."

R.&B. Beat
(Continued from previous page)

signed with Shaw Artists Corporation.... Tenor man Zoot Sims, whose new Prestige long player is causing a stir in modern music circles, reportedly breaking it up at Birdland with the Kai Winding-Bill Harris group.

Ruth Brown opened at the Apollo Theater, New York, Friday (22) for a week's engagement. Others on the bill are the Tiny Bradshaw ork with Tiny Kennedy and the Milt Buckner Trio.... The Clovers, Atlantic Records artists, go into the Earle Theater, Philadelphia, on February 5, the Howard, Washington, on February 13, and then to New York to cut some new sides.... "I Cried Last Night," tune waxed by newcomer Bill Heyman on the Sittin' In label, reported catching on in Philadelphia.... The Al Grey All-Stars, with Clarence Gatemouth Brown, are doing a string of one-nighters thru the Southwest. Paul Monday, well known pianist with the Grey unit, who also carries some of the band's vocal chores along with chirp Rosetta Perry, has come out with a new release for Peacock titled "I Promise" and "I Can't Forget About You".... B.B. King, with the Bill Harvey ork, is on one-nighters thru the South. Johnny Ace has formed an ork and will soon be on one-nighters....Charles Brown has ordered a specially made mink necktie to add to his already famous wardrobe. A strong contender for best-dressed honors in the show-biz world, Brown recently acquired a $2,500 wardrobe including imported tweed suits, pastel Tartan plaid jackets, and 15 pairs of shoes. Brown added that if he approves of the mink tie, he'll consider adding several other kinds of furs, including ermine.

"Heavenly Father" gal Edna McGriff was ordered to bed last week after medics declared the 17 year-old thrush's health would be seriously endangered if she did not cancel all engagements for the next two weeks. Edna was slated for a series of p.a.'s in Virginia and Delaware territory. She'll resume her sked with a concert at the Brooklyn Academy of Music on January 22, and will join the Buddy Lucas band in New Jersey the following day for a series of one-nighters.... Savoy a.&r. man Lee Magid leaving for Detroit to wax sessions with Varetta Dillard and T.J. Fowler. Thrush opens at the Flame Show Bar on the 19th,

then moves to New York's Apollo Theater on January 30. Varetta will also catch the inauguration crowd when she plays the Club Kovaks, Washington, D.C., on February 9. Following her Capitol stint, the Savoy chantress will combine with Wynonie Harris and Larry Darnell for a tour.... Robert Henry seeking talent for the W.C. Handy Theater, Memphis.... Tenor saxman Lynn Hope is reported running up big takes at all clubs. Sold to a promoter at a flat figure, Hope has been consistently coming out with $150.00 to $225.00 over guarantee. This on his 60 percent of the door.... The Orioles and Paul Williams

FATS DOMINO

orch. in Detroit for Washington's birthday, jump on down to Texas for six dates. Then the Orioles switch over to Fats Domino for a bunch of one-nighters to carry thru the spring. This will hike the price on Fats, who so far has been working only with his small band. The added attraction of a singing group is a nice plus for the rotund little entertainer.... Deejay Stan Pat (Pat Pagnotta) doing a great job on station WTNJ, Trenton, N.J. The genial spinner, whose show is aired Tuesdays, Thursdays and Saturdays, has hit on the commercially smart idea of mixing his musical styles, with half his show going to r.&b. and half going to the pop disks. As a result, his audience is larger and his sponsors happier.... Blues and rhythm spinner Jack Holmes, of station WLOW, Norfolk, Va., holds the distinction of being the first Negro disk jockey in Virginia. He started at the station in 1949 with one half-hour seg per day. Known as one of the best salesmen in Southern radio, Holmes says he has over 100,000 listeners and averages more than 500 pieces of mail weekly.

CHICAGO TIDINGS: Thrush Chubby Newsome, formerly with RCA Victor, and now on Chance label, working this week at Kansas City's Orchid Room. A unit being talked about for spring dates will comprise Miss Newsome, along with Al Smith's band and chanter Charles Gonzales, who hits the disk stalls under the monicker of Bobby Prince. Latter's newest slicing is a swingin' hand-clapper titled "Tell Me Why, Why Why".... Johnny Sellers, remembered for his spiritual singing some years ago, is now out on Chance label with a moving number

titled "Mighty Lonesome".... The Flamingos vocal group has also signed on with Chance Records. A fabulous sight act, the group is busy looking for what their manager thinks is the right material for etching.... Sugar Ray Robinson is reported doing a bang-up job on club dates and really knocked 'em cold the other nite on Jackie Gleason's TV airer. The boxer turned dancer-singer is eyeing a big chateau in Europe, where he may live.... Promoter Howard Lewis booking disk stars Little Walter and Eddie Boyd and his band into Houston, Texas on January 21 to begin a series of Southwest dates.... Blues veteran Tampa Red, who continues to write and record good blues sides for RCA Victor, says that in certain locations his disks are not getting the airplay necessary to make for bigger royalty checks. With youngsters coming out of left field and climbing fast into the $500 to $700 per week class, it has a tendency to make the old-timers think that they should be getting a bigger take.... Songstress Nellie Lutcher gave one of her greatest performances recently when her life story was told on the Hazel Bishop TV seg.

HEARD IN HOLLYWOOD: Percy Mayfield (Specialty) is back at work after a five-month convalescence from a serious auto accident. Ben Waller, Los Angeles agent, has him working Coast dates.... Jesse Belvin (Recorded in Hollywood) is doing his first personals for Waller thru New Mexico, Arizona and Texas.... B.B. King (RPM) has inked a new three-year pact with the Bihari brothers. He is now touring Texas.... Amos Milburn, after dates in Seattle and Tacoma, Wash., last week, now beginning a slow trek eastward, winding up for a March 16 opening at Pep's Musical Bar, Philadelphia.... Need a good piano player? We've got one that's available for weddings, bar mitzvah's and confirmations—name of Leo Mesner—a guy that plays some pretty good two-beat. Leo and his brother Eddie will shortly be doing pop versions of their Aladdin r.&b. hits with Ike Carpenter's band.... Specialty's Camille Howard continues to beat out those wonderful drivin' boogie woogie tunes on her piano. She's booked in the West by Ben Waller and by Universal in the East.... Jake Porter's Combo label riding high with Chuck Higgins' "Pachuko Hop" which is creating all sorts of noise here.... Frank L. Harper, Vogue Records prexy, says his firm's poised to enter the rhythm and blues field shortly.

January's Record Roundup

RATING SYSTEM
•••• Excellent ••• Very Good
•• Good • Fair

Week of January 3

Territorial Tips
NEW YORK
Rock, Rock, Rock--Amos Milburn--
Aladdin 3159
LOS ANGELES
The Bells--Dominoes--Federal 12114
WASHINGTON, D.C.
Story From My Heart and Soul--B.B.
King--RPM 374
CINCINNATI
Soft--Tiny Bradshaw--King 4577
Please, Baby, Please--Swallows--
King 4579
CHARLOTTE
How Long--Fats Domino--Imperial 5209

New R.&B. Releases
BOOTS BROWN/Victor 20-5110
•••• Block Buster
••• Shortn'in Bread
ELMORE JAMES/Meteor 5000
•••• I Believe
••• I Held My Baby Last Night
BEP BROWN ORCH./Meteor 5001
••• Round House Boogie
••• Kickin' the Blues Around
HENRY HAYES ORCH./Savoy 878
• Forgive Me, Baby
••• Over Here, Pretty Baby
BIG BILL BROONZY/Mercury 70039
••• Leavin' Day
••• South Bound Train
JOHNNY OTIS ORCH. (ADA WILSON)/
Mercury 70038
••• Why Don't You Believe Me
••• Wishing Well
CHARLES BROWN/Aladdin 3163
••• Moonrise
••• Evening Shadows
CLARENCE (GATEMOUTH) BROWN/
Peacock 1607
••• Dirty Work at the Crossroad
••• You Got Money
LITTLE WILLIE LITTLEFIELD/
Federal 12110
••• K.C. Loving
•• Pleading at Midnight
THE TRENIERS/Okeh 6932
••• Poon-Tang!
••• Hi-Yo Silver
BILL DOGGETT ORCH./King 4591
••• Mistreater
••• Early Bird
ARNETT COBB ORCH./Okeh 6928
••• Linger Awhile
••• "Lil" Sonny
BASIL SPEARS/MGM 11406
••• You Make Me Feel So Good
•• I Want a Man to Gimme Some Luck

THE BLUES CHASERS/MGM 11409
••• Old Fashioned Blues
•• Birmingham Special
BERYL BOOKER/Mercury 70041
••• Why Do I Love You
••• When a Woman Loves a Man
BABS GONZALES/Babs 6402
••• Cool Whalin'
•• Sugar Ray
EDDIE CARTER QUARTET/MGM
11405
••• Don't Turn Your Back on Me
•• Eat 'Em Up
IRENE REDFIELD/MGM 11408
•• Whalin' Away
•• Never Trouble Trouble
AL GREY ORCH./Peacock 1609
•• Trombone Interlude
•• Over and Under
JACKIE DAVIS TRIO/Victor 20-5111
•• Do, Baby, Do
•• Coffee Time
GABRIEL BROWN/MGM 11407
•• Cold Mama
•• I'm Just Crazy
LEROY LANG ORCH./Rockin' 502
•• Combo's Boogie
• A Tenor Wails the Blues

New Spiritual Releases
THE BARONS/Orange 1014
•• Ezekiel Saw De Wheel
•• This World Is in Bad Condition

Week of January 10

Territorial Tips
CINCINNATI
Baby Don't Do It--"5" Royales--
Apollo 443

New R.&B. Releases
WYNONIE HARRIS/King 4593
•••• Bad News, Baby
••• Bring It Back
JOHNNY OTIS ORCH./Mercury 70050
••• The Love Bug Boogie (vo. Ada
Wilson, Mel Walker)
••• Brown Skin Butterball (vo. Mel
Walker)
BIG JAY McNEELY/Federal 12111
••• Just Crazy
••• Penthouse Serenade
JAY McSHANN ORCH./Mercury 70040
••• Reach
••• You Didn't Tell Me
LUCKY MILLINDER ORCH./King 4589
••• Old Spice
••• When I Gave You My Love (vo.
Corky Robbins, Johnny Bosworth)

New Spiritual Releases
ORIGINAL FIVE BLIND BOYS/
Peacock 1706
•• I Was Praying
•• Will Jesus Be Waiting for Me
SISTER JESSIE MAE RENFRO/
Peacock 1707
•• No Room in the Hotel
•• I'll Be Satisfied Then

Week of January 17

Buy o' the Week
**Cross My Heart b/w Angel--Johnny-
Ace--Duke 107**
Action instantaneous. "Cross My Heart"
already on St. Louis territorial. Initial
reaction in Philadelphia, New York and
sections of South is strong.

Buy o' the Week
**Dream Girl b/w Daddy Loves Baby—
Jesse and Marvin—Specialty 447**
A sleeper which is getting some solid
movement in a number of areas such as
Chicago and St. Louis. Kids particularly
are going for it in Chicago. New York
distrib shows good action.

Territorial Tips
CHICAGO
Baby Don't Do It--"5" Royales--
Apollo 443
I Believe--Elmore James--Meteor 5000
CHARLOTTE
Story From My Heart and Soul--
B.B. King--RPM 374
ST. LOUIS
Dream Girl--Jesse & Marvin--
Specialty 447

New R.&B. Releases
LLOYD PRICE ORCH./Specialty 452
•••• Tell Me Pretty Baby
•••• Ain't It a Shame
JOHNNY ACE/Duke 107
•••• Cross My Heart
•••• Angel
PERCY MAYFIELD/Specialty 451
•••• The River's Invitation
••• I Dare You, Baby
JOE LIGGINS ORCH./Specialty 453
••• Freight Train Blues
•• Blues for Tanya
EMANON TRIO/Swing Time 322
••• Mr. Johnnie Long Donn Is Dead
••• My Man Is Gone (vo. Geneva Vallier)
CLIFF BUTLER/States 112
••• Benny's Blues (pno. Ben Holton)

••• Adam's Rib
THE FIVE CROWNS/Rainbow 202
••• Keep It a Secret
•• Why Don't You Believe Me
LLOYD (FAT MAN) SMITH/
Peacock 1611
••• No Better for You
•• My Clock Stopped
JACK (SCAT) POWELL/Nucraft 1010
••• Hipsters Jump
•• Boom Bah
DEXTER GORDON/Swing Time 323
••• My Kinda' Love
••• Citizen Bop
THE JETS/Rainbow 201
••• Drag It Home, Baby
•• The Lovers
PAUL MONDAY/Peacock 1608
••• I Can't Forget About You
•• I Promise
PAULA GRIMES & TEACHO
WILTSHIRE BAND/Prestige 801
••• Miss My Daddy
•• Sighin' and Cryin'

New Spiritual Releases

THE BELLS OF JOY/Peacock 1708
•••• Leak in This Old Building
••• Echoes From Heaven
THE CARAVANS/States 109
••• Get Away Jordan
••• He'll Be There
THE VETERAN SINGERS/States 105
••• On the Battlefield
••• Lord Is Riding

Week of January 24

Buy o' the Week

**Nobody Loves Me b/w Cheatin'—Fats
Domino—Imperial 5220**
This one looks solid. Both sides are getting good action, tho "Nobody" is showing
in more areas. Strongest reports came
from the South, Philadelphia and
Cincinnati.

Territorial Tips
NEW YORK
**Cross My Heart--Johnny Ace--
Duke 107**
I Believe--Elmore James--Meteor 5000

New R.&B. Releases

FATS DOMINO/Imperial 5220
•••• Cheatin'
•••• Nobody Loves Me
WILLIE JOHNSON & THELMA/
Savoy 881
•••• Thrill Me Baby
••• Don't Tell Mama
ILLINOIS JACQUET/Mercury 89021
•••• The Cool Rage
•••• Lean Baby
AL SEARS ORCH./Victor 20-5131
••• Huffin' and Puffin'
••• Mag's Alley

LIL' SON JACKSON/Imperial 5218
••• Black and Brown
••• Sad Letter Blues
BUDDY JOHNSON ORCH./Decca 28530
••• Just to Be Yours (vo. Nolan Lewis)
••• Somehow, Somewhere (vo. Ella
Johnson)
MELLO MOODS & TEACHO
WILTSHIRE BAND/Prestige 799
••• Call On Me
•• I Tried and Tried and Tried
BOBBY PRINCE/Chance 1128
••• Tell Me Why, Why, Why
•• I Want to Hold You
T-BONE WALKER/Imperial 5216
••• Blue Mood
•• Got No Use for You
FAT MAN MATTHEWS/Imperial 5211
••• Later Baby
•• When Boy Meets Girl
STEVE GIBSON/Victor 20-5130
••• Do I, Do I, I Do (vo. Damita Jo)
•• Big Game Hunter

New Spiritual Releases

MARIE KNIGHT/Decca 28545
•••• Jesus Walk with Me
•••• Get Away Jordan
SPIRITUAL HARMONIZERS/Glory 4004
••• Do You Know Him
•• God Leads His Children
SPIRIT OF MEMPHIS QUARTET/
King 4575
•• God's Amazing Grace
•• Toll the Bell Easy

Week of January 31

Buy o' the Week

**(Mama) He Treats Your Daughter-
Mean—Ruth Brown—Atlantic 986**
Smash potential here. Philadelphia and
Chicago reported it took off immediately.
New York and Buffalo reported good
activity. The Carolina report stated much
heavier initial action than on her last
disk. Flip is "R.B. Blues."

Territorial Tips
NEW YORK
Be True--Vocaleers--Red Robin 114

New R.&B. Releases

RUTH BROWN/Atlantic 986
•••• (Mama) He Treats Your Daughter
Mean
••• R.B. Blues
RAY CHARLES ORCH./Atlantic 984
•••• Jumpin' in the Mornin'
••• The Sun's Gonna Shine Again
JIMMY WITHERSPOON/Modern 895
••• Slow Your Speed
••• Baby, Baby
SMOKEY HOGG/Modern 896
••• River Hip Mama
••• Too Late, Old Man
ROSCOE GORDON/RPM 379
••• Just in From Texas
••• I'm in Love
THE BLUE BELLES/Atlantic 987
••• The Story of a Fool
••• Cancel the Call
BEN BURTON/Modern 894
••• Lovers Blues
••• Cherokee Boogie
LITTLE SON WILLIS/Swing Time 304
••• Operator Blues
••• Bad Luck and Trouble
JOE MORRIS' BLUES CAVALCADE
••• That's What Makes My Baby Fat
(vo. Fay Scruggs, Joe Morris)
••• I'm Goin' to Leave You (vo. Fay
Scruggs)
LIGHTNING HOPKINS/RPM 378
••• Candy Kitchen
••• Another Fool in Town
JIMMY NELSON ORCH./RPM 377
••• Right Around the Corner
••• Little Miss Teasin' Brown
PAUL GAYTEN/Okeh 6934
•• Don't Worry Me
•• Yes You Do--Yes You Do
ANNIE LAURIE/Okeh 6933
• Give Me Half a Chance
• Stop Talkin' and Start Walkin'

Decca to Reactivate Brunswick Label; Talent Signings Announced in Jazz, R.&B.

NEW YORK, Jan. 31—The reactivation of Brunswick Records as a productive r.&b. and jazz label is now underway by the Decca subsidiary. Firm has already signed several new artists, bringing its productive roster to five, and set a regular release schedule of new disks. It is also digging more intensively into old Decca and Signature masters for suitable reissue material.

In the jazz field, Brunswick has signed Jimmy McPartland. Jackie Paris has just been inked to cut vocals in his pop-jazz style. And the Five Bills and Gayle Brown have been pacted to join Mabel Scott in the firm's r.&b. division. There will be two releases of Brunswick wax monthly, each to consist of two or three singles and at least one album.

The diskery's first regular release, turned out to market next week, will contain singles by the Five Bills and Gayle Brown, plus the first in a new album series called "Battle of Jazz." The latter, to be made available only as a 10-inch LP, contains early blue label Decca etchings by the Bud Freeman and Joe Marsala orks.

Unlikely Success Story for Brunswick Pair

NEW YORK, Feb. 7—There's an interesting story behind Brunswick label's new r.&b. team of Gayle Brown and Sarah McLawler, who have just cut a terrific disk, "Gone Are the Days" for that label.

While in their early teens, the boy-girl pair sang together in a traveling religious group. Brown subsequently entered Fisk University and was later tapped by Uncle Sam for the army, while Miss McLawler completed her formal education and began her stint as a vocalist with Lucky Millinder's band. Her smooth piping soon won her a King Records recording contract. Sarah also formed an all-girl band that created quite a stir in r.&b. circles.

Brown meanwhile received his discharge, studied for three years at the McArthur Conservatory of Music in Indianapolis, Ind., and for eating money joined "The Brown Inspirational Group" headed by his mother.

The chanter then decided to pack his bags for New York, where he met up with old friend Johnny Hartman, who records for RCA Victor. The latter put Brown in touch with Phil Rose, Coral Records' a.&r. man, who set up an audition for the lad. To celebrate the occasion, Gayle and his wife went out on the town, winding up at a Brooklyn night spot known as the Arlington Inn. Who should be working there but the Sarah McLawler (whom Gayle hadn't

(Continued on next page)

Slay Disk Causing Sensation for Savoy

NEW YORK, Feb. 7—When Lee Magid, traveling a.&r. man for Savoy Records, left an acetate he cut with an unknown r.&b. combo in Detroit with a prominent deejay in Cleveland, little did he suspect he'd be launching what looks to be one of the biggest records in the field this year.

Reports started to trickle into the office late last week that "My Kind Of Woman" by the Emitt Slay Trio had broken wide open in Cleveland. Ohio Record Sales' Nate Kulkin reported on the telephone that

(Continued on next page)

Johnny Ace singing "CROSS MY HEART" on DUKE-107

DUKE RECORDS
4104 Lyons
Houston, Texas

Royals Can't Impersonate "5 Royales," Court Rules

NEW YORK, Feb. 14—A Superior Court injunction was granted last Saturday (7) at Muscogee County, Georgia, which prohibits the Royals, an r.&b. singing group, from further impersonating the Five Royales in the state of Georgia. A temporary injunction had been issued earlier in the case.

The Royals are prevented from using either the name Five Royals or Five Royales, and the group is also prohibited from using the pictures of the Five Royales in their promotion or inferring that they have recorded the songs "Baby, Don't Do It," the Five Royales' current hit, or any other of the latter group's disks.

The apparent misrepresentation was uncovered by Carl Lebow, a.&r. head for Apollo and personal manager of the Five Royales, and Ben Bart, head of Universal Attractions, which is the booking agent for the Five Royales. The Royals had been doing a series of theater dates thru the South under the billing of the Five Royales and/or Five Royals. Newspaper ads and placards made use of the pictures of the Five Royales. The Royals are now packaged in a show which includes Anna Mae Winburn and her ork, the Fou Chez dancers and Bobby Wallace. The Royals have been the headline attraction.

The tour has been promoted by Spizzy Canfield. The road manager is Eustace Pilgrim, husband of Miss Winburn. When the impersonation was discovered, registered letters were sent to all the known theaters on the tour asking that the Royals' act be cancelled. One theater in Newport News is kown to have done this. Others, however, followed thru with the booking. Canfield, along with D.P, Nesbitt, manager of the Liberty Theater in Columbus, Ga., were named as co-defendants, along with the Royals.

The hearing for a separate damage action against the Royals for $10,000 was set for the first Monday in June.

SAUNDERS GETS 15th ANNIVERSARY SALUTE

CHICAGO, Jan. 31—One thousand Chicagoans paid tribute to Red (Hambone) Saunders last week at the Club DeLisa, where Red celebrated his 15th year as drummer and orchestra leader. Celebrities attending the affair included Duke Ellington and singers Jimmy Grissom and Debbie Andrews. Disk jockeys Al Benson, Daddie-O Daylie, Sid McCoy and Vivian Carter; columnist Dan Burley, singer Joe Williams and Paris Club's Freddie Gordon acted as emcees.

RED SAUNDERS

Ellington, honorary chairman of the affair, presented Saunders with an award which was followed by a $1,000 check from club owner Mike DeLisa. The presentation was made by producer Sammy Dyer. A trophy award was presented by sales representative Dr. Jive Cadillac of the Canadian Ace Brewery. Saunders received 200 telegrams of congratulations, including one from Pearl Bailey and Louis Bellson. From the musicians' union, Local 208, came a basket of flowers. Tribute was also paid to contortionist-dancer Viola Kemp, in private life Mrs. Saunders.

Brunswick Pair

(Continued from previous page)

seen for 15 years) and her group. Their impromtu reunion resulted in their cutting a test disk, which they took to Phil Rose, who signed both immediately.

The "Gone Are the Days" etching, which is the first for Brown, features the chanter's solo backed with a strikingly different accompaniment by Miss McLawler on the Hammond organ, making for a highly unusual side with loads of commercial potential.

Slay Disk

(Continued from previous page)

he had rushed an order for 5,000 disks after a tremendous reception received following the disk's airing by Cleveland r.&b. spinner Alan (Moon Dog) Freed on his nightly WJW program. The original acetate that Moon Dog played was left behind by Magid after he had cut the Slay Trio in Detroit.

Savoy prexy Herman Lubinsky reported that orders from his Texas distrib are in excess of 5,000 for the disk, while orders from St. Louis totalled 3,000. His combined figure for two days has reached 18,000. "All this without distribs having received a single sample disk," Lubinsky stated. "All the business was done by playing the etching on the long-distance telephone."

14

Herb Abramson to Join Army Dental Corps

NEW YORK, Jan. 31—Hot and cool jazz luminaries, men of note in the rhythm and blues field, and many others who make their way in the ordinary pop music field gathered Wednesday (28) to pay homage to Herb Abramson, who leaves his exec post at Atlantic Records to do a turn as first lieutenant in the U.S. Army's dental corps.

Abramson switches his milieu next week. The transition is not as abrupt as it appears to be. Jerry Wexler, who emceed the luncheon, pointed out that Abramson, between recording sessions, has been practicing dentistry quietly on his blood relatives and Ahmet Ertegun, his partner in Atlantic. He will not commit this on the troops, Wexler noted.

Abramson, who leaves Wednesday (4), is likely to be stationed in Europe, from whence he is expected to return with a new line for Atlantic. One wag noted: "He's the first dentist to enter the service equipped with a 45 r.p.m. drill."

VICTOR PACTS R.&B. NAMES

HOLLYWOOD, Feb. 21—Jack Lewis, young manager and buyer for California Music, one-stop record outlet here, is reportedly seeking out and negotiating with new artists for Victor's r.&b. department.

Talent signed by Lewis includes the Robins, five-voice vocal group with Savoy previous to going into the service two years ago; Boots Brown, whose disking of "Block Buster" has shown signs of making it; Milton Trenier, kid brother of the Trenier twins, Columbia warblers, and Shorty Rogers, jazz trumpeter and arranger, who will cut bop albums for Victor.

REPUBLIC MUSIC GETS "YES, I KNOW" DITTY

NEW YORK, Jan. 31—"Yes, I Know," the r.&b. ditty which rocketed to hit status via a Linda Hayes disking on the Recorded in Hollywood label, has been turned over to Republic Music by the diskery's publishing subsidiary. The transfer was made without protest on the claim by Republic that the opus was a near carbon copy of the hot r.&b. property, "I Don't Know."

Meanwhile, Sammy Kaye, who owns Republic and who built his reputation on "sweet" music, is gaining new renown as a purveyor of r.&b. material. Hal Fein, Republic professional manager, has made a point of searching out items suitable for conversion into the pop idiom, and to date has an unusual record of successes.

"I Don't Know," a big hit in the r.&b. market via the Chess record by Willie Ma-

(Continued on next page)

HERALD LABEL LAUNCHED IN N.Y.

NEW YORK, Feb. 14—A new rhythm and blues diskery, Herald Records, was announced this week. Al Silver and Jack Braverman, co-owners of the Silver Record Pressing Company, and Fred Mendelsohn, former head of Regal Records, have joined forces to form the new firm. First releases will include some sides cut by Southern blues chanter Little Walter.

Mendelsohn is reported lining up a stable of r.&b. stars and will cut some new sessions in the latter part of February. He and Silver will then leave for a month-long Southern trek to line up distribs and additional talent.

Goldner Sets Rama, New Tico Subsid

NEW YORK, Feb. 14—George Goldner, general manager of Tico Recording, Inc., Latin American and mambo diskery, has activated Rama Records, a new label which will specialize in r.&b. and jazz wax. Goldner, who also heads the new enterprise, has taken on vibist-arranger Bert Keyes as musical director.

First group signed by Rama is the Five Budds, a vocal combo managed by Cliff Martinez. Their first platter, coupling "Midnight" and "I Was Such a Fool," has just been released by Tico Distributing, thru which Rama disks will be promoted to retailers. The label expects to sign other talent soon.

Republic Music
(Continued from previous page)

bon, is out in three current pop waxings, with another due for release soon. The Republic ditty, "I Played the Fool" is a best seller in the Atlantic recording by the Clovers. Bill Darnell has cut the tune pop and a cover waxing by Cathy Ryan and the Art Mooney ork is due out next week.

Parking Tix Costly to Cleffers

NEW YORK, Jan. 31—Cleffer and RCA Victor r.&b. artist Lincoln Chase came a-cropper in the traffic courts this week when he was fined $2,205 for ignoring 45 parking tickets here. Chase received the dubious distinction of being fined the most of any music man to date, beating out Teddy Reig, a free-lance a.&r. man who was also fined for ignoring parking tickets recently, by at least a grand. Chase's first waxing for RCA Victor, a tune he penned, is 'The Vultures," but does not refer to this courtroom incident.

On the r.&b. cleffing trail for about a year, Chase has gained some attention for his tunes, tho not nearly as much publicity as he received via the 45 mislaid summonses. He is the writer of "Must I Cry Again," "Rain Down Rain," "Salty Tears," "Tear Down the Sky," "Silly Heart" and "Mend Your Ways." His pact with RCA Victor is as a singer. He is signed to Dave Dreyer's Raleigh music firm as a writer.

Notes from the R.&B. Beat

DEEJAY POLL SHEDS LIGHT ON R.&B.: A recent Disk Jockey Poll conducted by a leading trade publication reveals some interesting facts about the percentage growth of r.&b. programs on the air and the number of hours that r.&b. disks are played by stations across the country. In this category, 25 percent of stations reported that they are playing more r.&b. disks now than a year ago; 59 percent that they are playing the same amount as last year, and 15 percent report a decrease. That there is still room for much more r.&b. programming is evident by the replies to the number of hours devoted to such disks per week as against popular, c.&w., etc. R.&B. disks are played a total of 2.5 hours per week by all stations. Pop records are first, with 31 hours per week; c.&w. second, with 11.5 hours per week; classical third, with 4 hours per week.

(Continued on next page)

R.&B. Beat
(Continued from previous page)

GOTHAM GAB: Buddy Johnson's ork is now playing at the Savoy Ballroom, New York.... Atlas Records, New York, pacted thrush June Davis to a long-term contract and also signed the Freddie Washington ork to the label.... Harlem's new Dawn Casino club is located on the site of the once-famous Bamboo Inn, where the community's social set mingled in droves during the 1920s.... Bop warbler Babs Gonzales says he has his "Shuckin' and Jivin'" and "Lullaby of the Doomed" set for release on his Babs label.... Bull Moose Jackson and his ork open at the Savoy Ballroom in New York on February 19.... Tenor sax star Joe Holiday, who rose to fame with his Prestige etching of "This Is Happiness," into the Apollo Theater January 30 to engage in a battle of the saxes with Big Jay McNeely.... Tommy (Dr. Jive) Smalls, of WWRL, Woodside, N.Y., to premiere the Five Crowns newest one for Rainbow titled "Alone Again" on his show this week.

PHILLY FLASHES: Station WHAT adds another r.&b. disk jockey in George Woods, taking over the mike for the afternoon "Snap Club" sessions.... Southern Records, new Philadelphia diskery helmed by Jerry Halpern and Ed Krensel, has just issued their initial disk. A new vocal group, the Buccaneers, is featured on both sides, titled "Dear Ruth" and "Fine Brown Frame." Backing on the "Ruth" side is provided by the Joe Whalen Trio, while Matthew Child and his Drifters take over the instrumental chores on the flip.... Philadelphia's Earle Theater will pass out of the picture next month, when the Warners chain is due to return the property to W.T. Grant and Company, who will convert the site into a department store. Songstress Wini Brown, along with the Earl Bostic crew, will be featured acts at the Earle's finale. Miss Brown will also appear at the Powelton Cafe beginning February 23.... Orkster Todd Rhodes coming East for a February 16 date at the Show Boat.... The Swallows of King Records were recently involved in an auto mishap in Lancaster, Pa. Group wound up entertaining convalescents in a nearby hospital while their car was undergoing repairs.... Hal Singer reported saxsational at Pep's Musical Bar, Philadelphia.

Jolly Joyce Agency, Philadelphia and New York, has placed the Three Peppers at the new Singapore Lounge in Miami Beach.... Gene Ammons back at Pep's Musical Bar in Philadelphia. In the same town, Skippy (Sheik) Williams moves in at the Butler Cafe with the Ray-O-Vacs moving close by to Bill & Lou's.... Newest musical spot is the Chateau Club with the Top Notes, featuring Beulah Frazier.

Michelle and his Swing Organ Trio are at Emerson's Grill, Philadelphia, around the corner from the Glen Hotel's Carver Bar, where Johnny Sparrow and his Bows and Arrows bow on a return trip. In West Philadelphia, Lonnie Bell takes over the booking chores at Powelton Cafe with Vi Burnside coming in this week to kick off a new musical policy.... The Blue Note sets up February bookings to make it a Progressive Jazz Month with Charlie Parker, Dave Brubeck, Bud Powell and Buddy DeFranco coming in a week apart. Ray Abrams is new at the Butler Cafe.... Walter (Foots) Thomas, former Cab Calloway sideman who is agenting Vi Burnside, Myrtle Young, Bill Doggett, "Doc" Bagby and Wild Bill Davis, plans to move his office from New York to Philadelphia.... New Philadelphia booking has Bill Darnell coming into Lou's Moravian, with Tamara Hayes bowing out after a long run; the coming of Coatesville Harris to the Butler Cafe, and the Bill Doggett trio with Mildred Anderson at Pep's Musical Bar.

D.C. DOINGS: When Max Silverman, owner of the Quality Record Shop here, was visited by Ruth Brown last week, he had to call the riot squad to escort the Atlantic recording star back to the Howard Theater, where she was appearing. Adoring fans practically disrobed her in the street as they clamored for her to sing "Mama".... A new spot, the Club Afrique, opens in Washington. First group in is Johnny Hodges and his trio. Club is owned by Paul Menn, who formerly owned the Club Bengasi.... Bette McLaurin does a week at the Howard in Washington on February 27, then plays a week at the Royal in Baltimore on March 6.... Laverne Baker, Miss Sharecropper, starts at the Booker T. Washington Restaurant on February 13 for two weeks.... Joe Holiday and his combo start at the Comedy Club, Baltimore, on March 9.... Arnett Cobb in a festive mood as press and public affectionately bestowed trophy, placques and gifts upon him during his playdate at the Hill Top, Washington, D.C., on Friday, February 20. Cobb's latest release for Mercury is "Poor Butterfly".... Charlie Fuqua's Ink Spots return to the Hill Top on February 27.... Dual trumpet man Frank Motley, newly signed by Specialty Records, has just completed a six-weeker at the Flamingo Room here. Motley's "real gone" combo consists of Jimmy Crawford, piano; Johnny Walker, drums; Russell Mason, sax; and Billy Taylor, bass. Motley's latest slicing of "Frantic" and "Heavy Weight Baby" was just released by Specialty.

Savoy Records' newest disk sensation, the Emitt Slay Trio, whose "My Kind of Woman" has really begun to take off in a big way, is now playing at the Plantation Room in Detroit.... Warbler Walter Spriggs was signed to Apollo Records. Carl Lebow of the diskery is personal manager of the

singer.... Choker Campbell's ork, a new crew out of Cleveland which toured with the Dominoes last spring, will go out on a Midwestern trek with the Clovers, starting March 13. The ork is signed with the Shaw Agency.... Ivory Joe Hunter is now on a Texas tour thru March 1.... Roy Brown, formerly with De Luxe, is now with King. Warbler is reportedly drawing capacity crowds with the Five Royales on a Ralph Weinberg tour.... Rudy Render, once with London, has been inked for Decca by Gordon Jenkins.... Linda Hayes, whose waxing of "Yes, I Know" is now moving up on the r.&b. charts, was signed by the Shaw Agency this week. She will be sent out on one-nighter treks and location dates.... The Gale Agency will send out a giant package

(Continued on next page)

R.&B. Beat
(Continued from previous page)

consisting of Larry Darnell, Wynonie Harris, Varetta Dillard and the Frank Humphries ork starting March 7. Unit will play one night theaters and dance dates thru April 15.

Eddie Boyd and Little Walter will be at the Royal Peacock, Atlanta, March 20 to 23.... Charlie Singleton a hold-over at Eddie Levine's, Boston.... Fats Domino concludes a string of one-nighters thru Texas on March 20.... The Orioles will start on a Ralph Weinberg trek thru the South with either the Paul Williams ork or the Griffin Brothers on March 16 thru April 6.... Sepia stars Dusty ("Open the Door, Richard") Fletcher, Eddie South (The "Dark Angel" of the Violin), Phil Moore, Una Mae Carlisle, Sugar Chile Robinson and former heavyweight champ Joe Louis are among entertainers spotlighted in "Holiday in Harlem," an all-Negro film spectacle.... Mercury Records has signed saxist Arnett Cobb and the Buddy Johnson orchestra for wax sessions.... Among packages getting big play from promoters: Tiny ("Mr. Soft") Bradshaw with Wini Brown, the Ink Spots with Cootie Williams' Orch., Little Esther with H-Bomb Ferguson and Tab Smith, and the Johnny Otis revue with vocalists Jimmy Witherspoon and Willie Mae Thornton.... Earl Bostic's recent one-nighter at Township Auditorium, Columbia, S.C., drew a reported 15,070 admissions.... Varetta Dillard following her Washington, D.C. stint with a stay at Chicago's Regal Thater. Savoy Records' a.&r. man Lee Magid is raving about Varetta's new one on that label titled "Getting Ready for My Daddy." While in Detroit recently Magid also cut T.J. Fowler's band. Coupling ready for issue is "Camel Walk" and "Gold Rush," with the latter being on a "Mule Train" kick.

TONGUE-TIED HE ISN'T: Some weeks back we reported to you the momentous story of Charles Brown and his genuine mink necktie. As proxy for Brown, who is currently touring on the West Coast, Nipsey Russell modelled the tie in the New York offices of Billy Shaw. The tie was created especially for Brown by fashion designer Elizabeth Meyers. Commented Russell, after soulfully gazing at the silver and blue neckwear, "This new cravat craze should go well—especially with bald-headed men. The tie can double for a toupee".... Atlantic disk stars the Clovers currently one-nighting thru the Carolinas, Georgia, Alabama and Virginia for the next few weeks. Group's waxing of "I Played the Fool" has been cut in pop versions by Art Mooney for M-G-M and Bill Darnell for Decca.... Faye Scruggs, new chirp with the "Joe Morris Blues Cavalcade" show, creat-

ing a tremendous stir with her appearances.... Wini Brown dishes up a real torcher in her latest Mercury offering titled "Can't Stand No More".... Duke Hampton's orch. inked for Cincinnati's Cotton Club beginning February 16.... Bill Doggett into the Casino, Baltimore, Md.

CHICAGO CHATTER: Lew Simpkins, United Records prexy, signed four new vocal acts this week, Billy Ford, the Dozier Boys, Jimmy Coe and Debbie Andrews. Miss Andrews has been with Decca, while Ford has etched for RCA Victor, Coe

(Continued on page 20)

February's Record Roundup

RATING SYSTEM
•••• Excellent ••• Very Good
•• Good • Fair

Week of February 7

Territorial Tips

NEW YORK
Yes I Know--Linda Hayes--Recorded in Hollywood 244
PHILADELPHIA
(Mama) He Treats Your Daughter Mean--Ruth Brown--Atlantic 986

New R.&B. Releases

LINDA HAYES/Recorded in Hollyw'd 244
•••• Yes! I Know (What You're Putting Down)
••• Sister Anne (Que Martyn combo)
ROY BROWN ORCH./King 4602
•••• Hurry Hurry Baby
•••• Travelin' Man
DANNY OVERBEA ORCH./Checker 768
•••• Train, Train, Train
••• I'll Wait
AMOS MILBURN/Aladdin 3164
•••• Let Me Go Home Whiskey
••• Three Times a Fool
LYNN HOPE ORCH./Aladdin 3165
••• Blues for Anna Bacoa
••• September Song
CHRISTINE KITTRELL & GAY CROSSE/Republic 7026
••• Gotta Stop Loving You
•• Slave to Love (C. Kittrell)
WINI BROWN/Mercury 70062
••• Can't Stand No More
••• Tear Down the Sky
SCAT MAN CARUTHERS/Recorded in Hollywood 401
••• Easy Money
••• Waiting for My Baby
THE BUCCANEERS/Southern 101
•• Fine Brown Frame
•• Dear Ruth

New Spiritual Releases

SISTER ROSETTA THARPE/Decca 28557
•••• I Just Couldn't Be Contented
••• How Well Do I Remember
BRO. JOE MAY & SALLIE MARTIN SINGERS/Specialty 841
••• Working on the Building
••• It's a Long, Long Way
THE GLORY TONE SINGERS/Tuxedo 2502
••• In the Wilderness
••• Leaning on the Everlasting Arm
THE RADIO FOUR/Republic 7018
•• Help Me to Run This Race
•• Never Too Late

Week of February 14

Buy o' the Week

Train, Train, Train—Danny Overbea—Checker 768
Not yet received in many parts of the country. Where it has been received (with the exception of Cincinnati) it is showing real signs of activity. Chicago reports say strong, as does St. Louis and Tennessee. Action beginning in New York. Flip is "I'll Wait."

Territorial Tips

DETROIT
Person to Person--Eddie Vinson--King 4582
PHILADELPHIA
Let Me Go Home Whiskey--Amos Milburn--Aladdin 3164

New R.&B. Releases

VARETTA DILLARD/Savoy 884
•••• Three Lies
••• Getting Ready for My Daddy
THE VOCALEERS/Red Robin 113
•••• Be True
••• Oh! Where
THE FIVE BILLS/Brunswick 84002
••• Till I Waltz Again with You
•• Can't Wait for Tomorrow
THE RAVENS/Mercury 70060
••• Don't Mention My Name
••• I'll Be Back
GAYLE BROWN/Brunswick 84003
••• Gone Are the Days
•• Gee Baby
LITTLE ESTHER/Federal 12115
••• Hollerin' and Screamin'
••• Turn the Lamps Down Low (Little Esther-Little Willie)
THE FIVE KEYS/Aladdin 3167
••• Come Go My Bail Louise
•• Can't Keep From Crying
THE DU DROPPERS/Red Robin 108
••• Can't Do Sixty No More
•• Chain Me Baby
TAMPA RED/Victor 20-5134
••• Too Late Too Long
••• All Mixed Up Over You
ELMORE NIXON/Mercury 70061
••• Playboy Blues
••• Million Dollar Blues
TERRY TIMMONS/Victor 20-5163
••• Please Don't Leave Me Now
••• My Heart Belongs to Only You
MEMPHIS SLIM/Mercury 70063
••• Drivin' Me Mad
••• Train Is Comin'
THE ORIOLES/Jubilee 5107
••• I Miss You So
••• Till Then
LITTLE SYLVIA & HEYWOOD HENRY ORCH./Savoy 873
••• It's a Good Good Morning
••• Bump, Bump, Bump (Heywood Henry Orch.)
FREDDIE WASHINGTON ORCH./Atlas 1026
••• 8-9-10 (vo. June Davis)
••• Two Faced Woman (vo. June Davis)
PETE (GUITAR) LEWIS/Federal 12112
••• The Blast
•• Chocolate Pork Chop Man

New Spiritual Releases

THE KINGS OF HARMONY/Tuxedo 2507
••• Rushing In
••• Someday, Somewhere
THE ORIGINAL HARMONETTES/Specialty 839
•• He's Right on Time
•• I Shall Know Him

Week of February 21

Buy o' the Week

Blues for Anna Bacoa—Lynn Hope—Aladdin 3165
Tho movement does not indicate smash potential, reports from such spots as Philadelphia, Buffalo, the Carolinas and Los Angeles show it to be a good mover both at the retail and operator level. There's jazz business in this disk, too. Flip is "September Song."

Territorial Tips

DETROIT
Hold Me, Thrill Me, Kiss Me--Orioles --Jubilee 5108
ATLANTA
I Dare You, Baby--Percy Mayfield--Specialty 451

New R.&B. Releases

EMITT SLAY TRIO/Savoy 886
•••• My Kind of Woman
••• Brotherly Love
JOHN GREER/Victor 20-5170
•••• You Played on My Piano
••• I'll Never Let You Go
FLOYD DIXON & JOHNNY MOORE'S THREE BLAZERS/Aladdin 3166
••• Broken Hearted Traveler
••• You Played Me for a Fool

Record Roundup
(Continued from previous page)

ANNISTEEN ALLEN ORCH./King 4608
••• Yes, I Know
•• Baby I'm Doin' It
IKE CARPENTER ORCH./Aladdin 3172
••• Sandu
••• Pachuko Hop
RED CALLENDER SEXTETTE/
Victor 20-5172
••• Hollywood Drive
••• Early Times
LINCOLN CHASE/Victor 20-5173
••• I've Got You Under My Skin
•• The Vulture Song
BROWNIE McGHEE/Red Robin 111
••• Don't Dog Your Woman
•• Daisy
BIG BOY CRUDUP/Victor 20-5167
••• Keep On Drinkin'
••• Nelvina
ERSKINE HAWKINS/King 4597
••• Fair Weather Friend (vo. Lou Elliott)
••• The Way You Look Tonight
THE ORIOLES & BUDDY LUCAS
ORCH./Jubilee 5108
••• Teardops on My Pillow
••• Hold Me, Thrill Me, Kiss Me
SONNY THOMPSON/King 4595
••• Chloe
•• Last Night (vo. Lula Reed)
SKIPPY BROWN/Chance 1129
•• So Many Days
•• Tale of Woe

Week of February 28

Buy o' the Week

Baby I'm Doing It—Annisteen Allen—King 4608
In the growing trend of answers to current top hits, this disk broke wide open this week. It's strong in Detroit, Chicago, St. Louis, Cincinnati and the south. Flip is also an answer, "Yes I Know."

Buy o' the Week

Crawlin' b/w Yes It's You—Clovers—Atlantic 989
Shapes up as another big one for the group, and it looks like a good two-sider. "Crawlin'" has the edge in New York, New Orleans and Baltimore-Washington. Other key Southern points plus Chicago are selling "Yes It's You."

Territorial Tips
NEW ORLEANS
Crawlin'--Clovers--Atlantic 989
PHILADELPHIA
You're Mine--Crickets--MGM 11428

Dear Ruth--Buccaneers--Southern 101
CHICAGO
24 Hours--Eddie Boyd--Chess 1533
ST. LOUIS
Woke Up This Morning--B.B. King --
RPM 380

New R.&B. Releases
THE CLOVERS/Atlantic 989
•••• Crawlin'
•••• Yes, It's You
SONNY BOY WILLIAMSON/
Trumpet 166
•••• Nine Below Zero
••• Mighty Long Time
SONNY TIL/Jubilee 5112
••• Have You Heard
••• Lonely Wine
THE CRICKETS/MGM 11428
••• You're Mine
••• Milk and Gin
EDNA McGRIFF & BUDDY LUCAS
ORCH./Jubilee 5109
••• Why, Oh Why
••• Edna's Blues
THE THREE DUKES/Triple A 2505
••• Hey, Mrs. Jones
••• The Duke's Boogie
HADDA BROOKS/Okeh 6939
••• When I Leave the World Behind
••• Brooks Boogie
TITUS TURNER/Okeh 6938
••• My Plea
•• It's Too Late Now
BUDDY LUCAS ORCH./Jubilee 5111
••• Organ Grinder's Swing
••• Laura

R.&B. Beat
(Continued from page 18)

for Mercury, and the Doziers with Columbia and Chess. Simpkins reports the Dozier Boys' first United slicing, "I Keep Thinking of You" has already begun to click in the pop field.... Paul Williams' first waxing for Norman Granz' JATP label will be released by Mercury Records next week.... Little Walter and Eddie Boyd complete their Texas one-nighter tour February 11, and then do a two-week trek thru the South. After that both warblers return to Chicago.

HEARD IN HOLLYWOOD: The Bihari brothers, who head the Modern and RPM diskeries, have added another new label, Music Masters. Platters will be semi-microgroove and will contain four tunes instead of the usual two.... Savannah Churchill opens at the Club Alabam in Los Angeles on February 26 for two weeks.... Central Record Sales, headed by Jim Warren, has announced the opening of its new and larger facilities at 2102 West Washington Blvd., Los Angeles. New firm will handle the distribution of the Okeh and Plymouth lines, in addition to others expected to be added in the near future. Features of the new headquarters include two new three-speed phonographs equipped with twelve-inch Concert-Tone speakers, tiled floors, a battery of eight giant fluorescent lighting fixtures, formica counters and rest rooms for the firm's patrons.

EARL HOOKER TRIO/King 4600
••• Race Track
•• Blue Guitar Blues
TODD RHODES ORCH./King 4601
••• Lost Child (vo. LaVerne Baker)
•• Thunderbolt Boogie
BEULAH BRYANT/MGM 11427
••• Bed Bug Blues
••• Fat Mama Blues
MILLIE BOSMAN/MGM 11429
••• Dream Street
•• You Ain't Had No Blues
SMOKEY HOGG/Federal 12117
••• Your Little Wagon
••• Penny Pinching Mama
JAMES WILLIAMSON/Chance 1131
••• The Woman I Love
•• Homesick
LOU BLACKWELL/Chance 1130
••• I'm Blue Without You
•• How Blue the Night
BIG JOHN BOUIE/Ember 100
•• Stump Juice
•• Deep Deep Sleep
AL (TENOR SAX) KING/MGM 11430
•• Royal Crown Blues
•• Big Wind

Prestige Inks Billy Valentine

NEW YORK, Feb. 28—Prestige Records has announced the pacting of Billy Valentine, the young chanter who rose to fame when his waxings of "Walkin' Blues" and "New Drifting Blues" with Johnny Moore's Three Blazers achieved national popularity, to an exclusive recording contract.

(Continued on next page)

ATLANTIC'S CLOVERS "CRAWLIN'" TOWARD SIXTH STRAIGHT HIT

NEW YORK, March 7—The Clovers, Atlantic Records' sizzling hot rhythm and blues vocal group, continued their unbroken string of hits this week when their latest disking, "Crawlin'" hit the national best-selling R.&B. record charts. This marks the sixth straight time that the group has made the charts, a rarity in a field where artists most often find it difficult to follow-up even one hit. This accomplishment is even more impressive when one considers that three of the Clovers' smashes have been of the double-sided variety, instead of merely one-sided hits.

The strength of the group in R.&B. circles is pointed up by the fact that every cutting they have released to date has sold more than 175,000 copies, and a number of their disks have gone well over the 200,000 mark, a figure that would have been respectable enough even in the pop field. In addition, nearly half a dozen of the tunes done by the group have been re-waxed by pop artists or bands after the Clovers made the tunes hits via the R.&B. market.

The list of tunes cut by the Clovers which have made the best-selling charts include the following: "Don't You Know I Love You," "Fool, Fool, Fool" (also cut by Kay Starr), "One Mint Julep" (also done by Buddy Morrow), "In the Middle of the Night," "Ting-a-Ling," "Wonder Where My Baby's Gone," "Hey, Miss Fannie" and "I Played the Fool" (also sliced by Bill Darnell). Their latest offering, "Crawlin'" and "Yes, It's You," has sold close to 100,000 copies since being released three weeks ago.

Two years ago the four voices and the guitar which make up the group were unknown kids in Washington, D.C. Their first Atlantic waxing, "Don't You Know I Love You," was issued in early 1951, and was so strong that no follow-up was issued by the label until five months later, when "Fool, Fool, Fool" was released.

MODERN SHELLS OUT FOR MASTERS

HOLLYWOOD, March 21—Modern Records paid $5,000 this week for eight masters from Class Records, new r.&b. diskery recently started by Leon Rene.

Sides purchased include "Honey Jump," a tune penned by Rene and his son Rafael with the Oscar McLollie ork, and "That's All," "The Boomerang," "Rain," and "You Can't Bring Me Down," all with the McLollie crew, and a Jimmy Lunceford ork cutting of "When the Swallows Come Back to Capistrano," which was taken from a ballroom concert tape.

Modern also took over the contract of the McLollie band with the acquisition of the masters.

Prestige Inks
(Continued from previous page)

Born in Birmingham, Ala., in 1926, Valentine attended school in that city until he was called into the navy at the age of 17. Following his discharge, he returned to Birmingham to attend Moorehouse College, where he made several recordings at jam sessions. One of these recordings came to the attention of the owner of a local radio station, who liked what he heard so much that he gave the young singer his own daily show on WBGE, on which Valentine appeared for two years while attending school.

BILLY VALENTINE

After graduation, Billy decided to try his luck as a bandleader, organizing a group known as the Harlem Nighthawks. After touring the country, the band broke up and Billy left with one of the members of his band for Ft. Worth, Texas. This Texas jaunt proved to be the turning point in Valentine's career, for it was here that he shortly received a call from Johnny Moore, who asked him to replace Charles Brown with the Three Blazers. The rest, of course, is history.

Valentine's first session for Prestige was cut recently in New York and the chanter's first release for the label, "I Wanta Love You" and "Gamblin' Men," will be released shortly.

BASIE-MOONDOG UNIT PLAYS OHIO DATES

AKRON, O., Feb. 28—The swinging Count Basie orchestra plus singer Danny Overbea and the Moonglows drew 2,468 at the Akron Armory Friday (20). Same package followed with a 2,244 draw at Stanbaugh Auditorium, Youngstown, O., on Saturday (21).

The "Moondog" radio show was included in the unit, which is produced by Alan Freed of Canton. Package is planning a tour of several midwestern and Ontario arenas and auditoriums.

Sun Record Label Launched in Memphis

MEMPHIS, Tenn., March 14—A new indie rhythm and blues label, Sun Records, was launched here recently. The outfit is headed by Jim Bulleit and Sam Phillips.

Both Bulleit and Phillips have quite a background in the disk business. Bulleit is currently bossman of J.B. Records and Bulleit Records, while Phillips has worked with Modern, Chess and other labels. He scouted, recorded and presented to the public such outstanding artists as Jackie Brenston, B.B. King, Howlin' Wolf, Joe Hill Louis, Roscoe Gordon, Wilie Nix and many others.

The Sun company plans to give every opportunity to untried artists to prove their talents, whether they play a broom stick or the finest jazz sax in the world. First releases were issued February 15 and already one of these, "Seems Like a Million Years," has stirred up action in Chicago and looks like a real blues money-maker.

Notes from the R.&B. Beat

THE SHOW MUST GO ON: Billy Ward's Dominoes, whose harmony and sock showmanship keeps them in demand week in and week out, were called upon to perform some new heroics this week. Reports had been trickling in that the Sugar Ray Robinson-Louis Armstrong package which had been touring the Midwest was doing some disappointing biz and that a hypo was sorely needed. Joining the Robinson-Armstrong show at the Fox Theater, Detroit, the Dominoes managed to turn the house topside down at every performance. In one instance Armstrong himself was stalled in the wings for five minutes while stagehands frantically replaced Billy Ward's piano on stage so the group could return for a fifth encore. The audience put on such a stormy demonstration that owner David Lidzell had to go out and plead with the crowd to allow the show to continue. Booking agent Joe Glaser, in town to catch the proceedings, called the demonstrations "something which happens to an act once in a lifetime."

Ruth Brown, whose fabulous career seems dogged with ill-fortune, almost didn't get off on the current tour with Billy Eckstine. Two days before she was due to start on the road, the energetic Ruth was taken with the urge to do some spring cleaning. All went well up to the handing of new curtains. During this phase, Ruth took a nasty fall and sustained a fractured foot. In spite of this, she reported for rehearsals and took off with Mr. B. for a Southern one-nighter swing.... Freddie Cole, the "Crown Prince" of the family which has a "King" called Nat, this week inked a long-term booking pact with the Shaw Artists Corporation. Freddie plays piano and sings in a manner all his own which resembles Nat's technique only slightly. Initial bookings at top clubs are already set for April.... Joe Morris adds a new blues singer to his Cavalcade, "Rev." Stringbeans from New Orleans.... Atlantic has announced the signing of singer-guitarist Chuck Norris to a wax pact.... Chance Records, Chicago waxery, has inked Big Boy Spires, country blues warbler formerly with Chess, and the Al Smith orchestra to disking pacts.

ANSWER ME THIS: The so-called "answer" record craze is still going strong in the r.&b. field. This week a new diskery came out with an answer to Peacock's smash waxing of "Hound Dog" with thrush Willie Mae Thornton. "Hound Dog" was released only about three weeks ago and has turned out to be one of the fastest-breaking hits in recent years. It has already popped into the best-selling r.&b. charts. The answer to "Hound Dog" comes from Sun Records, Memphis, Tenn., diskery, a wild thing called "Bear Cat" sung by Rufus Thomas Jr. It used to be that the answers to hits usually waited until the hit had started on the downward trail, but today the answers are ready a few days after records start moving upwards. This has led some to remark that the diskeries soon may be bringing out the answers before the originals are even released! Elsewhere in the field, Ruth Brown's latest smash waxing for Atlantic, "Mama, He Treats Your Daughter Mean," has called for one answer already, with two more in the offing. Gotham Records has just released "Papa, She Treats Your Son So Mean" with Benny Brown. Recorded in Hollywood and Rainbow Records have also prepped answers to the waxing. Another disk that broke wide open is "Baby, Don't Do It," the Apollo etching by the "5" Royales. After this disk was obviously a blazing success, King Records submitted its follow-up, "Baby, I'm Doing It" by Annisteen Allen. This bit follows on the heels of the many answers to "I Don't Know" spurred by the great success of the Willie Mabon slicing on Chess.

Savoy Records prexy Herman Lubinsky stopped off at Memphis, Tenn., on his way back from the Coast and ran into Joe, Jules and Les Bihari of Modern Records, and Irving Marcus of Duke. With Modern racking up sales with B.B. King's "You Know I Love You," Duke coining heavy with Earl Forest's "Whoopin' and Hollerin'" and Johnny Ace's "Cross My Heart," and Savoy hot with Emitt Slay's "My Kind of Woman," the colorful Hollywoodian expletives must have been something to be-

(Continued on next page)

Mesners, Toombs Unveil 7-11 Label

HOLLYWOOD, March 7—7-11 Records, newly informed subsid of Aladdin Records, broke with their first release here this past week, with advance orders indicating an excellent start for the label.

The firm issued two pairings, "Cheap Old Wine and Whiskey" and "I Need You, I Want You" by Jack Parker; and "Gomen Nasai" and "Volcano" by the Jets.

Firm's principals include Rudy Toombs, well-known song scribe, Eddie Mesner, artist and repertoire director for Aladdin Records, and Leo Mesner, prexy of the Aladdin label.

FORMER RAY-O-VACS SINGER DEAD AT 33

NEW YORK, Feb. 28—Les Harris, 33, RCA Victor r.&b. artist, and a former member of the Ray-O-Vacs group, died after a prolonged illness at the City Hospital, Newark, N.J., Wednesday (25). He had entered the hospital seven weeks ago with pneumonia, and a week ago complications set in.

Born in nearby Hackensack, N.J., Harris began his disk career some years ago. His first records with the Ray-O-Vacs were with the Coleman label. Decca soon signed the group where it had such disk successes as "Besame Mucho." Less than a year ago Harris split from the group to sign a recording contract with RCA Victor. His current disk of "The Bull Walked Around, Olay" has stirred considerable territorial action and has been cut by three pop labels.

Harris is survived by his wife, his mother and a sister.

4 BUDDIES BACK TO WAX WHIRL

NEWARK, N.J., March 7—The Four Buddies, once one of the top money-earning groups of the Savoy Records stable, were back in the recording studio recently with saxist Hal (Cornbread) Singer following the recovery of several of the group's members from a long illness.

One of the tunes sliced, titled "Ooh-Ow" has the Savoy execs excited, as they feel it has the hit potential of another "My Kind of Woman," current click on the label by the Emitt Slay Trio.

R.&B. Beat
(Continued from previous page)

hold.... The Buffalo Booking Agency has pacted the Deuces of Rhythm, the Tempo Toppers Quartet and Little Richard.... Willie Mae Thornton, who has a big one on Peacock with "Hound Dog" is on a one-nighter trek with warbler Johnny Ace and his ork.... Buffalo Booking's Evelyn Johnson was given a surprise party in Houston, Texas recently by Lloyd ("Lawdy Miss Clawdy") Price, Gatemouth Brown, Marie Adams, B.B. King and the staff of her office. Occasion marked the third anniversary of her entry into the booking biz.... Varetta Dillard, Wynonie Harris and Larry Darnell are the latest package set for a long string of one-nighters on the road. The unit will play thru the South for two months.... The Joe Loco ork was booked into the Hi-Hat Club in Boston, starting next week, by Shaw Artists.

Jack Angel, former owner of the Craft

Record Pressing Corporation for five years, and with a background of nine years in the disk business, announced the formation of a new diskery tagged Ember Records. Angel has already released several disks.... The Marylanders, on the strength of their latest Jubilee release, "Good Old 99," have been booked into the Royal Theater, Baltimore, for a week, to be followed by a series of one-nighters in the South.... Joan Shaw (Coral) endured a mishap last week when her truck, which has been built to act as her wardrobe and dressing room, turned over when passing thru Rockford, Alabama. The chirp went on anyway, performing in slacks, and did a bang-up job.... Atlanta's Royal Peacock club signed the Little Esther-H-Bomb Ferguson unit for March 27-29....RCA Victor's Big John

LITTLE ESTHER

Greer takes his new seven-piece combo out for two weeks, beginning in Hartford, Conn., March 6.... Paul Van Loan, formerly of the Ravens group, will perform as a single.... Paul Livert's band inked for Harlem's Press Ball in October at the Dawn Casino.... Duke Hampton, who heads that very versatile boy-girl musical combo, set the best record ever at Harlem's Apollo when he played two spectacular appearances, plus a midnite benefit show.

Hampton will play a return engagement at the Cotton Club, Cincinnati, March 30 for two weeks with vocalist Wini Brown.... Ivory "Deek" Watson will leave the Charlie Fuqua Ink Spots for Bill Kenny's version of that group shortly. Watson's replacement will be Antoine Leon.... Eddie Boyd's newest Chess release, "24 Hours," indicates he must be visiting a numerologist. Boyd's initial click, of course, was titled "Five Long Years".... Larry Darnell beseiged by bobby-soxers backstage at Harlem's Apollo last week, so much so that local gendarmes had to be called in to calm the disturbance.

Linda Hayes, whose "Yes, I Know" on the Recorded in Hollywood label, is one of the big platters of the new year, is set for the Apollo Theater, New York, for the week of March 13. This marks the singer's first appearance in the East. Miss Hayes then teams up with the Lynn Hope ork for three days of one-nighters from April 5 to 8, playing the Washington area....Fats Domino is heading for California. The singer opens at the 5-4 Ballroom on March 27 for a three-day stay.... Valleydale Music has picked up the copyright for "Train, Train, Train," a new ditty coming up via the Danny Overbea waxing on Checker, and already covered for the pop market by the Buddy Morrow orch.... Bill Beasley announces that his Republic label is taking over several masters formerly released on Tennessee Records.... Ben DeCosta's Arthur Prysock-Marie Adams-Edgar Blanchard package recently blazed through Texas, turning in a $6,850 gross in seven days.... Aladdin Records' star Peppermint

Harris and his Blues and Rhythm Show of '53, featuring Jay Franks' Orch., Jimmie Lee and Jo-Jo Brown, is due for a one-nighter tour thru the South in early March.

JOCKEY JIVE: Jack Walker, who does publicity for Atlantic Records and Shaw Artists, has taken over the midnight deejay show from the Palm Gardens, New

BRYANT AND CARROLL

York, over station WOV each night. The show is called "Life Begins at Midnight." Ralph Cooper used to handle the seg.... WHOM's Willie Bryant and Ray Carroll will feature the Top 20 r.&b. tunes every Saturday at 12 midnight from their new perch at the Birdland club, New York. Willie turned down a lucrative Coast offer to take this job.... Hal Jackson, r.&b. deejay over WMCA, New York, is running stage-shows on week-ends at the Northwest Casino, Washington. He has Floyd Dixon and Margie Day set for March 13-14 and Ruth Brown is set for April 3-4.... Jockey Jack's "Jockey Club" is now being beamed five hours daily from WMBM, Miami Beach.... Bill Cook's "Musical Caravan" on WAAT, Newark, N.J., has been extended an additional hour, and is now aired daily 9 p.m. to midnight.... Clarence Hamann, WJMR, New Orleans, and Larry Regan, WTPS, same city, are making plans for a trip to New York the end of June.

The Babs Gonzales orch. was pacted by Shaw Artists last week. The crew will play the Ebony Club, Cleveland, March 9 to 15.... The Billy Eckstine-Ruth Brown-Count Basie tour, which started on a six-week one-nighter trip two weeks ago, has racked up strong grosses to date on its road trek. At Atlanta this week, the doors had to be closed at 8:45 and over 2,000 fans were turned away at the doors. After the Eckstine-Brown-Basie tour is over, the warbler and the thrush, with Johnny Hodges, Timmie Rodgers and Coles and Atkins, will play a week at the Circus for Underprivileged Children, the annual fund-raising affair for the benefit of the Negro YMCA in St. Louis on April 27. This is the first appearance of Eckstine and Ruth Brown at the "Y" Circus.... Charles Brown starts off on a tour on March 30, opening at Lubbock, Tex., and winding up in Tulsa, Okla., on April 25. Every day is booked for the Brown trip.... Floyd Dixon and Margie Day will star at the Carolina Ball, to be held at the Hunt's Point Palace, New York, March

21.... Henry Stone, of Rockin' and Glory Records, was in Chicago last week to visit jocks.... Teddy Reig, now with Shaw Artists in the location department, just waxed four tunes for Roost Records with Sonny Stitt.... The Five Royales are playing to S.R.O. crowds at Top Hat club, Dayton, O., with Hal Singer due into the same spot April 6.... Farm Dell Club, Dayton, has Sonny Thompson booked for April 14. It will be the first time that Sonny's missed a Dodger opener in years. Willis Jackson moves into the Farm Dell on April 20.

Milt Buckner and his bouncy combo opened at the Club Afrique, Washington, D.C., on February 24, in place of the Johnny Hodges crew, who were originally skedded, but changed plans and opened at the Spa in Baltimore instead. Trombonist Lawrence Brown and trumpeter Emmett Berry are two of the ex-Ellingtonites who joined forces with Hodges when he broke away from the big orchestra a couple of years ago.... The Clovers will go on a one-nighter tour thru Florida after they finish their present Southern tour. Then the group heads for Texas and California. The Choker Campbell ork will accompany the group.... Bill Cook, deejay over WAAT, Newark, N.J., is now managing Little Mr. Blues, Rainbow recording artist.... Rainbow Records has added Duke Anderson's All Stars to its r.&b. stable.... Gotham Records' Andrea music subsidiary has changed affiliations from Broadcast Music, Inc., to SESAC.

PHILLY FLASHES: Charlie Gaines gets the call at the Germantown Tavern.... Rene Hall's now made it a quintet instead of a trio and last week played to capacity crowds at Philly's Powelton Cafe.... The Jackie Davis Trio is back in town this week at Emerson's Grille.... Chris Powell and The Five Blue Flames come back at the Showboat, with Joe Morris set for a return trip in the same boite starting March 30.... New floor space addition to Pep's Music Bar, Philadelphia, will be known as the Terrace Room, opening up this week with the Milt Buckner Trio and Cecil Young's Quartet.

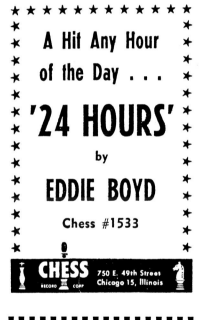

March's Record Roundup

Week of March 7

Buy o' the Week

Whoopin' and Hollerin'—Earl Forest—Duke 108
Out several weeks and just recently beginning to get some action. It's hot currently in Cincinnati, St. Louis and has been good for a number of weeks on the West Coast. it's just beginning to start in New York and in some Southern areas. Judging from the number of reports that had not heard about the record, there's still plenty of life ahead for it.

New R.&B. Releases

LINDA HAYES & RED CALLENDER ORCH./Recorded in Hollywood 407
•••• Atomic Baby
••• What's It to You, Jack
RAY CHARLES/Swing Time 326
•••• Misery in My Heart
••• The Snow Is Falling
OSCAR McLOLLIE ORCH./Class 501
••• You Can't Bring Me Down (vo. Paul Clifton)
••• The Honey Jump
PEE WEE CRAYTON & RED CALLENDER SEXTET/Recorded in Hollywood 408
••• Crying and Walking
••• Pappy's Blues
THE FIVE BUDDS/Rama 1
••• Midnight
••• I Was Such a Fool (To Fall in Love with You)
JIMMY WITHERSPOON/Federal 12118
••• Jimmy's Blues (Parts 1 & 2)
LLOYD GLENN/Swing Time 324
••• It Moves Me
••• Night Time
LITTLE CAESAR/Recorded in Hollywood 238
••• Do Right Blues
••• Your Money Ain't Long Enough
EARL BOSTIC ORCH./King 4603
••• Steamwhistle Jump
••• The Sheik of Araby
MAURICE SIMON'S ORCH./Recorded in Hollywood 404
••• I Don't Know Why
••• Big Apple Hop
LOWELL FULSON/Swing Time 325
••• Let Me Ride Your Little Automobile
•• Upstairs
STUMP AND STUMPY/MGM 11444
••• Loud Woman
••• Two-Thirds Dead

JULIAN DASH/Mercury 70087
••• Fire Water
•• Deacon Dash

New Spiritual Releases

THE SOUL STIRRERS/Aladdin 2037
••• My Journey to the Sky
••• Does Jesus Care?
THE ZION TRAVELERS/Aladdin 2036
••• Charge to Keep I Have
••• Need You, Lord
THE TRUMPETEERS/Score 5033
••• Run On
••• Live the Life I Sing About
THE SIMMONS-AKERS TRIO/Score 5018
••• Open Up the Pearly Gates
•• I Want a Double Portion of God's Love
SILVERETTE GOSPEL SINGERS/Hi-Lo 1417
••• I Want to Join the Band
••• Jesus Is Mine
REV. WM. MORRIS O'NEIL/Hi-Lo 1418
•• Stand By Me
•• My Expectations

Week of March 14

Buy o' the Week

24 Hours—Eddie Boyd—Chess 1533
Buffalo, L.A., Chicago and St. Louis reported sales jumps during the week. Also on several territorials. Only negative report received from those who had record in stock came from Philadelphia. Shaping up as a big one. Flip is "The Tickler."

Territorial Tips

CHARLOTTE
Hurry Hurry Baby--Roy Brown--King 4602
Nobody Loves Me--Fats Domino--Imperial 5220
NEW YORK
You're Mine--Crickets--MGM 11428
ST. LOUIS
Don't You Remember, Baby--Roy Milton --Specialty 455
ATLANTA
I Believe--Elmore James--Meteor 5000

New R.&B. Releases

WILLIE MAE THORNTON/Peacock 1612
•••• Hound Dog
••• Night Mare

EDDIE BOYD/Chess 1533
•••• 24 Hours
••• The Tickler
JOHNNY MOORE'S 3 BLAZERS/Rhythm & Blues 100
•••• I Don't Know Yes I Know (vo. Mari Jones-Lex-Nelson)
••• Too Bad (vo. Mari Jones)
B.B. KING ORCH./RPM 380
•••• Woke Up This Morning
••• Don't Have to Cry
GRANT (MR. BLUES) JONES/States 114
•••• Stormy Monday
••• Heartache Blues
KENZIE MOORE/Specialty 456
••• Don't Know Why
••• Let It Lay
ROY MILTON ORCH./Specialty 455
••• Don't You Remember, Baby?
••• Someday
THE FLAMINGOS/Chance 1133
••• Someday, Someway
••• If I Can't Have You
SLIM GAILLARD/Mercury 89031
••• Gomen Nasai
••• Potato Chips
FRANK MOTLEY/Specialty 454
••• Frantic
••• Heavy Weight Baby (vo. Jimmy Crawford)
JIMMY RUSHING/King 4606
••• Somebody's Spoiling These Women
••• She's Mine, She's Yours
CARL GREEN ORCH./Meteor 5002
••• My Best Friend
••• Four Years, Seven Days
MANZY HARRIS ORCH./Rockin' 506
••• You're Gonna Know (vo. Harold Young)
••• Crawlin' Around (vo. Harold Young)
ROOSEVELT WARDELL/Rockin' 508
••• Lost My Woman
•• So Undecided
JIMMY LEE AND ARTIS/Modern 899
••• All Right Baby
••• Why Do You Make Me Feel Blue?
EDDIE BOYD/J.O.B. 1009
••• It's Miserable to Be Alone
•• I'm Pleading
GAY CROSSE/Republic 7027
••• Easy Rockin'
••• G.C. Rock
JOHNNY SHINES/J.O.B. 1010
••• Evening Sun
••• Brutal-Hearted Woman
YOUNG JOHN WATSON/Federal 12120
••• No, I Can't
••• Highway 60
STICKS McGHEE/King 4610
•• Little Things We Used to Do
•• Head Happy with Wine

New Spiritual Releases

ORIGINAL FIVE BLIND BOYS OF ALABAMA/Specialty 842
•••• When I Lost My Mother
••• Oh Lord--Stand By Me
REV. A. JOHNSON/Glory 4011
••• God Don't Like It
••• If I Could Hear My Mother Pray Again
THE SOUTHERN WONDERS/Peacock 1711
••• There Is Rest for the Weary
••• The Gambling Man

Week of March 21

Buy o' the Week

Nine Below Zero b/w Mighty Long Time—Sonny Boy Williamson—Trumpet 166
Reported on the Atlanta chart with several other Southern areas showing good action. L.A. and Chicago were strong. Most reports favor "Nine Below Zero."

Buy o' the Week

Steam Whistle Jump b/w Shiek of Araby—Earl Bostic—King 4608
Gathering momentum in L.A. and Chicago, with good sales reported in Cincinnati, Buffalo and Philadelphia. Both sides moving in last named.

Buy o' the Week

So Long b/w What's the Matter Now?—Lloyd Price—Specialty 457
Off to a quick start. Southern reports are good. Also in Chicago, Philadelphia and L.A. Washington, D.C. favors flip.

Buy o' the Week

You're Mine—The Crickets—MGM 11428
Strength scattered. The disk is strongest in New York, Philadelphia, Washington, Baltimore, Chicago and the South. Buffalo and Cincinnati reports just fair.

Territorial Tips

NEW YORK
Red Top--King Pleasure--Prestige 821
PHILADELPHIA
Red Top--King Pleasure--Prestige 821
ST. LOUIS
Whoopin' and Hollerin'--Earl Forest--Duke 108
NEW ORLEANS
Hound Dog--Willie Mae Thornton--Peacock 1612

New R.&B. Releases

LLOYD PRICE/Specialty 457
•••• So Long
••• What's the Matter Now?
SHIRLEY AND LEE/Aladdin 3173
••• Shirley, Come Back to Me
••• Baby
PIANO RED/Victor 20-5224
••• I'm Gonna Tell Everybody
••• She's Dynamite
JIMMY FORREST/United 145
••• Mrs. Jones' Daughter
••• Mr. Goodbeat
JACK PARKER ORCH./7-11 2100
••• I Need You, I Want You (vo. Emmett Davis)
••• Cheap Old Wine and Whiskey (vo. Emmett Davis)
MR. SAD HEAD/Victor 20-5230
••• Hard Luck and Traveling
••• I'm High
TERRY TIMMONS/Victor 20-5227
••• He's the Best in the Business
••• Evil-Eyed Woman
MAXWELL DAVIS/Aladdin 3174
••• Hot Point
••• Gomen Nasai
THE ROYALS/Federal 12121
••• I Feel So Blue
•• The Shrine of Saint Cecilia
NAT FOSTER/MGM 11445
••• Lonely Soldier Blues
•• Tall, Tall Woman
TEDDY WILLIAMS/MGM 11446
•• Bar and Grill Blues
•• Why Do You Do Things to Cause Me Sorrow?
THE JETS/7-11 2102
•• Volcano
•• Gomen Nasai
MARI JONES/Recorded in Hollywood 409
•• There Is No Greater Love
•• Drifting Blues
BOOTS BROWN ORCH./Victor 20-5228
•• Breakfast Ball
•• Blue Fairy Boogie
ARDEL CARL/Hi-Lo 1419
•• Morning Blues
• My Mother's Eyes

New Spiritual Releases

THE SOUL STIRRERS/Specialty 845
•••• Blessed Be the Name of the Lord
•••• Jesus Paid the Debt
THE ORIGINAL GOSPEL HARMON-ETTES/Victor 20-5231
••• In the Upper Room
••• He's All I Need
THE SENSATIONAL NIGHTINGALES/Peacock 1709
••• I Thank You, Lord
••• A Sinner's Plea
LITTLE JOE/Brunswick 84005
••• Let Us Pray
•• Will You Be Glad to See Your Son Come Home?

THE GOSPEL PILGRIMETTES OF ATLANTA/Brunswick 84006
••• My Lord Won't Deny Me
•• This Heart of Mine

Week of March 28

Territorial Tips

LOS ANGELES
You're Mine--Crickets--MGM 11428

ATLANTA
Nine Below Zero--Sonny Boy Williamson--Trumpet 166

CHICAGO
Daughter (That's Your Red Wagon)--Sax Kari--States 115

New R.&B. Releases

THE SWALLOWS/King 4612
•••• Laugh (Though You Want to Cry)
••• Our Love Is Dying
SWINGING SAX KARI/States 115
•••• Daughter (That's Your Red Wagon)
••• Down for Debbie
BENNY BROWN/Gotham 293
•••• Pappa
••• Slick Baby
ARNETT COBB ORCH./Mercury 70101
••• Poor Butterfly
••• Congratulations to Someone
TIMMIE ROGERS/Capitol 2406
••• Saturday Night
••• If I Were You, Baby, I'd Love Me
LAZY SLIM JIM/Savoy 887
••• One More Drink
••• Wine Head Baby
ROY BROWN ORCH./King 4609
••• Grandpa Stole My Baby
••• Money Can't Buy Love
CARMEN TAYLOR/Mercury 70105
••• I'm Comin' Back to You
••• Lookin' for You
DORIS BROWNE/Gotham 290
••• Oh, Baby!
••• Please Believe Me
RALPH WILLIS/King 4611
••• Why'd You Do It?
•• Do Right
WILLIE NIX/Sun 179
••• Seems Like a Million Years
•• Baker Shop Boogie
JOE HILL LOUIS/Sun 178
•• She May Be Yours
•• We All Gotta Go Sometime

CLOVERS IN CLOVER NOW; HIT TWO MILLION MARK

NEW YORK, April 11—Atlantic Records honored the Clovers this week as the two millionth copy of their wax work was sold. Each member of the sensational group was presented with a gold record to mark the event.

While in New York to collect their honors, the Clovers will work a session in the Atlantic studio to turn out their spring releases. Johnny Bailey, Matthew McQuater, Hal Lucas, Harold Winley and guitarist Bill Harris are the Clover personnel.

"Record Show" Closes; Nat Cole Hospitalized

New York, April 18—"The Record Show," the Gale Agency package which set forth without the services of Nat Cole, closed Monday (13) after nine performances.

The road unit was originally set with Cole, Sarah Vaughan, the Billy May ork, and supporting acts, but Cole was hospitalized opening night. The Gale Agency tried to get Sugar Chile Robinson to replace the warbler, but were unable to do so, and decided to close the show instead.

Cancellation of "The Record Show" is costly, both to the Gale Agency, and to the promoters who were working on selling the show. Estimates run from $10,000 to $30,000 dropped in prepping and advertising the package for its one-night stands. Cole, who is still hospitalized, is expected to take a long rest in California after he leaves the hospital.

Meanwhile another Gale Agency production, the spring edition of "The Biggest Show of '53" is racking up solid grosses as it wends its way Eastward. Package features Frankie Laine, Ella Fitzgerald, Louis Jordan and the Woody Herman ork. It racked up $15,000 in Milwaukee Saturday (11), $14,000 in Minneapolis Sunday (12), $14,000 in Fort Wayne, Ind., Tuesday (14), and $10,600 in Columbus, Ohio, on Wednesday (15). The Columbus date was the weakest so far, due to bad weather. The show ran into a blizzard in Denver on Friday (10) and did not go on 'til 11 p.m., but 7,000 faithful waited until the performers arrived. There is already $20,000 in the till for the St. Louis engagement, which takes place tonight (18).

Indie Label "Answers" Drawing Fire As More Pubbers Seek Legal Action

NEW YORK, March 28—So-called "answer" records are increasingly becoming targets for lawsuits by publishers in the Rhythm and Blues field.

In an effort to combat what has become a rampant practice by small labels—the rushing out of "answers" which are similar in melody and/or theme to ditties which have become smash hits—many pubbers are now retaining attorneys and some have sought the aid of Harry Fox, publishers' agent and trustee.

Common practice, of course, is to regard the answer as an "original." Currently, however, publishers are putting up a fight to protect their originals from unauthorized or infringing answers. Attorney Lee Eastman has been retained by Republic music to protect that firm against what it considers infringements on "I Don't Know." Republic bought the tune from Chess when that firm's Willie Mabon

(Continued on next page)

Indie "Answers"
(Continued from previous page)

disk began hitting.

Meanwhile another firm, Fred Fisher Music, has retained Jack Pearl to protect against infringements of the copyright of "Mama, He Treats Your Daughter Mean."

Don Robey, Peacock Records' chief, stated this week that he was taking measures to protect his copyright of "Hound Dog," which was waxed by Willie Mae Thornton on Peacock. Robey stated he would follow the case right thru the courts, if necessary. Peacock's publishing affiliate is Lion music.

Republic's "I Don't Know," following Willie Mabon's original on Chess, was recorded via license by Bill Darnell on Decca, Tennessee Ernie on Capitol and Buddy Morrow on Victor. It appeared in answer versions on various labels, including: "Yes I Know" by Linda Hayes on Recorded in Hollywood, "You Can't Bring Me Down" by Oscar McLollie on Class and Little Caesar on Recorded in Hollywood; "I Don't Know—Yes, I Know" by Johnny Moore's Three Blazers on Aladdin.

Answer versions to "Mama," which first clicked on Atlantic via Ruth Brown, include: "Mama Your Daughter's Done Lied on Me" by Wynonie Harris on King; "(Daughter) That's Your Red Wagon," by Gloria Irving on States; "Papa" by Bennie Brown on Gotham and Scat Man Crothers on Recorded in Hollywood; and "Mama, Your Daughter Plays It Cool" by George Terry on Rainbow. Chief answer version to Peacock's "Hound Dog" disk is Rufus Thomas' "Bear Cat" on Sun.

Eastman is co-operating with attorneys on the Coast in an effort to establish the principle that the answers to "I Don't Know" are bastardizations, and tantamount to infringements of the original copyright. "If someone does not stop this practice, it will spread to fields other than rhythm and blues," he added.

The labels which have cut answers have been put on notice and Eastman indicated legal action would be taken promptly if an out-of-court settlement did not materialize. Eastman, by the way, took the lead in "answer" litigation about four months ago when he instituted suit in Southern District Court here on behalf of Lew Chudd's Commodore Music, publishing affiliate of Imperial, which holds the copyright "The Wild Side of Life." Named as defendants, in connection with the answer, titled "It Wasn't God Who Made Honky Tonk Angels" are Peer International, Decca, Columbia and RCA Victor. This case is still pending—with the defendants basing their defense on the contention that "It Wasn't God" isn't an answer.

Don Robey of Peacock this week stated he notified Harry Fox to issue sun a license on "Bear Cat," in order that Robey might

collect a royalty. Robey indicated that Sun was refusing the license. "I will follow thru with a court procedure if they refuse a license," he said.

Previously answer versions on tunes were often assigned to the publisher of the original tune. In the r.&b. field the growing practice has been to consider an answer as safe from claims of infringement. It is likely that with the r.&b. field becoming of such importance to pop publishers, some clarification of the problem will be forthcoming as a result of litigation and disputes now shaping up.

RCA Victor to Market New Record Label Via Indie Distribs

NEW YORK, April 4—RCA Victor will introduce a brand new record label next September, it was reported this week. The new label, as yet unnamed, will be competitive in every field except classical with its parent label, RCA Victor, and will be sold thru independent distributors thruout the country. It will be priced at 89 cents, including federal tax.

The final decision to introduce this new line, called label "X" for the purpose of this story, came this week with the agreement by RCA President Frank Folsom to the proposal submitted by Manie Sachs, recently appointed head of RCA Victor's record department. The project has been classified as top secret within the organization for some weeks while every angle, including all legal aspects, was investigated.

It was reported that organizational plans for the new label are only on paper at this point, but label "X" will operate completely independent of the parent label. It will have its own sales force, recording staff and artist roster. In the artist field, label "X" will bid for established disk names as well as build new record talent.

It is planned that label "X" will also be physically removed from the Victor offices in Radio City. Present thinking favors locating the subsidiary in the company's 24th Street building, where the Victor recording studios are housed. Staffwise, Sachs plans to bring in most, if not all, of the personnel from the outside rather than shift present RCA Victor personnel.

The only agreement reached thus far about the name for label "X" is that it will not be Bluebird. Bluebird has been RCA Victor's subsidiary label for some years, but has always been marketed by regular RCA Victor distributors. The elimination of Bluebird from consideration is believed to be because this label is presently used both for low-priced classic and kiddie records.

The decision by RCA Victor to issue a

(Continued on next page)

Vincent to Head Specialty Southern Branch

HOLLYWOOD, Mar. 28—John Vincent will head Specialty's new Southern office located in Jackson, Miss., it was reported this week. As part of the deal Specialty also acquired Vincent's Champion Records label.

Specialty's purchase of the Champion line, including acquisition of its 20 rhythm and blues and hillbilly masters, presages the label's first major expansion. Vincent, inked by Specialty prexy Art Rupe, will represent the diskery in the south as a distributor, artist and repertoire agent, and record artists in the area. This is the first time Rupe has delegated recording chores to anyone.

There are no plans for continued use of the Champion label, Rupe said. Two of four artists signed by Vincent for Specialty formerly recorded for Champion. They are Joe Dyson, young Jackson college band leader, and Ben Branch of Memphis. Others inked to a year's exclusive Specialty contract, with usual options, are vocalist Kenzie Moore, also of Jackson, and Frankie Lee Sims, Dallas blues singer.

Vincent, in addition to his exclusive duties for Specialty, will act as a roving good-will ambassador among distribs, d.j.'s and retailers. His headquarters, located at 241 North Farish Street, Jackson, bring to three the number of offices Specialty now has, the other two being in Hollywood and Philadelphia.

Vincent has been in the disk business for the past six years. He originally was with Allen Distributors, then went to Delta Music Sales, both New Orleans, before operating his own Griffin Distributing Company in Jackson. Griffin is now inactive.

VICTOR OFFICIALS MULL 2 NEW LABELS, 1 R.&B.

NEW YORK, April 18—RCA Victor is reportedly mulling the introduction of two new labels, one to be exclusively concerned with rhythm and blues records, the other, sponsored by RCA Victor's custom pressing division, would deal solely with jazz LP reissues from old RCA Victor masters.

These developments come in the wake of news that active work on label "X" is set to begin Monday (20), when Joe Carlton takes over as a&r director. Label "X" is an RCA Victor subsidiary which will be wholly owned by RCA Victor but distributed thru independent distributors. In this respect it will be similar to Decca's Coral and Columbia's Okeh.

Meanwhile the proposed r.&b. label, also still without an official name, would substitute for the present RCA Victor line

(Continued on next page)

Victor to Market
(Continued from previous page)

subsidiary label thru independent distributors is a major change for the company, which previously has worked exclusively thru its franchised distributors, but it is a question that has been given close thought sporadically during the last three years. In 1950, for example, serious consideration was given to a label for indie distributors, primarily geared to make the company a stronger factor in the rhythm and blues field.

ECKSTINE, BASIE AND RUTH BROWN ROCK "BAND BOX"

NEW YORK, April 11—Bill Levine's Band Box club is the latest jazz spot on the site of the now defunct Iceland and it's doing a phenomenal business. Caught on a 3 a.m. show on Wednesday, April 8, the room was literally packed. That Billy Eckstine was responsible for the business was obvious, tho the Count Basie band also accounted for some of the draw.

The show started with Basie's outfit rolling and rocking to the roars of approval from audience. If Basie has had a better band in the past, it must have been tremendous, because this one is magnificent.

The moment that Eckstine strolled on, the din became overpowering. It seemed there was nothing he could do that didn't meet with enthusiastic approval. He started off with "Until Eternity" (a Russ Columbo tune), a strange opener where a fast bright number was indicated. Nevertheless, it registered big. Then in rapid succession came "Rhythm in the Riff," "Sophisticated Lady" and "Coquette," his M-G-M disk now breaking out, and he was in by a mile.

For a "surprise" finisher (set up earlier) Eckstine brought on Ruth Brown for a reprise of their concert tour smasheroo song, "I Don't Know," for about 10 verses, and pandemonium broke out. It was one of those nights, and Eckstine took full advantage of it. On stage he was as effective a male singer as there is around today. He phrased his ballads delightfully. When it came to his typical stylings, he had a ready-made audience out front to sell it to. On straight melodic items, or those with off-beats, he was just as competent.

R.&B. artist Ruth Brown was equally superb. Her warm, full voice, her inflections and style deserve considerably more than such a limited audience which is now familiar with her.

The Band Box's capacity is 840 persons. Price policy is $3.50 minimum, with shows scheduled at 10:30, 12 and 3 a.m.

Officials Mull R.&B.
(Continued from previous page)

of r.&b. releases. It would have no effect on label "X," which would have its own r.&b. records, according to an RCA Victor spokesman.

The conception of an exclusive r.&b. line stems from the determination of RCA Victor to throw more emphasis into this field. Should the project receive top level blessing it is reported that the label would operate with a separate a.&r. and sales staff, so that greater concentration could be achieved. Victor's r.&b. operations, both in the a.&r. and sales areas, are now dovetailed with the hillbilly field under the supervision of Steve Sholes and Bob McCluskey, respectively.

Should the label projected by the custom-pressing division materialize, it would be dubbed the Camden label. This would, as previously mentioned, delve into old jazz masters, and be exclusively available on LP.

By drawing on old Victor masters, this label could conceivably compete with both the parent label and label "X." Several weeks ago, for example, George Frazier was appointed to head up special projects for RCA Victor, with part of his responsibilities being to cull the catalog for suitable re-issues. Should Camden be approved, it is believed that Orrin Keepnews and Bill Grauer, owners of the Riverside label and publishers of Record Changer, would be retained as consultants.

THIEVES VICTIMIZE LINDA HAYES

NEW YORK, March 28—Disk star Linda Hayes was robbed of $5,000 worth of clothing, jewelry and musical arrangements here last week as she was preparing to begin a Southern tour.

The "Yes, I Know" gal's belongings were taken in a two-part robbery. The thieves first session was backstage at the Apollo Theater, where Linda had just completed her successful debut to a Gotham audience. They played an encore several hours later by helping themselves to the things she had packed in her automobile.

Most difficult to replace will be the singing star's repertoire of musical arrangements and orchestrations which were the result of months of work and several thousand dollars worth of labor. Her gowns were all chosen with great care under the stagewise advice of Dinah Washington, who has been keenly interested in Linda's budding career.

Despite the unhappy occurrence, Linda was able to leave on schedule for her date in Baltimore.

Federal Adds to R.&B. Roster

LOS ANGELES, April 11—Federal Records' a.&r. director Ralph Bass this week added a flock of new talent to that firm's rhythm and blues artist roster.

Signed to term recording pacts were Camille Howard, Jimmy Nelson, Eleanor Franklin, Happy David and Cecil "Count" Carter. Of the new names signed, Miss Howard is the most prominent, having achieved fame via her waxings for Specialty Records through the years.

PHILLY FANS GO LOCO FOR JOE

PHILADELPHIA, April 11—The tremendous appeal and popularity of Tico Records artist Joe Loco with the younger set in Philadelphia was made evident here this past week.

When Bob Horn, who runs "Bob Horn's Bandstand" show over WFIL-TV, Philadelphia, arranged to have Loco appear on his program, he advertised the fact to his listeners two or three days before the piano stylist's scheduled appearance. One of the top jocks in the Quaker City, Horn features mambos on his show and has built himself quite an audience of Latin tempo fans.

Upon driving up to the WFIL studios with Tico a.&r. head George Goldner, Loco was astounded to find the street literally mobbed with thousands of teeners awaiting his appearance. After the show, Loco spent the remainder of the day signing autographs for the youngsters.

Loco's latest release on Tico is "The Song From the Moulin Rouge" backed with "Can Can Mambo."

INJUNCTION DENIED ON FUQUA'S INK SPOTS

NEW YORK, Mar. 28—A temporary injunction to stop Charles Fuqua and Universal Attractions from using the name "Ink Spots" with his quartet was denied this week when New York Supreme Court Justice Ernest Hammer ruled that there was no ground to issue the injunction requested by the Gale Agency, Inc., in advance of the trial to determine who has the right to the name.

"Ink Spots" title is said to belong to Fuqua and Bill Kenny as a partnership, and according to the plaintiff, they have an exclusive booking contract with Gale to run until July 1954.

Kenny and Fuqua split and latter signed with Universal Attractions, also under the "Ink Spots" title. Kenny and his "Ink Spots" record for Decca.

PROMOTION VETERAN RALPH WEINBERG DIES

NEW YORK, April 4—Ralph Weinberg, a well-known promoter in the rhythm and blues field, died Friday morning (3) while traveling in his car from Columbia, S.C., to Charlotte, N.C. He had been in ill health for the last few months. Weinberg, who was 57 years old, is survived by his widow and his son, Eli. The funeral will be held Sunday (5) at his home in Princeton, W. Va.

Active in the promotion field for about 35 years, Weinberg had handled key sports events, including boxing and wrestling matches during the first decade of his career and turned to music promotions about 20 years ago. Weinberg's tours thru Virginia, West Virginia, North and South Carolina, Georgia and Florida were well-known to jazz units, r.&b. packages and other performers over the last decade. He handled important one-nighter tours for the major booking agencies, his last promotion being the Billy Eckstine-Ruth Brown-Count Basie unit thru the South.

Eli Weinberg, who has been working for his father for the past few years, is expected to continue his father's promotion business.

MIAMI'S RIVIERA REOPENS

MIAMI BEACH, March 28—Bill Miller's Miami Beach Riviera reopened last night after a two-week shutdown and hopes to garner some of the spring business with Larry Steele's "Smart Affairs of 1953."

A cast of 40 includes Butterbeans & Susie, the Three Chocolateers, Flick Montgomery, Olivette Miller, Conrad and Estelle, and a line of girls. Jimmy Tyler's orchestra will handle the bandstanding.

Notes from the R.&B. Beat

"HOUND DOG" CREATING A SENSATION: The attention of tradesters this week is focused on two mighty strong waxings that are slugging it out for top honors in the field. The disks are Ruth Brown's "Mama" on Atlantic, still in the top slot on the juke box chart, and "Hound "Dog" with Willie Mae Thornton on Peacock, which moved to No. 1 on the best-selling chart this week. Not in the longest time has a record hit with such a startling and crashing impact as "Hound Dog." Willie Bryant (WHOM-N.Y.) tells us that the switchboard at the station lit up like Broadway and 42nd Street after one playing on the air. Irv Marcus, Peacock sales manager, has set up three new pressing plants to assist in the production of the record. Jake Friedman of Southland distributors in Atlanta has placed a phenomenal order of 10,000 for the platter. Meanwhile Essex Distribs in Newark report that they can't get away from the phone. Someone is always clogging up the board with orders for the "Hound Dog" side. In just three short weeks, "Hound Dog" has become the top record in five of the most important cities of the blues field. Incidentally, this is the first time in quite a while that the women have led the field with the strongest r.&b. platters. Atlantic has also come thru with another solid hit with the new Clovers slicing of "Crawlin'," which is in the top five on both national r.&b. charts.

Stan Lewis, of Stan's Record Shop down in Shreveport, La., is a little fellow who knows how to draw the big ones down. In the last ten days nine manufacturers dropped into the shop to sell him. Art Rupe and his new addition to the Specialty

LEONARD CHESS

staff, John Imradulio; Joe Bihari of RPM; Leonard Chess, Chess Records; Art Sheridan, Chance; Morty Shad, Sittin' In; a couple of bigwigs from RCA Victor; and Jim Bulleit of the new Sun label, who arrived to chase Willie Mae Thornton's "Hound Dog" with his punchy new answer, "Bearcat" by Rufus Thomas, Jr. .... Bob Weinstock, Prestige mahoff, leaving on a Southern trip to promote King Pleasure's "Red Top" with Charlie Ferguson's tenor sax backing, which has already broken thru in places like New York and Philly.... Ernie Young, prexy of Nashboro and Excello Recording Companies, has just inked two new blues artists who will wax for Excello. They are Del Thorne and her trio and "Little Maxie" Bailey. Ted Adams, assistant manager at The Record Mart, Nashville, reports that Excello waxed a Boyer Brothers session on Thursday, April 2. The group is now holding down the second spot in the Pittsburgh Courier spiritual group poll.

The Emitt Slay Trio, Savoy wax stars, are knocking 'em in the aisles at the Apollo Theater, Harlem. This is no one-disk act that dies on p.a.'s after they dish up their current hit, "My Kind of Woman." Matter of fact, the boys are great on stage. They follow their Apollo stint with dates at the Howard in Washington and then on to the Royal in Baltimore. Lee Magid, Savoy a.&r. man, has a follow-up side planned for the trio's next recording session in a few days.... Margie Day joins the Paul Williams one-nighter unit, May 1.... Amos Milburn will be at the Howard Theater, Washington, from May 15 to 21.... Laverne Baker plays the Palace, Harrisburg, Pa., opening April 6.... Varetta Dillard goes into the Downbeat Club, Providence, R.I., May 4.... Saxster Ben Webster romantically linked with Clara Millinder, ex-Cotton Club beauty. Webster joined the Johnny Hodges group for two JATP sessions and his booming tenor gives the Ellington sound to that group.... Rama Records, new r.&b. indie, has signed the Crows, vocal group, and Viola Watkins, former M-G-M chantress. The Crows were signed after they won in the finals of the Apollo Theater's amateur show. Viola handled the arrangement and direction as the group etched "Seven Lonely Days" and "No Help Wanted," with Miss Watkins singing on the "Lonely" side. George Goldner and Jack Waxman of Tico Records

are busy decorating their new offices which they'll move into shortly. Jack's reportedly in a daze trying to figure out how many golf balls he could've bought with what it's going to cost.

Philadelphians will be able to see thrush Bette McLaurin at Powelton's, beginning April 6.... Erskine Hawkins and his ork open at the Farm Dell, Dayton, O., April 13.... The Freddy Mitchell ork, now waxing for Mercury, has signed with the Gale Agency....Eddie Boyd is now heading out for his first swing thru the East. He will play one-nighters with thrush Linda Hayes, starting in Boston, April 3, and continuing in the territory thru April 26.... The Blenders have been signed by Joe Davis for M-G-M r.&b. waxings. First releases will be rushed out in two weeks...Joe Davis sent out 1,000 toy plastic racing cars as a tie-up on the new Paula Watson M-G-M etching "I Love to Ride." M-G-M Records has also released platters this week by warbler Lem Johnson and the Birmingham Boogie Boys combo.... Peacock Records has pacted, to a long-termer, jazz pianist Phineas Newborn. The label has also signed the Spirit of Memphis Quartet, for its spiritual division. The group was formerly on the King label.... Jack Bergman, head of Tempo Distributors and Discovery Records, has pacted thrush Joan Shaw and last week cut six original tunes for his new r.&b. label. Ben DeCosta, Miss Shaw's manager, reportedly handled the session.... Jax Records' Morty Shad walking around these days with a big smile as his Bob Gaddy disking of "No Help Wanted" began to take hold in cities like Charlotte, New Orleans and Chicago.

Ben Blaine of Jubilee Records is elated over the success of the Orioles' newest release on the label, "Dem Days." Group's previous two disks, "Till Then" and "Hold Me, Thrill Me, Kiss Me" are still among firm's top sellers, he notes. Jubilee has also signed Andrew Wiedman, 12-year-old blues singer who was discovered via National Broadcasting TV's "Star Time" show.... Douglas (Jocko) Henderson, deejay over WHAT, Philadelphia, is doing a guest show in New York every Saturday over WLIB.... The Cap-Tans, Dot Records artists, will do a series of one-nighters after they kick off at the Blue Mirror, Washington, next week.... Tuxedo Records has pacted Woody Smith to a term contract. Smith appeared on Broadway in "Peter Pan" and "Four Saints in Three Acts." He has a deejay show over WWRL, Long Island, and was soloist with the American Negro Opera Guild.... Rainbow Records has purchased the master of "Fine Brown Frame" and "Dear Ruth" by the Buccaneers, which was originally issued on Southern Records.... Brunswick has signed James Allen, Southern blues singer, for the label.... The Kings, a Joe Louis discovery, are waxing the "Joe Louis Mambo" on

Jubilee. Hal Allen is personal manager of the group.... Coral Records has pacted The Cincinnatians, a new spirituals group, to a long-term contract.... Lew Simpkins, head of United Records, is at the Mayo Clinic in Rochester, Minn., for treatment.

PHILLY FLASHES: Lenny Sloan is launching a name policy at his Emerson's Show Bar, Philadelphia, with a package including Jackie Davis Trio, Johnny Hartman and Connie Carroll.... Steve Gibson and The Redcaps, with a new RCA Victor contract under their belt, plus a new waxing binder for vocalist Damita Jo, return to the local scene at the Rendezvous, after a private club date on Sunday (12) at the Erie (Pa.) Social Club.... The Jolly Joyce Agency, with offices here and in New York City, has the Three Peppers, who after wintering at the Singapore, Miami Beach, open Monday (13) at the Esquire Sho-Bar, Montreal. The agency also has the Top Notes at the Holiday Tavern, Toronto, and returns Chris Powell and the Blue Flames on Monday (13) to Philadelphia for a stay at Bill and Lou's.... Paul Quinichette, ex-Count Basie tenorman, is making his first local appearance this week at Bill and Lou's where Jimmy Turner, formerly at Club 421, is the new house manager.... Earl Plummer, formerly singing with Steve Gibson and the Red Caps until stepping out several months ago as a single, has formed the Earl Plummer Quartet, with Joe (Rip) Sewell, ex-Tiny Grimes tenorman, featured. They make their bow at Spider Kelly's.

Newest sensation in the r.&b. deejay field is Douglas (Jocko) Henerson. "Jocko," who's behind the mike at Phily's WHAT all week, comes to New York every Saturday to do a one-shot via WLIB. Doug's tag is "From the Big P to the Big M".... Henry Marcus, Columbia, S.C., who had been associated with the late Ralph Weinberg for many years, has joined with Eli Weinberg in a new promotion firm to be called Weinberg and Marcus. They will do southern bookings for the r.&b. agencies, taking out tours thru Dixie. First booking for the new firm is the Amos Milburn-Clovers package.... Raleigh Music is the pubber of the Five Bills' latest tunes on Brunswick Records. The ditties are "Waiting, Wanting" and "Til Dawn and Tomorrow"....
Miriam Abramson and Ahmet Ertegun at Atlantic inform us that Ruth Brown now has a telephone installed in her car, and whenever she is anywhere within a hundred miles of the New York office she calls in every five minutes. Ruth opens at the Town Casino, Buffalo, May 18. The chantress had her tonsils out this week and is feeling well.... Lowell Fulson, T-Bone Walker and Lloyd Glenn start on a Southwest tour, April 30, beginning in Houston, and ending May 23 in Albuquerque, N.M. They return to California via Denver.... Amos Milburn starts at the Howard Thea-

(Continued on next page)

R.&B. Beat
(Continued from previous page)

ter, Washington, May 15.... Amos Milburn, Linda Hayes and the Orioles grossed $2,500 for promoter Teddy Powell in Newark, N.J., Saturday (11).

CHICAGO TIDINGS: Checker Records harmonica ace Little Walter has been bedded for the past couple of weeks due to head injuries suffered in an auto mishap.... Latest Chess label offering is titled "Wine Head Willie, Put That Bottle Down" and is performed by Elder Beck, who not only sings but plays the organ as well.... Tommy Brown into Martin's Corner here for a comfortable 12-week stay.... Danny Overbea, originator of "Train, Train, Train" smash on Checker label, now being featured at the Paris Club.... Cy House of King reports nice reaction to Wynonie Harris' disking of "Mama, Your Daughter Done Told a Lie on Me"'.... Charlie Michaels says "Mama, Your Daughter," etc. by the Five Keys on Aladdin is clicking for him.... Johnny ("Duke's Blues") Hodges and his all-stars will soon hit the Capitol Lounge here for two weeks, followed by Big Jay McNeely.... Johnny Holiday has a new United release, "Why Should I Cry" b/w "With All My Heart." Disk so far has been released only in Chicago, but reaction has been very favorable, according to reports. Lew Simpkins, United-States boss, has a hot one in "Daughter, That's Your Red Wagon" by Swingin' Sax Kari.... Floyd Dixon and the Orioles set for the Pershing Ballroom April 19.... New diskery popped up this week, Co-Ben Recording Co., headed by former M-G-M's Brother Brown, who shouts "Half Past" on one disk. On a second coupling, Herbert Beard and his four-piece combo do "Luxury Tax Blues" b/w "Oh Rhythm." Herb is well-known in these parts, having played top North, South and West Side spots. This all Chi setup cutting at Universal.... Bobby Prince heads for Louisville after date at the Flame Club in Detroit.

(Continued on page 38)

April's Record Roundup

Week of April 4

Territorial Tips
LOS ANGELES
K.C. Loving--Little Willie Littlefield --
Federal 12110
WASHINGTON--BALTIMORE
Good Old 99--Marylanders--
Jubilee 5114
CINCINNATI
Person to Person--Eddie Vinson--
King 4582

New R.&B. Releases
RUFUS THOMAS, JR./Sun 181
•••• Bear Cat
••• Walking in the Rain
SCAT MAN CROTHERS/Recorded in Hollywood 142
•••• Papa (I Didn't Treat That Little Girl Mean)
••• Till I Waltz Again with You (Red Callender Sextet)
DOLLY COOPER & HAL SINGER ORCH./Savoy 891
•••• I Wanna Know
••• I'd Climb the Highest Mountain
LITTLE ESTHER/Federal
•••• Street Lights
••• You Took My Love Too Fast (vo. Bobby Nunn-Little Esther)
ILLINOIS JACQUET ORCH./Mercury 89036
••• What's the Riff?
••• Blues in the Night
THE SHA-WEEZ/Aladdin 3170
••• Early Sunday Morning
••• No One to Love Me
JIMMY AND WALTER/Sun 180
••• Before Long
••• Easy
THE FIVE CROWNS/Rainbow 206
••• I Don't Have to Hunt No More
••• Alone Again
CAROL KAY/Recorded in Hollywood 424
••• You Can't Do the Boogie in School
••• A Good Man Is Hard to Find
LIGHTNIN' HOPKINS/Sittin' In 660
••• Mad Blues
••• Why
THE MARYLANDERS/Jubilee 5114
••• Good Old 99
••• Fried Chicken
SONNY THOMPSON/King 4613
••• Insulated Sugar (vo. Rufus Junior)
••• Clean Sweep
IVORY JOE HUNTER/MGM 11459
••• If You See My Baby

••• I Had a Girl
HAL SINGER/Savoy 890
••• Hometown
•• Easy Living
PAUL WILLIAMS ORCH./Mercury 89034
••• Easy Walking
••• Miami Drag
ELMORE NIXON & HENRY HAYES ORCH./Savoy 889
••• Sad and Blue
•• Elmore's Blues
LITTLE MR. BLUES/Rainbow 208
••• Mama--Your Daughter Plays It Cool
•• Rough and Rocky

New Spiritual Releases
ANGELIC GOSPEL SINGERS/Gotham 729
•••• My Lord and I
••• Jesus Will Carry You Through
ROBERT PATTERSON SINGERS/Gotham 731
•••• After Awhile
••• I Will Walk with Jesus
ECHO GOSPEL SINGERS/Gotham 730
••• I Want to Thank My God in Person
••• This Is Like Heaven to Me
WARD SINGERS/Savoy 4044
••• I Just Can't Make It Myself
••• Since I Found the Light
EVENING STAR QUARTET/Gotham 732
•• Say a Prayer for the Boys in Korea
•• Make It In

Week of April 11

Buy o' the Week
**Bear Cat—Rufus Thomas, Jr. —
Sun 181**
The answer to "Hound Dog" broke loose this week with fury. Hit a number of territorial charts and also is registering strongly in Chicago and around Nashville.

Buy o' the Week
**I Wanna Know—Du Droppers—
RCA Victor 20-5224**
The label could have its first big hit in some years with this one. It's big in Detroit, Washington, Baltimore and is No. 1 at the moment in Durham, N.C. Philadelphia and Cincinnati also returned good reports.

RATING SYSTEM
•••• Excellent ••• Very Good
•• Good • Fair

Updates on Recent Territorial Tips

Daughter, That's Your Red Wagon—Gloria Irving—States 115
Made the national retail chart this week and also came within one place of making the national juke box chart. Strength is further indicated by its placing on six territorial charts.

My Hat's On the Side of My Head—Four Blazes—United 146
This one is beginning to register on the West Coast and continues to sell in Nashville, Cincinnati and Chicago. Eastern reports indicate that it is still weak there generally.

You're Mine—The Crickets—MGM 11428
Placed on the New York and L.A. territorial charts this week and still good in Nashville, Cincinnati and Chicago.

Territorial Tips
CINCINNATI
Hittin' on Me--Buddy Johnson Orch.--Mercury 70116
She's Got to Go--Ravens--Mercury 70119
Going to the River--Fats Domino--Imperial 5231
ST. LOUIS
Bear Cat--Rufus Thomas, Jr.--Sun 181
NEW ORLEANS
Hound Dog--Willie Mae Thornton--Peacock 1612
Bear Cat--Rufus Thomas, Jr.--Sun 181
Going to the River--Fats Domino--Imperial 5231
ATLANTA
Bear Cat--Rufus Thomas, Jr.--Sun 181

New R.&B. Releases
PAULA WATSON/MGM 11466
••• I Love to Ride
••• Put a Little Bug in My Ear
CHUCK WILLIS/Okeh 6952
••• Going to the River
••• Baby Has Left Me Again
WYNONIE HARRIS/King 4620
••• Mama, You're Daughter's Done Lied on Me
••• Wasn't That Good?
LEM JOHNSON/MGM 11467
••• I Got a Letter
••• It Takes Money, Honey
HOT LIPS PAGE ORCH./King 4616
••• What Shall I Do? (vo. Henry Mance)
••• The Jungle King (vo. Hot Lips Page)

LITTLE ESTHER/Federal 12126
••• Sweet Lips
••• Hound Dog
RED SAUNDERS ORCH./Okeh 6953
••• Mambo in Trumpet
•• Probably (vo. Joe Williams)
STOMP GORDON/Decca 48290
••• Devil's Daughter
•• Hide the Bottle
STAN GETZ/Jax 5007
••• As I Live and Bop
•• Diaper Pin
LOIS HINDS/Okeh 6951
•• That's Alright for You
•• It Must Have Been (Two Other People)
LARRY DARNELL/Okeh 6954
•• Crazy She Calls Me
•• I'll Be Sittin', I'll Be Rockin'

Week of April 18

Buy o' the Week
Going to the River—Fats Domino—Imperial 5231
Now on the Washington-Baltimore and New Orleans charts, disk also registered solidly in midwestern and Southern reports. Not too much yet in the East.

Buy o' the Week
She's Got to Go—The Ravens—Mercury 70119
Good to strong reports received from New York, Philadelphia, Cincinnati, Chicago and Detroit.

Territorial Tips
PHILADELPHIA
Is It a Dream--Vocaleers--Red Robin 114
NEW ORLEANS
Tell Me Mama--Little Walter--Checker 770
WASHINGTON--BALTIMORE
Play Girl--Smiley Lewis--Imperial 5234

New R.&B. Releases
THE ORIOLES/Jubilee 5115
•••• Dem Days
••• Bad Little Girl
DINAH WASHINGTON/Mercury 70125
•••• You Let My Love Grow Cold
••• Ain't Nothin' Good
THE ROCKETS & VAN WALLS ORCH./Atlantic 988
•••• Big-Leg Mama
••• Open the Door
ROY BROWN/King 4627
•••• Mr. Hound Dog's in Town
••• Gamblin' Man
THE "5" ROYALES/Apollo 446
•••• Help Me Somebody

••• Crazy, Crazy, Crazy
THE RAVENS/Mercury 70119
•••• Come a Little Bit Closer
••• She's Got to Go
EUNICE DAVIS/Atlantic 992
•••• My Beat Is 125th Street
••• Go to Work, Daddy
OSCAR McLOLLIE/Modern 902
••• The Honey Jump (Parts 1 & 2)
JIMMY McCRACKLIN/Peacock 1615
••• She Felt Too Good
••• Share and Share Alike
STICK McGHEE/Atlantic 991
••• Meet You in the Morning
••• New Found Love
ST. LOUIS JIMMY/Duke 110
••• Drinkin' Woman
••• Why Work?
THE FIVE BILLS/Brunswick 84004
••• Till Dawn and Tomorrow
••• Waiting, Wanting
IKE CARPENTER'S ORCH./Decca 28668
••• Crazy, Crazy (vo. Effie Smith)
••• (Mama) He Treats Your Daughter Mean (vo. Effie Smith)
TINY GRIMES ORCH./Atlantic 990
••• Begin the Beguine
••• The Man I Love
BONITA COLE/Duke 111
••• Gatemouth's Ghost
•• Life's Like That
THE FIVE KEYS/Aladdin 3175
••• Mama, Your Daughter Told a Lie on Me
•• There Ought to Be a Law (Against Breaking a Heart)
BUDDY JOHNSON/Mercury 70116
••• Hittin' On Me (vo. Ella Johnson)
•• Ecstasy (vo. Nolan Lewis)
MARIE ADAMS/Peacock 1614
••• I'm the Bluest Gal in Town
•• Ain't Car Crazy
JO JO JOHNSON/Victor 20-5262
•• I'm With You
•• Last Stop

New Spiritual Releases
SPIRIT OF MEMPHIS/Peacock 1710
•••• God Save America
••• Surely, Surely, Amen
THE FOUR INTERNS/Federal 12124
••• Do Unto Others
••• I'm Using My Bible for a Road Map
SWANEE SPIRITUAL SINGERS/Duke 200
••• God Spoke to Me One Day
••• Let Us Stand on That Rock

Week of April 25

Buy o' the Week
Crazy, Crazy, Crazy b/w Help Me Somebody—"5" Royales—Apollo 446
A two-sided hit. Most reports favor "Crazy," which received the initial plays.
(Continued on next page)

Record Roundup
(Continued from previous page)

However, "Help Me" broke wide open this week in North Carolina, and at a faster clip than "Baby Don't Do It," which clicked first in that area. All r.&b. reporting areas were enthusiastic about the record.

Territorial Tips

CINCINNATI
Shirley, Come Back to Me--Shirley and Lee--Aladdin 3173

WASHINGTON--BALTIMORE
Is It a Dream--Vocaleers--
Red Robin 114

PHILADELPHIA
Is It a Dream--Vocaleers--
Red Robin 114

New R.&B. Releases

LITTLE WALTER/Checker 770
•••• Tell Me, Mama
•••• Off the Wall
WILLIE MABON/Chess 1538
•••• I'm Mad
•• Night Latch
BIG MAYBELLE/Okeh 6955
•••• Just Want Your Love
••• Way Back Home
BOB GADDY/Jax 308
•••• No Help Wanted
••• Little Girl's Boogie
MILT TRENIER & HIS SOLID SIX/
Victor 20-5275
••• Rock Bottom
••• Squeeze Me
TAMPA RED/Victor 20-5273
••• Got a Mind to Leave This Town
••• I'll Never Let You Go
THE ROBINS/Victor 20-5271
••• All Night Baby
••• Oh Why?
FLETCHER SMITH/Swing Time 329
••• Mean Poor Gal
•• Brand New Neighborhood
CHARLIE (LITTLE JAZZ) FERGUSON/
Apollo 815
••• Bean Head
••• Big "G"
DEEP RIVER BOYS/Victor 20-5268
••• Oo-Shoo-Be-Do-Be
••• The Biggest Fool
CAMILLE HOWARD/Federal 12125
•• Excite Me, Daddy
•• I'm So Confused
JOHN GREER/Victor 20-5269
••• Ride, Pretty Baby
•• Don't Worry About It
LOWELL FULSON/Swing Time 330
••• The Blues Come Rollin' In
••• I Love My Baby
RENE HALL ORCH./Victor 20-5274
••• Seen Better Days (vo. Courtland Carter)

•• Voodoo Moon
LES HARRIS/Victor 20-5270
•• Amapola
•• Nobody Else But You
DO RE MI TRIO/Brunswick 80218
•• I'll Never Stop Being Yours
•• I'm Only Human
THE EMANON TRIO/Swing Time 328
•• The Emanon Blues
• E-e-e-e-zy
AL SEARS/Victor 20-5272
• Easy Ernie
• In the Good Old Summer Time
CHARLIE BRANTLEY ORCH./King 4619
• Movin On Now (vo. Clarence Jolley)
• Fog Horn

New Spiritual Releases

THE SPIRITUAL KINGS/Score 5039
••• A Letter to Jesus
••• Paul and Silas
ST. PETER'S GOSPEL SINGERS/
Apollo 271
••• The Battle Done Got Started Again
•• Lord, Hold My Hand
THE CARAVANS/States 116
••• Blessed Assurance
••• God Is Good to Me
THE ZION TRAVELERS/Aladdin 2038
••• Your Wicked Ways
••• Last Days
MYRTLE JACKSON/Brunswick 84007
•• Come, Ye Disconsolate
•• Do You Love My Jesus?

R.&B. Beat
(Continued from page 36)

Willie Mabon's new Chess slicing, "I'm Mad," sold 30,000 copies the first week. According to Phil Chess, diskery tried to keep this one quiet so they could satisfy their distribs' advance orders, but as soon as word got out of a "new Mabon disk" the orders came pouring in. As a result, Len Chess had to rush down to Memphis to Buster Williams' pressing plant to personally supervise and help ship orders. Meanwhile in Memphis, Len is also shipping Little Walter's "Off the Wall" on Checker, which looks like the chanter's third hit in as many releases.... Buddy Morrow making the rounds of local platter spinners with his latest for Victor, "Train, Train, Train".... Sax tootler Herbie Fields opened return engagement at the Preview Lounge, Chicago, April 15 for a four-week stay.... Al Benson (WGES) notes that the Du Droppers' "I Wanna Know" on RCA Victor getting plenty of requests.... Tom Edwards, WERE, Cleveland, wants to know the meaning of "Big Mamou," disk put out on Okeh by Link Davis. Edwards thinks it stands for "grandmother," a mistranslation from the French, and he says most of his listeners agree.... Jerry Kay, WWEZ,

New Orleans, has come up with another meaning for "Big Mamou." Says Kay, "Actually, I don't think there is any translation for the word. 'Mamou' is in reality a small town in the heart of the French Cajun country in Louisiana. Link Davis, who wrote the song, hails from there."

HEARD IN HOLLYWOOD: Modern Records' Saul Bihari jumped on the hit bandwagon via his purchase of "The Honey Jump," a hot platter waxed by the Oscar McLollie crew and originally released on the Class label. Modern reportedly paid veteran disk man Leon Rene the sum of $5,000 for the master and signed the McLollie group to an exclusive contract. Since releasing the disk only a short week ago, Modern already has been swamped to the tune of more than 25,000 back-orders. Reaction from all distribs indicates that not since the original "Honeydripper" on Exclusive some years back has there been a recording to rival the current disk. McLollie and his Honey Jumpers now are enjoying an extended engagement at the Stardust, Long Beach nitery.... Mr. and Mrs. Art Rupe, Specialty Records, busier than a pack of beavers with the new Mercy Dee waxing of "One Room Country Shack".... Big hoopla at the Pasadena Civic Auditorium for Duke Ellington and his orchestra, featuring drummer Louis Bellson.... Earl Bostic and his gang just closed at the Tiffany Club.... If there ever was a song sleuth in the r.&b. business, it's Eddie Ray over at Central Record Sales. Eddie has, by far, one of the most phenomenal intuitive methods for picking a hit. He's currently touting that fast-climbing "Wine Head Willie" etching by Elder Beck on Chess.... Lew Chudd's Imperial plattery comes up with a pair of great ones via the new Fats Domino "Going to the River" and the Smiley Lewis etching of "Play Girl."

John Dolphin, of the Recorded in Hollywood label, has announced the appointment of Lou Sowa as national sales manager of the firm. Sowa was formerly a distribber of M-G-M disks in Pittsburgh, Pa. and has many years experience in the field. He replaces Franklin Kort, who resigned his post this past week to form his own Bayou label with his own varied selection of masters he's acquired thru the years. Disclosure of the firm's first releases will be made shortly.... Floyd Dixon will return to California for an end-of-month wax session for Aladdin and a May 1 opening at the 5-4 Ballroom.... Little Willie Littlefield's "K.C. Loving" on Federal making lots of noise in this town.... and we still insist that the guitar work on "Hound Dog" sounds just like John Lee Hooker.... Rumors still persist re the possibility of a TV rhythm and blues stanza to preview new disks. Hunter Hancock and Bill Sampson have been mentioned as possible emcees for the seg.... Buddy Beason is handling an r.&b. show over KFOX, Long Beach.

JERRY WEXLER JOINS ATLANTIC AS PARTNER

New York, May 23—Jerry Wexler will join Atlantic Records as a partner beginning June 1, it was announced this week by Ahmet Ertegun, executive vice-president of Atlantic.

Wexler has resigned his post as publicity and advertising director of the Big Three publishing group (Robbins-Feist-Miller) effective May 29. Prior to joining the Big Three in November of 1951, he served on Billboard's music staff for some

(Continued on next page)

Explosive Growth of R.&B. Labels Seen as Industry Phenomenon

NEW YORK, May 16—The spate of new rhythm and blues labels that have shot up over the past year is one of the most sensational developments in the field in a decade, according to vet tradesters.

It's getting so that hardly a week goes by that two, three or more new r.&b. labels do not suddenly burst upon the scene, being either brand new labels or subsidiaries spawned by r.&b. or jazz platters already in the field. Indeed, it almost appears these days that an r.&b. label that does not have at least one or two subsidiary labels (and there is one that now has five) loses face in the market.

Amazingly, the entire r.&b. market is said to comprise only 5.7 percent of the entire record business. Its percentage is topped by the pop, classical, kiddie and country markets, and the only fields it is really ahead of are the jazz, Latin American and international categories. Still, this market now consists of close to 100 active labels, and major firms such as RCA Victor and Columbia are actively competing for sales with the indies in the r.&b. field.

Labels that have subsidiary labels in the r.&b. markets include Chess (with its Checker subsidiary), Aladdin (Score), King (Federal and its semi-subsidiary labels Rockin' and Glory) Peacock (Duke), Modern (RPM, Rhythm and Blues, Meteor), United (States), Roost (Scooter), Tennessee (Republic), Tico (Rama) and Gotham (20th Century). The majors also have their subsidiary lines, such as Decca (Brunswick, the r.&b. subsid of Decca's Coral line), Columbia (Okeh) and the forthcoming RCA Victor label, still unnamed, which will be the subsidiary of the firm's new indie line. Mercury and M-G-M are the lone exceptions among the majors, who continue to issue r.&b. waxings under their own label.

Among the few r.&b. diskeries who seem to be satisfied with one label is Atlantic, which is also one of the few r.&b. firms with two such consistent hit-makers as Ruth Brown and the Clovers. Specialty has another label, Fidelity, which, however, is not active. Savoy, whose other labels are in the pop field, Imperial, a firm that believes in putting out pop, c.&w. and r.&b. on the same label, Recorded in Hollywood, Jubilee and Apollo are others presently without an active subsid line.

With the explosive growth of r.&b. labels over the past year or so, there has also been a great increase in the number of artists waxing in the field. In fact, it is probably easier today for an unknown r.&b. artist to get on wax than it has been for years, owing to the proliferation of la-

'53 May Be Biggest Year in History of One-Nighter Package Field

NEW YORK, May 2—This will be the biggest season in the history of the one-nighter packages, if all plans now being formulated for fall road shows materialize. Plans are currently being drawn up by four agencies for over a half-dozen major road shows, even before the "Biggest Show of '53" and the Gene Krupa (Goodman ork)-Louis Armstrong packages have finished their road trek.

The Associated Booking Corporation, for example, which books the Krupa-Armstrong package, is currently working on a couple of arena-auditorium units for the fall. One will feature the Lionel Hampton ork plus another big band, and another will spotlight Duke Ellington, a name singer, plus other attractions.

A third package will feature a complete show with ex-champ Sugar Ray Robinson. All of these shows, according to ABC head Joe Glaser, will be artist-owned packages, with ABC merely acting as agency and booker for the attractions. All of the key performers in these units will get a percentage.

Likewise the Gale Agency intends to send out another "Biggest Show of '53" this fall. As in previous Gale shows, this one will feature top record names, plus a big ork as well as other acts. The "Biggest Show of '52," with Nat Cole, Stan Kenton and Sarah Vaughan last year, hit the top gross of any package unit of this type to date—over $900,000 for 60-odd dates.

Another "Jazz at the Philharmonic" jazz unit will be sent out by Norman Granz this fall. Granz' JATP tours, which now play the Hawaiian islands and Europe in addition to the U.S., have been solid money-makers since they were started about five years ago and have been responsible for bringing to public attention some of the newer and hotter names in jazz.

A giant rhythm and blues package is being prepped by the Gale Agency, which will be sent out in the summer months and will play ball parks in addition to arenas and auditoriums. The unit will consist of Ruth Brown, Louis Jordan, The Clovers,

(Continued on next page)

Former Dominoes Lead Signed By Atlantic

New York, May 23—Clyde Lensey McPhatter, former lead singer with the Dominoes, has formed his own group, which is as yet un-named.

He has signed a long term contract with Atlantic Records and the diskery is planning to promote the group into the top spot in the A&R picture.

(Continued on next page)

Guardians Named for 'Hound Dog' Team

HOLLYWOOD, April 25—The mothers of Mike Stoller and Jerry Leiber, 20 year-old cleffing team currently riding high on the r.&b. charts, have been named their legal guardians. Superior Court Judge Victor R. Hansen okayed the guardianships of Mrs. Mary Stein for Leiber and Mrs. Adelyn Stoller for Mike.

Team wrote "Hound Dog," tune waxed by Willie Mae Thornton for Peacock label, which now occupies the top spot on the national best-seller list, and rated the second most frequently played r.&b. number in the nation's juke boxes. Since the original Peacock recording, "Hound Dog" has been cut by Little Esther for Federal, Billy Starr for Imperial, Jack Turner for Victor (a country and western version), Cleve Jackson for Herald, and three separate disks by Tommy Duncan, Betsy Gay and Eddie Hazelwood for Intro, Aladdin subsidiary.

Stoller and Leiber claim more than 43 song credits. "Hound Dog" is their most successful tune, which Peacock chief Don Robey estimates is approaching the 300,000 mark. Pair were also accepted into Broadcast Music, Inc., this week. Leiber and Stoller are agented by Les Sill, who took them under his wing in April 1951, when they still were attending Los Angeles City College. Boys have been together for almost three years.

'53 Biggest Year
(Continued from previous page)

Wynonie Harris, Erskine Hawkins' orch., Dusty Fletcher, Stuffy Bryant, Gordon and Gordon, plus other acts. Package will kick off July 17 and will be out for at least four weeks, with the possibility of two more weeks if it pulls strongly.

Explosive Growth
(Continued from previous page)

bels. And it has given old-timers a chance to re-emerge, whether under a new name or variation of the old one. Many artists have also taken the opportunity to wax for more than one diskery by using a pseudonym. There is now a blues singer who waxes for at least four labels and does not bother to change more than a letter or two of his name for each of the labels.

At the moment, the r.&b. field offers an equality of opportunity to a degree that is unknown in other fields of the record business. It does not necessarily take either an exceptionally strong artist or piece of material to break thru with a hit in the r.&b. category. Nor does it necessarily take a very large firm or one that has been in business a long time. While it is true that a well-known artist with a good commercial item gets acceptance immediately, there are so few accepted artists that stick around very long in the blues field that newcomers are always on the horizon.

An r.&b. hit can sometimes surpass the 300,000 mark, but such hits are rare. A so-so r.&b. disk may have a tough time selling over 1,000 platters, a poorer average than in other fields. A record that goes above 40,000 has to be considered a hit, and one that sells 100,000 is a big hit.

Even tho there are probably too many firms in the field today to have any substantial share of the small and intensely competitive market, the labels keep coming, keeping the r.&b. field alive and precarious as ever.

LEW SIMPKINS DEAD AT 35

CHICAGO, May 2—Lew Simpkins, head of the United Record Company, died Monday (27) at St. Mary's Hospital, Rochester, Minn. Simpkins, who was 35 years old, had been confined to the hospital for about five weeks. Death was believed to be caused by leukemia.

Simpkins formed United in partnership with Leonard Allen, who will assume the presidency of the firm. A few of United's recent releases are "My Hat's on the Side of my Head" by the Four Blazes, "Security Blues" by Roosevelt Sykes, and "Night Train" by Jimmy Forrest. The firm has dealt strictly in the r.&b. field.

Simpkins is survived by his widow, Eva, and two children, Randy and Pamela.

4-Star Acquires Big Town

HOLLYWOOD, May 2—Bill McCall's 4-Star Records, indie plattery heretofore concerned mainly with the country field, has acquired the Big Town r.&b. line from Bob Geddins and retained the latter as artist and repertoire man. Geddins was also signed to an exclusive seven-year deal for his songwriting.

In the purchase, McCall acquired 40 masters and the rights to use of Big Town's name. Geddins signed a three-year pact to serve as a.&r. rep for the label. In addition, he'll turn over all his tune cleffing efforts to 4-Star's pubbing firm. Diskery chief Bill McCall made deal this week and expects soon to release first record on rejuvenated label, "Tin Pan Alley" by Jimmy Wilson.

The 4-Star topper also disclosed a deal to lease all Trilon Records masters. McCall closed the deal with Rene Lamarre this week. Included is the original recording of "I Wonder, I Wonder, I Wonder," as done by the Four Aces in Oakland 10 years ago. McCall stated he would re-cut a new master on the tune for early release.

PHILLY "UPTOWN" TO SHOWCASE R.&B. FLESH

PHILADELPHIA, May 23—In an attempt to fill the gap left when Warner's Earle theater recently shuttered, Sam Stieffel's Uptown Theater in the North Philadelphia sector will be bringing in live rhythm and blues shows starting June 15. Lionel Hampton's band will be the initial offering, with probably the Joe Louis package show to follow.

The Uptown is equipped for stage offerings, altho when operated for many years by the Warner Brothers circuit, it was on straight pictures. It's a key nabe house, with a favorable location, altho removed from the main stem.

Staging the Uptown's shows will be Sid Stanley, originator of r.&b. band stage-shows here dating back to the Pearl Theater some decades ago.

Wexler Joins
(Continued from previous page)

four years.

He joins the company as vice-president in partnership with Ertegun and Herb Abramson, having purchased a substantial stock interest. With Abramson currently serving in the Air Force Dental Corps in Germany, Wexler will share duties with Ertegun in all phases of the Atlantic operation: A&R, sales, publicity and promotion, and production.

Notes from the R.&B. Beat

MORE ON MOONDOG: Injuries suffered by Alan (Moondog) Freed in an auto accident early this week were more serious than at first believed. The Cleveland deejay (WJW) is being treated for serious internal injuries, deep facial cuts and a broken arm.... Phil Kahl has worked out a partnership in Patricia Music with Morris Levy and will start next week as general professional manager of the firm. In addition, Kahl and Levy are setting up another BMI firm to be called Phil Kahl Music. Patricia Music, in addition to its music activities also handles Alan Dean, Francis Faye and Bud Powell. Kahl was formerly professional manager of Disney Music for three years.... Lou Krefetz, who has been sales manager for Atlantic Records for the past year, is leaving next week to devote more time to the management of the Clovers, one of the country's top vocal groups. The Clovers, who will be part of the forthcoming Gale Agency r.&b. package, have their sixth hit in a row for Atlantic with "Crawlin."

The Houston Press last week ran a story on the Peacock "Hound Dog" and Sun "Bear Cat" controversy. Article quotes Don Robey, Peacock owner, as saying "Hound Dog" by Willie Mae Thornton should easily outsell his biggest previous disking, "Let's Talk About Jesus" by the Bells of Joy.... A new r.&b. tune stirring up some action is "Paradise Hill" by the Embers. Originally released on the Ember label, the master was acquired by Herald Records who reports excellent results in Jersey and points south. Latest cities to come in strong are Atlanta and Baltimore.... Joe Morris' "Blues Cavalcade" show, with recent addition Mr. Stringbean of New Orleans, creating a stir wherever they've appeared.... Good sleeper disk is Jimmy McCracklin's "Share and Share Alike" and "She Felt Too Good" on Peacock. Disk started slowly, but has been catching fire, according to late reports.

WILLIE MAE THORNTON

COURIER POLL RESULTS: The Eighth Annual Theatrical Poll conducted by the Pittsburgh Courier ended this week, and the winners in the various categories were finally announced. In most cases the established favorites prevailed, but there were a few surprises. Here are the winners in the various categories: Big Band: Buddy Johnson ork, with Ernie Fields, Duke Ellington and Count Basie runners up; Trio: King Cole, with Wild Bill Davis and Bill Doggett's combos following; Small Combo: the Ray-O-Vacs, followed by Paul Gayten, Myrtle Young and Louis Jordan; Vocal Quartet: the Ravens, with the Clovers and the Dominoes close behind; Girl Singer: Dolores Parker, followed by Sarah Vaughan, Debbie Andrews and Ella Fitzgerald; Girl Blues Singer: Ruth Brown, with Dinah Washington, Little Esther and Julia Lee runners up; Male Singer: Arthur Prysock, with Nat Cole, Joe Medlin and Johnnie Ray next; Male Blues Singer: Nickie Lee, far ahead of Wynonie Harris, Larry Darnell and Charles Brown; Gospel Singers: the Ward Singers, followed by the Cincinnatians, the Boyer Brothers and Mahalia Jackson.

Prexy Ernie Young, of Excello and Nashboro labels in Nashville, Tenn., has just recorded three new artists. They are Good Rockin' Beasley, who waxed "Long Goody" and "Happy Go Lucky"; Kid King's Combo, who cut "Banana Split" and "Skip's Boogie"; and Shy Guy Douglas, etching "Detroit Arrow" and "New Memphis Blues".... Lewis Buckley of Buckley's One-Stop in Nashville predicts big things for Mercy Dee's "Please Understand".... Word has it that Rufus Thomas, Jr., who waxed the smash "Bear Cat" for Sun Records, is turning down many a one-nighter so he can remain mikeside at his WDIA deejay post.... Gem Records, New York, has just cut a session with a new group, the Four Bells, winners at the Apollo Theater here. Sides are "Please Tell It to Me" and "A Long Way to Go." Group will head for

(Continued on next page)

Palda-Essex Moves to New Location

PHILADELPHIA, April 25—Palda Records, manufacturers and marketers of the Essex line, has relocated its entire operation into a recently converted building at 3208 South 84th Street here. Pressing equipment, which when complete will have a capacity of 20,000 platters daily, has already been set in operation, according to firm's exec Dave Miller.

Essex performs a near-complete production job in its plant, which includes facilities for milling wax compound, printing and die cutting.

MILLER USES "HIDDEN TALENT" FOR RECORD DATE

PHILADELPHIA, May 2—Though it's generally conceded that there is no shortage of disk talent on the scene these days, circumstances recently were such that a distributor, a manufacturer, a promotion man and a porter all found their way onto a record.

Essex diskery chief Dave Miller was cutting the Bill Haley original of "Crazy, Man, Crazy" and had hired a group to handle the gang-sing shouts of "Go, Go, Go." The group didn't sound big enough to Miller and the engineer, so pressed into service as part of the gang-sing were Miller himself, his Essex label promotion man D. Malamud, distributor Jerry Blaine and the studio porter.

PETE DORAINE NAMED ALLEN SALES CHIEF

NEW YORK, May 16—Allen Records last week named Peter Doraine as national sales manager for the firm, and acquired four sides by purchasing masters from Bill Harrington, Buddy Kaye and Frank Stanton.

According to firm's chief, Victor Allen, Doraine is currently setting distribs for the label in many territories in preparation for issuance of singles and albums in the pop, r.&b. and light classical fields.

The four masters all feature Harrington on vocal. Tunes were written by the Harrington-Kaye-Stanton team. First release couples "Wedding Day," based on the MacDowell "To a Wild Rose," and "Give Me Love."

MODERN RELEASES WITHERSPOON'S 'STEP'

HOLLYWOOD, April 25—Modern Records this week released Jimmy Witherspoon's version of "Each Step of the Way," sacred song published by Fiesta Music. It is the song's tenth disk pressed since its publication 18 months ago.

At the same time Herman Music's "Lord Keep Your Hand on Me," featuring Little Ruth, was released by Modern. This is the sixth record for this song, which since its publication February 28 has sold 10,000 pieces of sheet music. Sheet music sales of "Each Step of the Way" have reached 50,000 copies. Redd Harper composed both numbers.

"Each Step of the Way" thus far has been recorded by Capitol, RCA Victor, International Sacred, Sacred, Sharon, Singspiration, Word, Cornerstone and two other small labels. "Lord Keep Your Hand on Me" previously was waxed by Capitol, RCA Victor, International Sacred, Sacred and Word.

Both tunes are taken from music of Billy Graham's motion pictures. "Each Step of the Way" is from "Mr. Texas," while "Lord Keep Your Hand on Me" is from "Oil Town."

R.&B. Beat
(Continued from previous page)

a two-weeker at Club Bill & Lou, Philadelphia.

RING GIMMIX FOR WIENER: Gold wedding bands are being sent out to deejays by George Wiener, of Wemar Music, to focus attention on the firm's new ditty, "The Ring." The tune has been cut by Linda Shannon on King, and by Little Sylvia on Jubilee.... Phil Rose, Coral-Brunswick staffer, covered deejays in Philadelphia, Baltimore and Washington this week, plugging recent releases by Bette McLaurin and Sarah McLawler.... George Treadwell, former jazz trumpet player who married Sarah Vaughan, has opened his own talent agency in New York. In addition to Miss Vaughan, his starting stable includes Ruth Brown and Dizzy Gillespie.... "Jocko" Henderson's "Big Swing Train" WHAT platter show at midnight, will soon originate from Pep's Musical Bar.... Brunswick Records has pacted the Cincinnatians, a gospel group heard frequently over station WZIP, Covington, Ky.

Bess Berman, Apollo bosslady who's at Doctor's Hospital, Manhattan, recovering from a heart attack, has organized hospital staff into the "5" Interns and is teaching

---

them the two Apollo smashes "Crazy, Crazy, Crazy" and "Help Me Somebody" as etched by her "5" Royales. Readers are invited to drop Bess a line.... Atlantic Records signed two new artists this week, LaVerne Baker (formerly Miss Sharecropper) and Carmen Taylor. Miriam Abramson of Atlantic expects big things from the newly inked thrushes.... Jack Walker, Atlantic promotion man, unveiled the new Ruth Brown platter "Mend Your Ways" on his deejay program in a sneak prevue. Jack reports that listener reaction was tremendous.... Herman Lubinsky and Lee Magid burning up the phone wires at Savoy Records

VARETTA DILLARD

with long-distance playings of Varetta Dillard's latest, "Mercy, Mr. Percy" and "You're No Kinda Good, Nohow."

The Gale Agency signed a flock of talent this week to booking contracts. Artists signed include the Sax Kari ork and Gloria Irving, now with the United label; The Ray-O-Vacs, with Jubilee, Debbie Andrews, with United, and John Lee Hooker, who has been associated with a number of diskeries. The Sax Kari ork and Gloria Irving start a theater tour thru the South starting May 16 and running till June 7. Debbie Andrews is set for the Orchid Room, Kansas City, starting May 21.... Lynn Hope and his ork play their first New York one-nighter at the Hunts Point Palace in the Bronx on May 1 for promoter Cecil Bowen.

Paul Williams in Gotham for a short visit. Margie Day joins the ork leader as a featured thrush on May 20 in Locklin, O. .... Erskine Hawkins plays two dates at Clemson College in South Carolina on May 8 and 9.... Erroll Garner opens at the Hi-Hat in Boston on May 4.... Savannah Churchill opens at the Stagecoach in Hackensack, N.J., on May 1.... The Emitt Slay Trio opens April 27 at the Farm Dell in Dayton, O. .... Arthur Prysock starts at the Orchid Room in Kansas City, Mo., Friday (8).... Varetta Dillard opens on Monday (4) at the Downbeat, Providence.... Savoy Records has pacted two new vocal groups, the Falcons, a New York group, and the Carols, from Detroit.... The Shaw Artists package, consisting of T-Bone Walker, Lowell Fulson and Lloyd Glenn, pulled a gross of

$5,600 in Houston, Thursday (30).... RCA Victor hit the national r.&b. charts for the first time in nearly a year with the Du Droppers' waxing of "I Wanna Know".... Andrew Wiedman, 12-year-old singing star of NBC's "Star Time," starts at the Apollo Theater, New York, May 15.

The Gale Agency is negotiating with Joe Louis to go with the r.&b. package being sent out in July by the agency. Louis broke in his vaudeville act at the Apollo Theater, New York, about a month ago. If the unit, which will feature Ruth Brown, the Clovers, Wynonie Harris, and the Erskine Hawkins ork, signs Joe Louis, it will make the package complete. If not, it is possible that Louis Jordan will go with the unit.... Ruth Brown, held over at the Band Box this week, will play a number of one-nighters with the Orioles and the Sonny Stitt crew. On May 28, the unit will play Glen Cove, L.I.; on May 29, they'll travel to The Armory in Troy, N.Y., for an Elks Convention; then, on May 30, Ruth, the Orioles and a mambo ork will perform at St. Nicholas Arena, New York, and on May 31 at Turner's Arena in Washington. After that, the Atlantic Records thrush will return to the Band Box for another engagement.

A new club has been opened in Jacksonville, Fla., called the El Sambo. First act featured is the Five Keys.... Fats Domino was unable to fulfill his one-nighter engagements in Louisiana, Alabama and Georgia from May 1 to May 6 due to illness. The singer has recovered.... Deejay Bill Williams, of WBOY, in Tarpon Spring, Fla., is presenting a one-hour r.&b. show daily, and is hoping diskeries will send him platters to spin.... Atlantic Records has pacted singers Hal Paige and Chuck Norris. Their first wax will be released next week.... LaVerne Baker plays the Royale in Baltimore on May 15 and the Howard in Washington, D.C., on May 29. In between these dates she will play theater one-nighters in Virginia.... Herald Records, the latest addition to the r.&b. field, has pacted the Embers, a new vocal group. The firm now has 20 distributors across the country and is releasing waxings on a regular basis. The head of the firm is pressing exec Al Silver.... Sarah McLawler opens at the Apollo, New York, on June 5 with her trio. The group will feature drums, violin and organ.... Willie Mabon will play a week at the same theater starting June 15.... The Orioles and the Paul Williams ork will do a Midwest one-nighter tour starting on July

3 in Louisville, and finishing on July 14 in Cincinnati.... Shaw Artists pacted blues shouter T-Bone Walker this week.... Lynn Hope and his ork will play a week of dates in Bermuda, starting June 2. This will be coronation week in the Islands.... La Verne

LYNN HOPE

Baker opened May 15 at the Royale, Baltimore; then plays the Howard in Washington May 29.... Big Maybelle, who has another hit on Okeh Records with "Way Back Home," will be at the Orchid Room, Kansas City, starting May 18.... Buddy Johnson's ork goes out on a Southern one-nighter tour starting next week. Ork will play thru the South and into Texas thru June.

PHILLY FLASHES: Johnny Sparrow and his Bows and Arrows will return to Atlantic City's Paradise Club for the summer season, opening May 20.... The Tilters make their first Philadelphia appearance at the Showboat. In the same city, the Orioles are new at Pep's Musical Bar.... Illinois Jacquet goes into Pep's on May 4 and into the Band Box, New York, on May 12.... Sarah Vaughan starts at the Rendezvous in Philadelphia on May 6 for 10 days.... Myrtle Young, former saxist with the Sweethearts and Darlings of Rhythm, has settled down in Philadelphia with her all-girl Rays combo.... Billy Gaines and his organ and band are back at Butler Cafe, Philadelphia.... H-Bomb Ferguson with the Guy Dickerson combo usher in the season at the Whispering Pines Inn, near Hightstown, N.J. .... Varetta Dillard plays a week at Wecke's Cafe in Atlantic City starting May 22.... T.N.T. Tribble and His T.N.T. Boys have been booked by the Jolly Joyce Agency for an indefinite run at the Flamingo Club, Washington.... Freddie Mitchell's orch. opens May 18 at Bill and Lou's in Philadelphia.... Jay Hawkins, former vocalist with Tiny Grimes, joins Johnny Sparrow at the Powelton Cafe.... The Famous Ward Gospel Singers, led by Clara Ward, lists Gertrude Ward as joint owner in registering that name in Pennsylvania; also setting up their own music shop in Philadelphia under the name of Ward's House of Music.

JOLLY REPORTS: Jolly Joyce, head of the Jolly Joyce Agency, Philadelphia and

New York, has set three major unit bookings for the summer season in Wildwood, N.J. Following their stay at New York's Cafe Society in June, Chris Powell and the Blue Flames open July 1 at Moore's Inlet Cafe, sharing the spotlight with the Three Peppers, opening the same night after spending the June month at the Brown Derby in Toronto.... Four Tunes, after the June month at the Maroon Club in Montreal, open July 1 at the Martinique Cafe, taking over the spot held for many seasons by Steve Gibson.... Joyce Agency also set The Top Notes or an indefinite stand at the Cadillac Club, Cumberland, Md. ... Tiny Grimes plays the Memorial Day Dawn Dance at the Met Ballroom in Philadelphia, same evening also providing a charity jazz concert at the Academy of Music with

(Continued on page 46)

May's Record Roundup

Week of May 2

Pop Best Buy

Crazy, Man, Crazy—Bill Haley—Essex 321

Strong for several weeks in Philadelphia and Pittsburgh and still building. This week solid progress was reported in Boston, Hartford, Cincinnati and Chicago. Record is particularly strong with ops. Mercury has just brought out a Ralph Marterie cover which follows the original very closely. Flip of Haley record is "Whatcha Gonna Do."

Buy o' the Week

Hittin' On Me—Buddy Johnson—Mercury 70116

Showing well in New York, Chicago, the South and the Midwest. Record is definitely building. Flip is "Ecstasy."

Buy o' the Week

One Room Country Shack—Mercy Dee—Specialty 458

Midwest reports good for several weeks. Now showing growth in new areas. Took a big jump in North Carolina and new action reported in Pittsburgh. East has been slow, but New York noted increased interest this week. Flip is "My Woman Knows the Score."

Buy o' the Week

Way Back Home—Big Maybelle—Okeh 6955

Big jump in Tennessee and Detroit this week. Action had been solid in Chicago, Cincinnati and Pittsburgh. East is slow, with some reports citing poor shipments from label.

Territorial Tips

ATLANTA
Tell Me Mama--Little Walter--Checker 770

DETROIT
Crazy, Crazy, Crazy--"5" Royales--Apollo 446

New R.&B. Releases

GEORGE GREEN/Chance 1135
•••• Finance Man
•• Brand New Rockin' Chair
EMITT SLAY TRIO/Savoy 892
•••• I've Learned My Lesson
(vo. Bob White)
••• You Told Me That You Loved Me
(vo. Bob White)
HENRY PIERCE/Specialty 461
••• Hey Fine Mama
••• Thrill Me, Baby
FLOYD DIXON/Aladdin 3111
••• Too Much Jellyroll
••• Baby, Let's Go Down to the Woods
FRANKIE LEE SIMS/Specialty 459
••• Lucy Mae Blues
••• Don't Take It Out on Me
JIMMY BINKLEY JAZZ QUINTET/Chance 1134
••• Midnite Wail
••• Hey, Hey, Sugar Ray
LYNN HOPE ORCH./Aladdin 3178
••• Morocco
••• Broken-Hearted
ELMORE JAMES/Meteor 5003
••• Baby, What's Wrong?
••• Sinful Woman
PERCY MAYFIELD/Specialty 460
••• The Lonely One
••• Lost Mind
PEPPERMINT HARRIS/Aladdin 3177
••• Wasted Love
••• Goodbye Blues
TITUS TURNER/Okeh 6961
••• Livin' in Misery
••• Big Mary's
BASIL SPEARS/MGM 11490
••• Don't Sing Me No More Blues
••• Leave Him Alone and He'll Come Home

Week of May 9

Buy o' the Week

I've Learned My Lesson—Emitt Slay Trio—Savoy 892

Off quickly in New York, Cincinnati, Philadelphia, Buffalo and Detroit. Flip is "You Told Me That You Loved Me."

Territorial Tips

ATLANTA
Help Me Somebody--"5" Royales--Apollo 446

NEW ORLEANS
Help Me Somebody--"5" Royales--Apollo 446

New R.&B. Releases

BILLY WARD & THE DOMINOES/Federal 12129
•••• These Foolish Things Remind Me of You
••• Don't Leave Me This Way
ANNISTEEN ALLEN/King 4622
••• Trying to Live Without You
••• My Baby Keeps Rollin'
WILLIE JONES/Atlas 1028
••• Jockey Jump
••• Sad Love
CHARLIE SINGLETON/Atlas 1029
••• Broadway Beat
••• Pony Express
CHARLES BROWN/Aladdin 3176
••• Take Me
••• Risin' Sun
EARL BOSTIC ORCH./King 4623
••• Cherokee
••• The Song Is Ended
THE CHAPTERS/Republic 7038
••• Goodbye, My Love
••• Love You, Love You, Love You
THE CROWS/Rama 3
••• No Help Wanted
•• Seven Lonely Days
ST. LOUIS JIMMY/Herald 408
••• Whiskey Drinkin' Woman
••• Your Evil Ways
SMOKEY HOGG/Federal 12127
••• Gone, Gone, Gone
••• I Ain't Got Over It Yet
ROBERT HENRY/King 4624
••• Something's Wrong with My Lovin' Machine
•• Miss Anna B
BLIND BILLY TATE/Herald 411
••• I Got News for You, Baby
• Love Is a Crazy Thing
SONNY TIL/Jubilee 5118
••• (Danger) Soft Shoulders
•• Congratulations to Someone
ANDREW WIEDMAN/Jubilee 5117
•• Mama's Little Boy Got the Blues
• I'm Not a Child Anymore
THE FIVE BUDDS/Rama 2
•• I Want Her Back
•• I Guess It's All Over Now
BOO BOO TURNER GROUP/Fortune 809
•• I Goofed
•• Cooling with Boo Boo
HELEN FOSTER/Republic 7037
• They Tell Me
• Somebody, Somewhere

New Spiritual Releases

SWAN SILVERTONE SINGERS/Specialty 844
•••• He Won't Deny Me
••• Man in Jerusalem

Week of May 16

Buy o' the Week
These Foolish Things Remind Me of You b/w Don't Leave Me This Way-- Dominoes—Federal 12129
Off very strongly, with every report this past week showing good activity. New York and Philadelphia favor "Don't Leave Me This Way."

Buy o' the Week
My Mother's Eyes—Tab Smith— United 147
Excellent in Chicago and L.A. Good in Cincinnati, Philadelphia and Detroit. Flip is "Cuban Boogie."

Territorial Tips
ST. LOUIS
Is It a Dream--Vocaleers-- Red Robin 114
CINCINNATI
These Foolish Things--Dominoes-- Federal 12129
LOS ANGELES
Can't Do Sixty No More--Du Droppers --Red Robin 108

New R.&B. Releases
JIMMY NELSON/RPM 385
•••• Married Men Like Sport
•••• Meet Me with Your Black Dress On
MEMPHIS MINNIE/Checker 771
••• Me and My Chauffeur
••• Broken Heart
TINY BRADSHAW/King 4621
••• The Blues Came Pouring Down
••• Heavy Juice
STICKS McGHEE/King 4628
••• Whiskey, Women and Loaded Dice
••• Blues in My Heart and Tears in My Eyes
THE FALCONS/Savoy 893
••• You're the Beating of My Heart
••• It's You I Miss
JOHN LEE HOOKER/Modern 901
••• Ride 'Til I Die
••• It's Stormin' and Rainin'
MELVIN DANIELS/RPM 383
••• I'll Be There
••• Boogie in the Moonlight
ROSCOE GORDON/RPM 384
••• We're All Loaded
••• Tomorrow May Be Too Late
SWINGING SAX KARI ORCH./States 117
••• Henry (vo. Gloria Irving)
••• You Let My Love Grow Cold (vo. Gloria Irving)
JOAN SHAW/Gem 205
••• You Drive Me Crazy
•• Why Don't You Leave My Heart Alone

GENE AMMONS/United 149
••• Red Top
•• Just Chips
THE CHECKERS/King 4626
••• Ghost of My Baby
•• I Wanna Know
SCHOOLBOY PORTER/Chance 1132
••• Lonely Wail
•• Small Squall
THE BLENDERS/MGM 11488
••• I Don't Miss You Anymore
•• If That's the Way You Want It, Baby
HADDA BROOKS/Okeh 6962
••• Dreamin' and Cryin'
• You Let My Love Grow Cold
IRENE REDFIELD/MGM 11489
••• Shakin' the Blues Away
••• The Cat's Evil
J.B. LENORE/J.O.B. 1012
••• How Can I Leave
•• The Mojo
KING CURTIS/Monarch 702
••• Wine Head
•• I've Got News for You, Baby
THE TRENIERS/Okeh 6960
••• Rockin' Is Our Bizness
•• Sugar--Doo
SARAH McLAWLER/Brunswick 84009
•• I'm Tired Cryin' Over You
•• Foolin' Myself
SNUB MOSLEY/Penguin 0065
• Baby's Paintin' the Town
• John Henry

New Spiritual Releases
LITTLE RUTH/Modern 904
••• Lord Keep Your Hand on Mine
••• Witness
JIMMY WITHERSPOON/Modern 903
••• Each Step of the Way
••• Let Jesus Fix It for You
ROBERTA MARTIN SINGERS/Apollo 272
••• After It's All Over
•• The Old Account (vo. Narsalus McKissick)

Week of May 23

Buy o' the Week
Heavy Juice—Tiny Bradshaw— King 4621
Bradshaw's follow-up to "Soft" is showing excellent potential. Strength increasing in the East as well as in numerous Midwest points. Flip is "The Blues Came Pouring Down."

Territorial Tips
LOS ANGELES
Is It a Dream--Vocaleers-- Red Robin 114

New R.&B. Releases
MITZI MARS & SAX MALLARD ORCH./ Checker 773
•••• Roll 'Em
•••• I'm Glad
LITTLE SAM DAVIS/Rockin' 512
••• 1958 Blues
••• Goin' Home to Mother
WILLIE JOHNSON/Savoy 894
••• Love Me 'Til Dawn
••• Sometimes I Wonder Why
MERCY DEE/Bayou 003
••• Please Understand
•• Anything in This World
BERT KEYES/Rama 4
••• Your Cheatin' Heart
•• Wandering Blues
JOE HOUSTON/Bayou 004
••• Sabre-Jet
•• Moody
KING SOLOMON'S TRIO/Big Town 102
••• Mean Train
•• Baby, I'm Cutting Out
RED CALLENDER/Bayou 001
••• The Honey Jump (Parts 1 & 2)
JOE HOUSTON ORCH./Recorded in Hollywood 423
••• Corn Bread and Cabbage
•• Jay's Boogie
GWEN JOHNSON/Peacock 1613
••• New Orleans
•• Never Again
JOHNNY MOORE & MAURI JONES/ Recorded in Hollywood 425
•• Keep Cool
• Blues in My Heart
RED CALLENDER SEXTET/Bayou 002
•• Soldier's Blues (vo. Duke Upshaw)
•• In the Meantime (vo. Duke Upshaw)
HAROLD YOUNG/Rockin' 511
•• You're Gonna Miss Me, Baby
•• I Love You for Myself
GEORGE LAWSON ORCH./Rockin' 510
•• Blue Memphis
• Honkin' the Blues
JIMMIE WILSON/Big Town 103
•• Call Me a Hound Dog
• Instrumental Jump

Week of May 30

Territorial Tips
ATLANTA
Don't Leave Me This Way--Dominoes -- Federal 12129
ST. LOUIS
I'm Glad--Mitzi Mars--Checker 773
NEW ORLEANS
One Room Country Shack--Mercy Dee-- Specialty 458
Lucy Mae Blues--Frankie Lee Sims-- Specialty 459

(Continued on next page)

Record Roundup
(Continued from previous page)

New R.&B. Releases

RUTH BROWN/Atlantic 993
•••• Wild, Wild Young Men
•••• Mend Your Ways
AMOS MILBURN/Aladdin 3168
•••• Long, Long Day
••• Please, Mr. Johnson
LUCKY ENOIS QUINTET/Modern 905
••• Crazy, Man, Crazy
••• Zig Zag Ziggin'
HAL PAIGE/Atlantic 996
••• Drive It Home
••• Break of Day Blues
THE CARDINALS/Atlantic 995
••• Lovie Darling
••• You Are My Only Love
KENZIE MOORE/Specialty 462
••• I'm Beggin' You Baby

••• My Baby's Gone Again
TASSO THE GREAT/United 150
••• My Sympathy
••• Ebony After Midnight
CHUCK NORRIS/Atlantic 994
••• Messin' Up
••• Let Me Know
ILLINOIS JACQUET ORCH./
Aladdin 3180
••• Destination Moon
••• For Truly?
ANNIE LAURIE/Okeh 6973
••• I Ain't Got It Bad No More
•• It's Been a Long Time
REUBEN MITCHELL/Okeh 6974
••• Mambo After Hours
••• Tropical Blues
THE BALLADIERS/Aladdin 3123
••• What Will I Tell My Heart?
••• Forget Me Not
CLARENCE BON-TON GARLOW/
Aladdin 3179
••• New Bon-Ton Roulay
••• Dreaming

THE FIVE KEYS/Aladdin 3190
••• These Foolish Things
••• Lonesome Old Story
PAUL GAYTEN ORCH./Okeh 6972
••• Time Is A-Passin'
••• It Ain't Nothin' Happenin'
EDNA McGRIFF/Jubilee 5119
••• Scrap of Paper
•• Be Gentle with Me

New Spiritual Releases

THE PILGRIM TRAVELERS/Specialty 847
•••• Amazing Grace
•••• Gonna Walk Right Out
THE ORIGINAL GOSPEL HARMONETTES/Specialty 846
••• The Railroad
••• Where Shall I Be?
BRO. HUGH DENT/Trumpet 181
••• Let Us Glory
••• I'm Growing in the Spirit

R.&B. Beat
(Continued from page 43)

Lester Young and Savannah Churchill in the leads, while the Clara Ward Gospel Singers headline the same holiday weekend at The Arena.

CHIGAGO CHATTER: McKie Fitzhugh is now a deejay on station WOPA, Chicago, with his own show daily.... Aladdin's Eddie Mesner has left for Chicago, where he's set waxing sessions for Charles Brown.... 7-11 a.&r. chief Rudolph Toombs has recorded four by a brand new artist, Dessa Ray, who hails from Newport News, Va....

EDDIE BOYD

Mercury's singing group, the Ravens, are current at the Chicago Theater. Their latest pairing is "She's Got to Go" and "Come a Little Bit Closer".... Mabel Scott currently appearing at the Club DeLisa and getting raves.... Eddie Boyd set for a Decoration Day appearance at the Union Park Temple.... Little Walter now touring California through the end of May, then into Texas.... Margie Day and Paul Williams set for a May 22 p.a. at Detroit's

Greystone Ballroom.... Lloyd Glenn and Lowell Fulson go into Milwaukee's Rendez-vous, May 31.... Evelyn Aron is replacing Margaret Frye as librarian at WIND, Chicago. Miss Frye is moving to WCFL as librarian.... Homer Harris has taken over "Jump! Jive! and B-Bop" on KWCB, Searcy, Ark., replacing Johnny Argo, who has moved to KVLC, Little Rock.

HEARD IN HOLLYWOOD: Specialty Records reports the reaction to Percy Mayfield's first etching since that tragic accident of a year ago, "The Lonely One," has been instantaneous.... One of the most personable of recording stars we've ever met, Fats Domino, is just knocking 'em over at the 5-4 Ballroom this week. Fats' latest on Imperial, "Going to the River," is clickin' like mad.... Franklin Kort looking ten years younger these days as he bows into the biz with a label of his own, Bayou Records. Firm has set four releases for their initial offering, with two by Red Callender and one each by Mercy Dee and Joe Houston to start the ball rolling.... Allied Record Sales' Paul and Irv Shorten are keeping their hit string in tact with Dolly Cooper's Savoy etching of "I Wanna Know".... Vivian Greene goes into Denver's Cherrelyn Inn next week.... Jim Johnson's Quartet now at the Katz 'n Kitten, Denver nitery.... Denver was visited by Joe Liggins' Honeydrippers ork last week when the crew played the Rainbow Ballroom there.... Selika is now playing organ at the Rossonian Lounge, Denver, and handling piano work as well.

Atlantic, King Both Claim McPhatter

NEW YORK, June 6—When Atlantic Records last month announced the signing of Clyde McPhatter, former lead singer of the Dominoes, the diskery created a situation in which both Atlantic and King Records (the company to whom the Dominoes are currently pacted) claim exclusive rights to the warbler.

McPhatter obtained his release from Dominoes' leader Billy Ward and Rose Marks, manager of the group. According to Atlantic officials, McPhatter then approached them, showed them his release and was signed to a long term contract. McPhatter has formed his own vocal group, as yet unnamed.

Syd Nathan, King and Federal Records prexy who was in New York at the time when advised of the signing by his Cincinnati office, placed the matter in the hands of his attorney for clarification. Said Nathan, "While it is true that McPhatter has a perfectly valid release from Billy Ward and Rose Marks, it is also true that McPhatter has an individual contract with Federal Records. He belongs to us."

A similar happening occurred about a year ago when Billy Brown was given his release from the Dominoes. Brown formed his own group called the Checkers and signed with King.

MABON SIGNED TO WRITER PACT

NEW YORK, June 13—Willie Mabon, high-riding r.&b. cleffer-chanter, has been signed to an exclusive writer's pact by Goday Music. Hal Fein, who recently joined Happy Goday as a partner in the publishing enterprise, brought Mabon into the fold. Fein has also inked the artist to a personal management pact.

Mabon, who first gained attention via his sock waxing of "I Don't Know," currently has one of the top r.&b. best-sellers in his Chess slicing of "I'm Mad."

Indie Diskers Gain Influence; Tin Pan Alley Takes Notice

NEW YORK, June 13—The importance of working with the smaller diskeries in getting a new tune started is being brought home to publishers via the current activity of the well-established indie labels, as well as some of the newer firms who have shown the ability to kick off a tune in today's market. The consistent performances recently of such labels as Dot, Derby, Rainbow and Essex in the pop field, and Abbott and Imperial in the c.&w. marts, are being viewed with growing interest by the publishers.

BROWN, LOUIS TO HEAD GALE ROAD UNIT

NEW YORK, May 30—The Gale Agency's rhythm and blues one-nighter package, skedded for an eight-week tour this summer, will be headlined by chantress Ruth Brown and champ Joe Louis and his group. In addition, the show will feature acts such as the Clovers, the Buddy Johnson ork, the Lester Young combo, Wynonie Harris, Dusty Fletcher and a dance act.

This new road unit is the first r.&b. package of its size to date and will take to the road about the middle of July. It will play ballparks, arenas and auditoriums. It marks the first time that Joe Louis has appeared with a road show package.

LITTLE CAESAR INKED BY BIG TOWN

PASADENA, Calif., June 6—Four Star and Big Town Records prexy Bill McCall, Jr., this week announced the signing of warbler Little Caesar to a term recording pact.

The Big Town label, newly revived via the purchase of original masters and contracts from the previous owners, is currently kicking up a fuss on the West Coast with "Tin Pan Alley" by James Wilson. Disk is the label's first rhythm and blues release and has firmly entrenched the firm as a solid entry in the field.

McCall stated that Big Town will issue R&B releases on a regular schedule. Acknowledging that heretofore the Four Star interests primarily dealt with country and western music, McCall stated that Big Town will make every effort to give R&B distribs releases they can sell. A policy of expansion is now in force, with additional announcements of new artist signings expected soon.

In recent times Dot has come up with three hits by the Hilltoppers, including "Trying," which sold over 500,000; "If I Were King," which did better than 200,000; and their latest, "I'd Rather Die Young" and "P.S.: I Love You," which has really taken off. Essex Records, which sold over 400,000 of the Don Howard waxing of "Oh, Happy Day" is back again with another big one in Bill Haley's "Crazy, Man, Crazy," which is approaching the 200,000 mark. Derby Records sold over 150,000 of Bob Carroll's "Say It With Your Heart" and has surpassed that figure with Trudy Richards' version of "The Breeze." Rainbow Records hit nearly 100,000 with the Esquire Boys' version of "Caravan" and has another one going with their revival of the "Sheik of Araby," with the Super Sonics. In addition, Allied Records, a new subsidary of Allied Record Manufacturers, has sold close to 100,000 of the Three Dons and Ginny slicing of "Say You're Mine Again."

In the country wax field, Abbott Records at present has the best selling disk with Jim Reeves' "Mexican Joe." This represents the first time an indie has captured top slot in this market since Imperial broke thru with Slim Whitman a year ago. Imperial has been able to continue issuing strong Slim Whitman waxings, with practically all of his disks doing nicely in the market.

A number of indie labels have shown not only that they can start a tune and introduce new artists, but that they can come up with hits on a more or less consistent basis, just as the major firms do. The fact that every strong indie label has one or occasionally two artists who can sell 100,000 records has proved to be important for the up-to-date publisher. For one thing, it means the pubber has another place to take his tune, if he is unsuccessful in attracting a top record artist with a major diskery. It also helps loosen the stranglehold that many pubbers feel the major a.&r. men have on the music business.

Rather than take a second-rate artist on a major label, many pubbers would

(Continued on next page)

Joe Davis to Launch Jay-Dee Label

NEW YORK, June 6—Joe Davis, who for the past year has been supervising the recording and merchandising of r.&b. disks for M-G-M Records, will sever his relations with the diskery in July, and start his own r.&b. label. The new label will be called Jay-Dee and will feature those artists who have been waxing under Davis for the M-G-M r.&b. line. The parting of the ways between Davis and M-G-M is a friendly one and has been in the works for some time.

Davis, who heads Beacon Music and is an old-timer in the r.&b. field, started to handle r.&b. platters for M-G-M last September, and he has cut all of the waxings released by the label in this market since last December. In addition to his a.&r. duties, Davis has corralled all of the r.&b. talent for the label and has merchandised this part of the line for the diskery, even going out on the road to visit distribbers to have them get behind the line.

Since Davis has begun working with M-G-M, he has come up with a hit r.&b. waxing, "You're Mine" by the Crickets, which sold well over 50,000 platters. It's now riding with another upcoming Crickets etching, "For You I Have Eyes."

Among the talent that Davis will take to his new label are the Crickets, the Blenders, Paula Watson, Beulah Bryant, Gabriel Brown, Lem Johnson, Irene Redfield, Basil Spears, Tommy Brown, Teddy Williams, Leslie Uggams Crayne, Al King and Nat Foster. All of these artists are under a waxing pact to Davis.

According to Davis' pact with M-G-M, all masters sliced by him for the label will revert to him if they are not released by the diskery in a certain amount of time. Indications are that M-G-M will release one more group of r.&b. platters cut by Davis in July. Davis will start out on his own about July 15 and is expected to release his first wax in August.

Pressing of the Jay-Dee line will be handled by the M-G-M plant. Distribs have not yet been set for Jay-Dee, but will be named sometime in July.

M-G-M has apparently not yet decided whether to start anew in the r.&b. field or to bypass the market for the nonce. The label has a few r.&b. artists pacted, including Ivory Joe Hunter, but its r.&b. releases, outside of the Davis etchings, have been few and far between.

King Prexy's Letter Leaves Pubs Pondering

NEW YORK, June 20—King Records chief Syd Nathan has issued a form letter concerning publisher relations with his diskery that has caused some raised eyebrows among publisher recipients.

Lecturing the pubbers with his pen, Nathan says: "Anywhere from 5 to 10 weeks after a record has hit the market, we will receive a letter and a copy of the tune, and the letter will very kindly advise us that the tune has been recorded by so-and-so on such-and-such a label, and that your company thinks it a good idea if we would cover the tune. My suggestion is that whoever in any company sends out this type letter should be immediately promoted--to janitor."

Claiming that "some a.&r. men have pet publishers," Nathan advises all "that this will not be tolerated by me. All we ask is to be given the truth and not presented with a tune, told it had not been shown to anyone else and then, before we can even consider it, find it has been recorded after being shown to everyone in the business." He added that publisher day will be held at King offices here every Tuesday.

Indie Diskeries
(Continued from previous page)

rather use a top artist with an indie firm. There reasons are that, first, the strong indie artist usually can outsell a second-rate warbler with a large diskery, and second, a tune that breaks on an indie label has a good chance to be covered by a potent name on a big label.

Pubbers who have continually worked with indie diskeries over the years will sometimes even put up the loot for a waxing session in order to get a large ork and the preferred arranger or conductor. In many cases they will share only part of the costs, since the indie firm is more than happy to work with a strong new tune.

A "HORRIBLE" RELEASE FOR RAMA RECORDS

NEW YORK, June 13—George Goldner, a.&r. head of Rama Records, this week announced his label was releasing the "worst" record ever perpetrated on the rhythm and blues market. The tune is "My Baby Started Cryin'" and is sung by John Perry and his group.

Goldner insists his company is not trying to copy the recently released Horrible Record which was done for the pop field and which was a take-off on some of the "horrible" sounds which are prevalent on so many of today's diskings. This latest goof was entirely unintentional, or to put it simply, a bad take. The singing was atrocious, the instrumentalizing worse and the technical production was a rank amateur job. But in spite of all this, Goldner says the record has something that will appeal to the public. That certain something that made "Oh Happy Day" such a big seller has been captured on this side, the Rama chief claims.

Notes from the R.&B. Beat

R.&B. DISKERIES SET FOR SUMMER DRIVE: The sluggishness that usually sets in from May to the end of June has slowed down sales in the r.&b. field as well as the pop and c.&w. markets. There hasn't been a real smash in the field since "Hound Dog," which is still on the national r.&b. charts after nearly three months. But with the slow season nearly at its close, the platteries are getting their big guns ready in search of that big summer hit. Next week Atlantic will bring out a new Clovers, and Peacock is due to issue another Willie Mae Thornton shortly. There is a new Ruth Brown waxing that is starting to grab some action, the Du Droppers' "I Found Out" is strong, and B.B. King's latest on RPM is also starting to ride. At the moment, the Five Royales on Apollo have the hottest waxing on the market with "Crazy, Crazy, Crazy" and "Help Me Somebody." Both sides of this disking are on the charts, making it the first double-sided r.&b. platter in a long, long time.

DEUCES WILD FOR PEACOCK: Early reports on Peacock's "Ain't That Good News" and "Fool at the Wheel" indicate the disk could really take off here. Platter presents an unusual combination of talent. The Deuces of Rhythm are a husband-wife team, Raymond and Mildred Taylor. Ray plays the piano, trumpet, trombone and organ, while Mildred's an ace drummer. The Tempo Toppers, who handle the vocals, are a terrific group of singers. Little Richard sings lead with the group.... Duke Records will release Johnny Ace's third slicing next week, titled "The Clock." Don Robey, label prexy, is cutting a new spiritual singer, Cleophus Robinson, in Memphis today.

TEMPO TOPPERS

Duke also recently signed the Sunset Travelers, a spiritual group.... The Dixie Hummingbirds have signed guitarist Howard Carroll for the group.... Progressive Records is the name of the new Peacock jazz label, and its first release will feature pianist Phineas Newborn, Jr. The label has also pacted Al Grey and His All Stars.

Moondog, otherwise known as Alan Freed, one of Cleveland's top r.&b. deejays, is back at work and just about completely recovered after a serious automobile accident nearly two months ago.... Phil Rose, a.&r. exec at Brunswick Records, has signed saxist Freddie Mitchell to a term pact. Mitchell, formerly with

(Continued on next page)

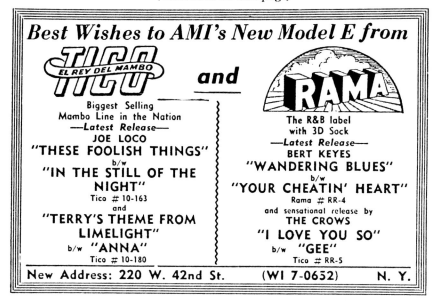
FLAIR RELEASES R.&B. PLATTERS

HOLLYWOOD, May 6—Flair Records, a division of Modern Records which heretofore waxed of only country and western tunes, this week entered the rhythm and blues field with release of two platters featuring Elmore James and Little Johnny Jones.

The releases also mark the departure of Joe Bihari from Modern to devote full time to Flair in his capacity as president and a.&r. chief. Bihari takes James with him, whom he had under personal contract. James previously recorded for another Modern subsidiary, Meteor Records.

Lubinsky Gives Advice to Record Distribs

NEW YORK, June 20—Savoy Records prexy Herman Lubinsky this week sent to his distributors another of his now famous letters in which he gives vent to his thoughts about the record business. Here, in part, is what he said:

"Webster says that inertia is passiveness, inactivity, sluggishness. We at Savoy say it is a distributor who's sitting on his ash can, talking about the heat, the weather in general, and the fact that business is dead. We just got a call from one of our distributors who had replaced one of his old salesmen with a new one. The results were astounding. Remember the adage, about the new broom sweeping clean? Maybe that's what some of our distributors ought to do—buy a new broom.

"If you are supporting some of these order-taker, robot salesmen on your payroll, you are losing money. Once in a while the boss gets off his fat fanny and gets out and sells. Possibly the boss doesn't know how to sell; then he hires someone who does. But if the boss is out playing golf or fishing, how in the h__ do you expect to help sell records? Try fishing on weekends. It might help.

"We know this letter will be on every distributor's bulletin board. We know, too, that we will be cussed up and down by the salesmen, but salesmen are like trolley cars. You miss one and another will come along. So don't let that worry you.

"There is no such thing as a 'summer slump.' We have proof of that time and time again. The slump has been started psychologically in the minds of salesmen, sales clerks, stores and distributors. A distributor who rolls up his sleeves and is determined to build up his billing is the man who reaps the golden harvest 12 months a year. He doesn't sell demand merchandise spasmodically; he creates demand so that there is a consistent, continual flow of traffic in and out of his establishment."

DOMINOES NEGOTIATE FOR PARAMOUNT

NEW YORK, May 6—Billy Ward's Dominoes, Federal Records' sock r.&b. group now featured at Loew's State Theater, Cleveland, are negotiating for an engagement at the Paramount Theater here for the fall. The Ward crew, which intends to move into the pop field via its next waxings for the King Record label, has been booked for the Michigan State Fair in September. Group played the spot last year as well.

Plans for a European tour in the fall are also being mulled, along with a one-nighter trek with a road unit here next winter. It was erroneously reported a few weeks ago that Clyde McPhatter, former lead singer of the Dominoes, had penned the r.&b. hit "Have Mercy Baby." Tune was actually penned by Billy Ward, Dominoes' topper, who has written over a dozen ditties for the group.

AUTO PLANT LAYOFFS COST DOMINO-HAMPTON PACKAGE

DETROIT, May 30—The Fox Theater's second consecutive week of stageshows, under a policy of rare spot bookings, proved a disappointment with the Lionel Hampton ork and the Dominoes, who grossed only $35,000. Hampton took in $40,000 when he played the house in March, 1949.

Primary reason for the drop below an anticipated $45,000 figure was a chain reaction of lay-offs in Ford, Chrysler and other major plants. Total lay-offs ran over 100,000 in the area. The shut-downs hit the rhythm and blues audience naturally attracted by Hampton. The week started off fairly strong, but began slipping when the Ford lay-off of 85,000 was announced.

R.&B. Beat
(Continued from previous page)

Derby and Mercury, has cut several sides for Brunswick which are skedded for early release.... Fats Domino will be at the Celebrity Club, Providence, from July 6 to 12.... The Crickets, M-G-M artists who were pacted by Shaw Artists this week, will be featured at the Apollo, New York, July 3, with Ruth Brown and the Sonny Stitt crew. Ruth, incidentally, will play the Hi-Hat in Boston from June 15 to 21.... Amos Milburn opens at Sportoree's in Youngstown, O., July 27.... Imperial Records has started a new subsidiary named Bayou.... Apollo Records also launched a new label—

Lloyds.

CLOVERS O.K. AFTER SHAKE-UP: The Clovers, Atlantic wax stars and one of the country's top r.&b. groups, were involved in an auto accident Friday (12) while traveling from Houston to Midland, Tex. One of the group's cars was struck and completely demolished by the trailer part of a trailer truck that had gone off the highway. Driving along in the dark hours of the early morning after having completed their Houston engagement, they passed the cab part of the truck, which was racing in the opposite direction toward Houston, when suddenly the truck went off the road and the trailer part whipped around, smashing into the Clovers' car from the rear. Accident was no fault of the boys and, tho one of the autos was badly damaged, only bass singer Harold Winley, who was cut around the eyes by flying glass, required any medical care. Upon being informed of the accident, manager Lou Krefetz flew down from Washington, D.C. The group rested in Houston for a few days, during which time Krefetz purchased a new car to replace the splintered vehicle. After having to cancel some of their one-nighters, the Clovers resumed their one-nighter tour in Phoenix and are now reported heading toward the West Coast.

Fats Domino goes into the Showboat, Philadelphia, July 6 to 11; then on a one-nighter trek. He will be accompanied by the Orioles on the tour, which will start in Oklahoma City July 31 and end in Amarillo, Tex., August 21.... Ruth Brown, now at the Hi-Hat in Boston, plays a week at Pep's in Philadelphia from July 22 to 27, and then does some one-nighters in the East before playing the Apollo Theater July 3. She kicks off with the Gale Agency r.&b. package July 17.... Edna McGriff, the Crickets, Bobby and Randy Waterman and the John English ork will be featured at a dance at the Bedford YMCA, Brooklyn, June 21.... Peacock and Duke are now stocking their 45's in Newark, N.J. in order to service the Eastern markets more quickly with their platters.... The Jackie Davis trio started a three-month engagement at Facks in San Francisco this week. The unit, which is managed by Lou Entin, just finished two weeks at the Band Box in New York.

Atlantic Records this week announced the pacting of Eva Foster and the Van Perry Quintet. The unit has been performing regularly at the Club 7 & T, Washington, D.C. First release, ready in about a week, will be titled "Waxin' for Maxie".... Frank Motley, dual trumpeter, out on a new DC label release on which he plays three trumpets. Frank plays "Caravan" and his version's really different.... Decca, which is prepping a new drive in the r.&b. field, has signed the Shadows, whose first disk is being readied for early release. The

group, formerly an active recording combo, is returning to wax after a five-year hiatus. Lead singer is Scott King.... The Flamingos, new vocal group on the Chance label, are at Gleason's in Cleveland, starting June 15.... Johnny Sellers, of the same label, opens at the New Era in Nashville for two weeks starting June 12.... Orkster Buddy Johnson will offer a $50 defense bond to the person who sends him the best title for a new tune which he has written in honor of Joe Louis. Titles should be sent to the Gale Agency in New York before July 10. Johnson starts out with the r.&b. road package with Ruth Brown and other stars on July 17.... Lee Magid, of Savoy Records, cut singers Earl Johnson, Huey Smith,

Billy Wright and Willie Johnson for the firm in New Orleans this week.... Larry Smith, formerly with Rainbow and Derby, has started his own r.&b. company, Tri-Boro Records. The staff will consist of Benny Wells as arranger and William Henry Miller as vice-president.

GOTHAM GLEANINGS: Tico-Rama Records, headed by George Goldner and Jack Waxman, celebrated the opening of their beautiful new offices and stock room at 220 West 42nd Street with a cocktail party at their new location on Tuesday (16). The party was one of the most congenial and light-hearted affairs attended in some time. Goldner, a.&r. head, and a lush senorita did a mambo that would do credit

to a professional team. However, some out of town distribs ran into quite a bit of trouble getting into town. Ivin Ballen and Matty Singer, of Gotham Distribs., Philadelphia, broke down several times and almost missed the party. Joe Cohen, Essex Distributors, Newark, N.J., was in a near fatal car accident. As he stopped to pay the toll at the N.J. Turnpike exit, a huge trailer truck, out of control, tore down at break neck speed, smashed his car and almost tore down the turnstiles and booths. Miraculously, while the plush convertible was reduced to a pile of junk, Joe escaped unhurt.... Fred Mendelsohn this week sold his stock in Herald Records to Jack Angel of Ember Records. The firm is now a three-way partnership comprised of Al Silver, Jack Braverman and Jack Angel. Herald announced the signing of a new group, the Rocketeers, with first release slated for next week.

New York is expected to gain another important jazz and r.&b. spot when Sugar Hill re-opens here in the fall. The club is being taken over by Ralph Watkins, who runs the Embers in Gotham. Meanwhile, the Band Box in New York is continuing with strong r.&b. and jazz shows thruout the summer, with the Woody Herman ork and Ruth Brown due in on June 9, the Lionel Hampton crew and Charlie Ventura's orch. on June 23, and the Count Basie orch., the Duke Ellington crew and the George Shearing combo to follow.... Sugar Ray Robinson, who is now an important figure in the entertainment world after retiring from the ring last year, cut two sides for King Records this week.

(Continued on next page)

R.&B. Beat
(Continued from previous page)

Robinson sings "I Shoulda Been on My Merry Way" and "Knock Him Down Whiskey." Sides will be released in a few weeks.

Bill Beasley, Republic Records, Nashville, wearing a big smile these days as a result of the reception to his disk, "I'll Help You, Baby" as sung by Christine Kittrell. Alan Bubis has resigned from Republic to devote more time to his other business interests.... Peacock sales manager Irv Marcus reports orders have been flooding in for Johnny Ace's new one on Duke, "The Clock." Matty Singer of Gotham Distribs., confirms the disk has broken wide open due to heavy airplay in Philadelphia and says he can't get sufficient quantities of the disk to meet the demand.

PHILLY FLASHES: Jimmy Tyler will be back on the bandstand at the Club Harlem, Atlantic City, this season, along with the Wild Bill Davis Trio, including Floyd Smith and Chris Columbus. Johnny Sparrow and his Bows and Arrows are booked at Grace's Belmont Inn at the resort. Also in Atlantic City, the Torch Club introduces Paula Watson and Roy Branker, piano single formerly with the Three Peppers.... Sam Stieffel, introducing stageshows at his Uptown Theater in Philadelphia, has the Joe Louis unit following Lionel Hampton's opening June 15 week. Billy Eckstine is booked in for the July 29 week.... In Philadelphia, Myrtle Young returns her all-gal unit to the Powelton Cafe, with Club Bill and Lou bringing in Al Hibbler plus the Lindy Ewell unit.

Wynonie Harris and Larry Darnell provided "Battle of the Blues" to usher in the new season at the Rosedale Beach Ballroom, Millsboro, Del., with Eddie Durham for the dancing.... Al Jenkins, operating Philadelphia's Showboat, has signed Lynn Hope exclusively for the year 1954....Elijah Sims is renovating his Sims Paradise, once

one of the most lavish cabaret spots in Philadelphia, to join the after-dark scene again next fall.... Pep's Musical Bar features Erskine Hawkins this week, while Arnett Cobb holds forth down the street at the Showboat and Al Hibbler holds the spotlight around the corner at the Emerson. Crosstown, Stuff Smith plus the Charlie Rice All-Stars attract attention to the Red Rooster, and out in West Philly, Powelton Cafe carries on with Eddie Vinson. Away from the Stem, Romaine Brown and his Romaines opened this week at the suburban Cafe De-Ray in Andalusia, Pa., while the Treniers remain in town at Sciolla's Cafe.

CHICAGO RUMBLINGS: Word out that Mahalia Jackson has auditioned for a 15-minute weekly TV show here before ABC bigwigs. Should plans go thru, show would be titled "Mahalia's House" and would have Mahalia hostessing name guests from world of music. It would be nation's first TV airer to feature a Negro gospel singer on a network basis.... Billie Holiday is currently featured at the Beaucoup Lounge here, sharing the spotlight with Ike Cole and his Quartette. Ike's the brother of Nat Cole, and this marks his first professional engagement....Leonard Chess just back from New York, where he cut four sides with Willie Mabon.... Louis Jordan goes on the boards of the Regal Theater for the week of June 19.

DENVER DOINGS: Duke Ellington packed Denver's Rainbow Ballroom on his one-nighter in the Mile High City last week. Always a favorite with Denver music lovers, the Duke was brought to Denver under the auspicies of Leroy Smith, talent representative who has been responsible for a tremendous jump in jive and blues concerts.... Selika, the Haiti-born Michigan State music grad, has hung out the s.r.o. sign at Joe Harrington's Rossonian Lounge in Denver during her limited engagement there, ending this week. From Denver she moves to Chicago to pick up her personally-designed, custom-built Hammond organ before continuing her first cross-country nitery tour....Vivianne Greene, former Apollo Theater organist, has opened for a limited time at suburban Denver's Cherrelyn Inn.

COAST CUTTINGS: The 9th Annual Cavalcade of Jazz that came off here a week ago Sunday was one of the best shows seen in some time. Approximately 15,000 music fans jammed the Wrigley Field ballpark to listen to the greatest aggregation of jazz greats ever assembled on one stage. Lloyd Price of Specialty Records was presented with an award for having won the 1952 Automatic Music Industry Poll for his "Lawdy Miss Clawdy," voted the best Rhythm and Blues disk of the year. Price, incidentally, stopped the show cold with his rendition of the hit tune and actually hypnotized a number of fans with his sock showmanship.

June's Record Roundup

Week of June 6

Buy o' the Week
She Felt Too Good--Jimmy McCracklin—Peacock 1615
Strong in North Carolina. Good in L.A., Philadelphia and St. Louis. Flip is "Share and Share Alike."

Buy o' the Week
Where You At? (Venice, BMI) b/w Baby Don't Turn Your Back On Me (Venice, BMI)—Lloyd Price—Specialty 463
Heavy action in Philadelphia and also good in a number of Midwest areas.

Buy o' the Week
I'm Glad b/w Roll 'Em—Mitzi Mars—Checker 773
Now riding the juke box chart with good reports from a number of Southern and Midwestern points.

Territorial Tips
CINCINNATI
Wild, Wild Young Men--Ruth Brown--Atlantic 993
NEW ORLEANS
Please Love Me--B.B. King--RPM 386

New R.&B. Releases
LLOYD PRICE/Specialty 463
•••• Baby, Don't Turn Your Back on Me
••• Where You At?
THE DU DROPPERS/Victor 20-5321
••• I Found Out
••• Little Girl, Little Girl
VARETTA DILLARD/Savoy 897
•••• Mercy, Mr. Percy
••• No Kinda Good, No How
THE CRICKETS/MGM 11507
•••• I'll Cry No More
••• For You I Have Eyes
CECIL CARTER ORCH./Federal 12130
••• What's Wrong with Me?
(vo. Ben Hughes)
••• Strange Blues (violin--Ginger Smock)

CHRISTINE KITTRELL/Republic 7044
••• I'll Help You Baby
••• L & N Special
JIMMY WITHERSPOON/Federal 12128
••• One Fine Gal
••• Back Home
THE FOUR PLAID THROATS/Mercury 70143
••• My Inspiration
•• The Message
ALLEN BUNN/Apollo 447
••• Baby I'm Going to Throw You Out
••• Wine
THE CAROLS/Savoy 896
•• Fifty Million Women
•• I Got a Feelin'
BEULAH BRYANT/MGM 11509
•• He's Got Plenty on the Ball
•• I'm Just Like the Bear
DUKE HAMPTON ORCH./King 4625
•• Please Be Good to Me (vo. Aletra Hampton)
•• The Push
JIMMY WRIGHT ORCH./Meteor 5007
• Porkey Pine
• Scotch Mist
(Continued on next page)

PIANO RED

"YOUR MOUTH'S GOT A HOLE IN IT"

and

"DECATUR STREET BOOGIE"

ANOTHER SMASH
IN RCA VICTOR'S
RED HOT R&B LINE

RCA VICTOR RECORDS 20/47-5337

RCA VICTOR
FIRST IN RECORDED MUSIC

Record Roundup
(Continued from previous page)

SUNNY BLAIR/Meteor 5006
• Please Send My Baby Back
• Gonna Let You Go
AL (TENOR SAX) KING/MGM 11508
• Flyin' with the King
• The King Is Blue
ALBERT AMMONS/Mercury 70158
• I Don't Want to See You
(vo. Jack Cooley)
• Swanee River Boogie

New Spiritual Releases
THE TRAVELING FOUR/Score 5040
••• I Ain't Gonna Study War No More
••• No Love Like Mother's

Week of June 13

Buy o' the Week
I Found Out (Park Ave., BMI)—Du-Droppers—RCA Victor 20-5321
Disk really broke out this past week and is already on a number of territorials. Flip is "Little Girl, Little Girl" (Park Ave., BMI).

Buy o' the Week
Please Love Me b/w Highway Bound—B.B. King—RPM 386
Now on the St. Louis chart and good in the South, Pittsburgh and New York. Except for a Chicago report, all action appears to be on "Please Love Me."

Buy o' the Week
Third Degree (Burton, BMI)—Eddie Boyd—Chess 1541
On Detroit chart and showing nice action in Chicago, Cleveland, Pittsburgh, and in sections of the South.

Territorial Tips
WASHINGTON--BALTIMORE
These Foolish Things--Dominoes--Federal 12129
DETROIT
Third Degree--Eddie Boyd--Chess 1541
LOS ANGELES
Tin Pan Alley--Jimmy Wilson--Big Town 101

New R.&B. Releases
EDDIE BOYD/Chess 1541
•••• Third Degree
••• Back Beat
DINAH WASHINGTON/Mercury 70175
•••• My Lean Baby
••• Never, Never
B.B. KING ORCH./RPM 386
•••• Please Love Me
••• Highway Bound
BUDDY JOHNSON ORCH./
Mercury 70173
••• That's How I Feel About You
(vo. Ella Johnson)
••• Jit Jit
T-BONE WALKER/Imperial 5239
••• Party Girl
••• Here in the Dark
ELMORE JAMES & BROOM DUSTERS/
Flair 1011
••• Early in the Morning
••• Hawaiian Boogie
DANNY OVERBEA/Checker 774
••• 40 Cups of Coffee
••• I'll Follow You
THE SWALLOWS/King 4632
••• Bicycle Tillie
••• Nobody's Lovin' Me

CHARLES BROWN/Aladdin 3191
••• I Lost Everything
••• Lonesome Feeling
LITTLE JOHNNY JONES/Flair 1010
••• I May Be Wrong
••• Dirty By the Dozen
BULL MOOSE JACKSON/King 4634
••• Meet Me with Your Black Dress On
•• Try to Forget Him, Baby
JIMMY COE/States 118
••• After-Hour Joint
•• Baby, I'm Back
LITTLE BUBBER/Imperial 5238
••• Never Trust a Woman
••• Runnin' Round
THE DU DROPPERS/Red Robin 116
••• Come On and Love Me, Baby
••• Go Back
LULA REED/King 4630
••• My Poor Heart
••• I'm Losing You
LYNN HOPE ORCH./Aladdin 3185
••• Tenderly
••• Just the Way You Look Tonight
DEUCES OF RHYTHM & TEMPO
TOPPERS/Peacock 1616
••• Ain't That Good News?
(vo. Little Richard)
••• Fool at the Wheel (vo. Little Richard)
PRESTON LOVE ORCH./Federal 12132
••• You Got Me Drinking (vo. Frank Evans)
•• Stay By My Side
LIL' SON JACKSON/Imperial 5237
••• Spending Money Blues
••• All Alone
BOBBY MARCHAN/Aladdin 3189
••• Just a Little Walk
•• Have Mercy
MILT BUCKNER ORGAN TRIO/
Scooter 306
••• Boo It
• Trapped
THE SERENADERS/Red Robin 115
•• I Want to Love You, Baby
•• Will She Know
RAY MILLER/Savoy 895
•• That's What Love Did to Me
•• Please Be Kind

New Spiritual Releases

THE DIXIE HUMMING BIRDS/
Peacock 1713
•••• Eternal Life
••• Lord If I Go
THE STARS OF HOPE/Peacock 1712
••• You Better Mind
••• Where Shall I Go

Week of June 20

Pop Best Buys

Crying in the Chapel (Valley, BMI)—Darrell Glenn—Valley 105
Just received for review, this disk has been getting some good action in some spots. It's a semi-religious number, and distribution is still far from complete. Action on this has sparked a number of major cover efforts. Flip is "Hang Up That Telephone."

Buy o' the Week

Tin Pan Alley—Jimmy Wilson—Big Town 101
Doing well in Cincinnati, L.A., Chicago, St. Louis and parts of the South. Not all areas have yet received this record. Flip is "Big Town Jump."

Buy o' the Week

I'll Cry No More (Beacon, BMI) b/w For You I Have Eyes (Beacon, BMI)—Crickets—M-G-M 11507
Good and up-and-coming reports from Philadelphia, Durham, Chicago, Cincinnati and Buffalo.

Buy o' the Week

If I Can't Have You—Flamingos—Chance 1133
Strongest selection this week. On the Philadelphia chart and good in Detroit, Cincinnati, Buffalo and St. Louis. Action is definitely increasing. Flip is "Some Day, Some Way."

Territorial Tips

NEW ORLEANS
Please Love Me--B.B. King--RPM 386
ATLANTA
Please Love Me--B.B. King--RPM 386
CHARLOTTE
Don't Leave Me This Way--Dominoes --Federal 12129
WASHINGTON--BALTIMORE
My Dear, Dearest Darling--"5" Willows--Allen 1000
CHICAGO
She Felt Too Good--Jimmy McCrack-lin--Peacock 1615

PHILADELPHIA
If I Can't Have You--Flamingos --Chance 1133
Mend Your Ways--Ruth Brown--Atlantic 993
LOS ANGELES
Highway Bound--B.B. King--RPM 386

New R.&B. Releases

SUGAR RAY ROBINSON/King 4641
•••• Knock Him Down Whiskey
••• I Shoulda Been on My Merry Way
DOLLY COOPER/Savoy 898
••• Alley Cat
••• I Need Romance
PINEY BROWN/King 4636
••• Whispering Blues
••• Walk-a-Block-and-Fall
BIG THREE TRIO/Okeh 6944
••• Be a Sweetheart (vo. Willie Dixon)
•• Come Here, Baby
IKE CARPENTER ORCH./Decca 28687
••• Ain't Nothin' Nothin', Baby, Without You (vo. Effie Smith)
•• Shoo My Blues Away (vo. Effie Smith)
THE ROYALS/Federal 12133
••• Get It
••• No It Ain't
WYNONIE HARRIS/King 4635
••• The Deacon Don't Like It
•• Song of the Bayou
THE JUMPING JACKS/Lloyds 101
••• Do Let That Dream Come True
••• Why, Oh, Why?
FRANK MOTLEY/DC 94-78
••• I Found Out
• Caravan
ARNETT COBB/Mercury 70171
•• Apple Wine
• The Traveler

New Spiritual Releases

LUCILLE BARBEE/Republic 7034
••• Where Could I Go?
••• I Just Can't Keep It to Myself

Week of June 27

Buy o' the Week

The Clock (Lion, BMI)—Johnny Ace—Duke 112
Off to a fast start, disk is already on the New Orleans chart, with good to strong reports from New York, Philadelphia, Detroit and Southern areas. Flip is "Aces Wild" (Lion, BMI).

Buy o' the Week

Mercy, Mr. Percy (Savoy, BMI) b/w No Kinda Good, No How (Crossroads, BMI)—Varetta Dillard—Savoy 897
Disk took off this week and is the strong-est of this week's selections. Heavy action on "Mercy, Mr. Percy."

Buy o' the Week

After Hour Joint (Pamlee, BMI) b/w Baby, I'm Gone (Pamlee, BMI)—Jimmy Coe—States 118
Strong in New York, Philadelphia, Chicago and Cleveland. Most action on "After Hour Joint."

Territorial Tips

ST. LOUIS
Early in the Morning--Roy Milton--Specialty 464
DETROIT
If I Can't Have You--Flamingos--Chance 1133

(Continued on next page)

Record Roundup
(Continued from previous page)

CHICAGO
40 Cups of Coffee--Danny Overbea--Checker 774
PHILADELPHIA
Paradise Hill--Embers--Herald 410
NEW ORLEANS
The Clock--Johnny Ace--Duke 112

New R.&B. Releases

JOHNNY ACE/Duke 112
•••• The Clock
••• Aces Wild
SHIRLEY AND LEE/Aladdin 3192
•••• Shirley's Back
••• So in Love
CAMILLE HOWARD/Federal 12134
•••• Hurry Back, Baby
••• I Tried to Tell You
EARL FOREST ORCH./Duke 113
••• Last Night's Dream
•• Fifty-Three
PIANO RED/Victor 20-5337
••• Decatur Street Boogie
••• Your Mouth's Got a Hole in It
CHUCK WILLIS/Okeh 6985
••• Don't Deceive Me
••• I've Been Treated Wrong Too Long

ROY MILTON/Specialty 464
••• Let Me Give You All My Love
••• Early in the Morning
THE CROWS/Rama 5
••• Gee
••• I Love You So
THE ORIOLES/Jubilee 5120
••• One More Time
•• I Cover the Waterfront
JOE LIGGINS/Specialty 465
••• Farewell Blues
••• Just Plain Blues
DESSA RAY/7-11 2103
••• Ain't Gonna Tell
•• Daddy
ROY BROWN/King 4637
••• Old Age Boogie (Pts. 1 & 2)
JIMMY WILSON/7-11 2104
••• Tell Me
••• Ethel Lee
JOHNNY SELLERS/Chance 1138
••• Newport News
•• Mirror Blues
THE "5" WILLOWS/Allen 1000
••• Rock Little Francis
• My Dear, Dearest Darling
EFFIE SMITH/Trend 56
••• Three Men in My Life
••• Cry, Baby, Cry
GEORGIE AULD & SARAH McLAWLER/
Brunswick 84014
•• The Blue Room

•• Let's Get the Party Rockin'
BERT KEYES/Rama 6
••• After All I've Been to You
•• Be With the One You Love
VICKI NELSON/Brunswick 84011
• I've Got to Keep Movin'
•• My Poor Life Blues
STOMP GORDON/Decca 48297
•• Pennies From Heaven
•• My Mother's Eyes

New Spiritual Releases

THE SUNSET TRAVELERS/Duke 201
•••• Yes, Yes, I've Done My Duty
••• My Number Will Be Changed
BROTHER JOE MAY/Specialty 848
•••• The Old Ship of Zion
••• Thank You, Lord, for One More Day
THE CINCINNATIANS/Brunswick 84012
••• Will You Be There?
••• Jesus My Friend
BILL LANDFORD QUARTET/Victor 20-5351
••• The Devil Is a Real Bright Boy
••• Jesus Love of My Soul
THE CHOSEN GOSPEL SINGERS/Specialty 849
••• It's Getting Late in the Evening
••• The Lord Will Make a Way Somehow

JULY 1953

DECCA STARTS R.&B. RETURN; SHAD APPOINTED A.&R. CHIEF

NEW YORK, July 11—The recent decision of Decca Records to re-enter the rhythm and blues field was augmented this week with the naming of Bobby Shad, now with Mercury, as Decca's new r.&b. chief. Shad's appointment was announced by Milt Gabler, Decca a.&r. director, and will take effect next Monday (20).

Shad's dual responsibilities with Decca will cover sales promotion as well as artists and repertoire. He will personally promote each new r.&b. release. In addition to handling artists and creative chores, it is expected that Shad will spend much of his time on the road covering key r.&b. territories.

W.D. (Dee) Kilpatrick, who handles country wax chores for Mercury, will take over Shad's slot with the label. Although Mercury has no big plans for heavy r.&b. expansion, veepee Art Talmadge said new attention will be paid to moving such wax in Southern areas. Kilpatrick already covers the South for Mercury.

Decca's intention to move back into the r.&b. specialty market was said to be largely to meet the demands of distributors located in areas where r.&b. wax constitutes a substantial segment of the sales volume. Like most majors, Decca, over the past few years, had gradually abandoned the market to small independent diskeries who concentrated their efforts on r.&b. material. Label execs indicated that Decca is also expanding its disk jockey coverage to include important r.&b. platter spinners.

The first batch of r.&b. records spearheading Decca's return to the field was released about a week ago, before Shad's appointment was announced. Included in that release were slicings by the Shadows, a group managed by Paul Kapp of General Music; saxist Coleman Hawkins; Little Donna Hightower, Tony Hollins and a spiritual disking by Sister Rosetta Tharpe

(Continued on next page)

Withdraw "Dragnet," Modern Told

HOLLYWOOD, July 18—Producers of the radio-TV melodrama "Dragnet" made their second demand within a fortnight this week for the market withdrawal of a record charged with using the drama's theme music, format and title without authorization.

Modern Records, which released "Dragnet Blues" by Johnny Moore's Three Blazers, were advised by attorneys for Dragnet Productions, Inc., that Modern cease what the show's producers claim is the unauthorized manufacture, release and distribution of the disk in question. They assert that use of "Dragnet's" name, music and format constitutes both copyright infringement and unfair competition.

Modern was asked to deliver all its master records, matrices, labels, sheet music and advertising matter on which the name "Dragnet" appears. Modern declined to comply immediately, altho attorneys for both parties met to discuss the matter. Another meeting is scheduled for Monday, when diskery's attorney is expected to suggest a compromise entailing change of disk's introductory music, the chief bone of contention.

Action against Modern follows closely the successful "Dragnet" demands against Bayou Records which first came out with a disk titled "Dragnet." Bayou withdrew the disk to the "Dragnet" firm's satisfaction.

Modern indicated it would continue to press the record pending a final settlement. Disk has given indications of getting sales action. Diskery denies infringement, claiming the only similarity "Dragnet Blues" has with the show's theme music are use of the latter's first four bars.

In the meantime it has become known that Buddy Morrow ork had waxed the "Dragnet" musical theme for Victor Records here with Steve Sholes supervising. Dragnet Productions negotiated with Walter Schumann, of Schumann-Bourne Music, for licensing of the eight-bar theme music for recording. The Victor disk, with the blessing of Dragnet Productions, is due for early release under the "Dragnet" title.

MERCURY PACTS FOUR NEW R.&B. NAMES

HOLLYWOOD, July 18—Four new artists were acquired this week for Mercury Records by W.D. (Dee) Kilpatrick in his new added capacity of artist and repertoire director for the label's rhythm and blues division.

Kilpatrick's quartet of artists all hail from the New Orleans region. They include Woo Woo Moore, Ray Johnson, Lollypop and Pat Valadear. Also signed was Tibby Edwards, male hillbilly singer from New Orleans.

BIG TOWN ADDS TALENT

PASADENA, Ca., July 11—Big Town Records, which launched its re-entry into the R&B field via a nationwide smash hit in "Tin Pan Alley," this week disclosed the signing of additional talent to its expanding artist roster.

Prexy Bill McCall, Jr. announced the signing to term pacts of Jesse Thomas and Sister Roseanne Winn. Both artists have already cut their initial wax, with releases due shortly.

Firm has also released their first Little Caesar wax titled "Big Eyes" and has indicated they already have a hit on their hands via distribs' initial and repeat orders. Meanwhile, sale of their "Tin Pan Alley" with Jimmy Wilson continues to soar, with distribs in the South and East regions increasing their orders substantially. Glen Allen Distributing Co., Memphis, Tenn., this week reported that "Tin Pan Alley" was rapidly overtaking all coming R&B tunes in the area.

McCall also noted the assignment of J.R. Fullbright, veteran A&R man in the blues and rhythm biz, who is currently scouting new talent and tunes for Big Town.

Notes from the R.&B. Beat

HOT BISCUITS: The virtual flood of topflight new releases from the indie r.&b. diskeries could give the industry a real shot in the arm this summer and help shake the traditional slowdown this time of year normally brings. Hot as the Coney Island fireworks show on July 4 are Johnny Ace's "The Clock" and Earl Forest's "Last Night's Dream" on Duke, the Tempo Toppers' "Ain't That Good News" and "Fool at the Wheel" on Peacock. Atlantic has the Clovers' seventh straight smash in "Good Lovin'" and Ray Charles' "Mess Around." Savoy comes up with a new Emitt Slay Trio offering titled "Male Call" that should stir up some action based on the novelty of the disk, and a solid hit in "Four Cold, Cold Walls" by Billy Wright.

Heat means nothing when Ruth Brown is the draw. Appearing last week at Harlem's Apollo Theater, Ruth chalked up another box office record for the summer season. The songstress goes into rehearsal for the big tour with the Clovers and Champ Joe Louis which tees off in mid-July.... Clyde McPhatter, newly pacted Atlantic artist, began rehearsing with his new group last week.... Bob Weinstock of Prestige Records reported to be on a honeymoon trip thru the South, will mix a little business with his pleasure by visiting some distribs along the way.... Bert Keyes' Rama slicing of "Your Cheatin' Heart" breaking wide open in Philadelphia, with the label's distrib in that area, Gotham, reordering in four figures.... New diskery, Old Town Record Corp., signed and waxed the Five Crowns, who had some good sides for Rainbow awhile back.

RUTH BROWN

The Gale Agency's giant r.&b. package starring Ruth Brown, the Clovers, the Joe Louis act and Wynonie Harris, as well as other key acts and a large ork, will kick off in Boston July 17. Here is the rest of the schedule for the first two weeks: Newark, N.J., 18; Baltimore, 19; Cleveland, 20; Detroit, 21; Cincinnati, 23; Evansville, Ind., 24; St. Louis, 25, , Kansas City, Mo., 26; Wichita, Kan., 27; Tulsa, Okla., 28; Oklahoma City, 29; Amarillo, Tex., 30. Unit is now almost completely booked thru August 18, and there is a good possibility that it will run until September.... Alan (Moondog) Freed will emsee the "Rhythm and Blues show" when it appears at the Cleveland Arena on Monday night (20). The WJW, Cleveland, deejay will be making his first public appearance since recovering from a se-

(Continued on next page)

HAZEL SCOTT INKED BY DORAINE

NEW YORK, July 11—Pete Doraine, a.&r. head of Allen Records, New York diskery, this week announced the signing of Hazel Scott to an exclusive recording contract with the indie label. Miss Scott, pianiste extraordinaire who formerly waxed for Decca and Capitol, never before recorded rhythm and blues material, which is what she will do for Allen. "You ain't heard her really sing until you've heard her do rhythm and blues," Doraine said.

Miss Scott left for Europe on July 7, where she will tour all the big cities of the continent, including an appearance at the London Palladium.

Savoy to Handle Dee Gee Line

NEW YORK, July 18—Prexy Herman Lubinsky, of the Savoy and Regent diskeries, has completed a deal with Dee Gee Records, Detroit-based jazz label, to handle national and world-wide distribution for the Dee Gee line. Deal involves over 200 masters, many of which are not yet released.

Lubinsky stated that the deal calls for maintaining the label's name and for Dave Usher, Dee Gee topper, to continue recording for the label. Usher will also handle artists and repertoire assignments in the Detroit area for the Savoy line.

Plans call for early release of additional Dee Gee masters on both LP and EP.

Decca Returns
(Continued from previous page)

and Marie Knight.

Shad's initial entry into the music business was as a partner in a mail-order record firm. He later formed his own diskery and also cut sides on a free-lance basis for several indie labels. A onetime a.&r. chief for National Records, Shad joined the a.&r. staff of Mercury in 1951.

CHESS SIGNS WASHBOARD SAM

CHICAGO, June 27—For the past two years, Leonard Chess, executive of Chess Records here, has been on the lookout for a character named "Washboard Sam," but to no avail. Suddenly, out of a clear sky, about three weeks ago, just as Chess was about to board a plane at Chicago's Midway Airport, he bumped smack into the singer. Quickly taking advantage of the chance meeting, Chess pacted Washboard Sam to a contract. Several sides have already been cut, the first of which should be ready in about two weeks.

"PARADISE HILL" RIGHTS TO MILLER

NEW YORK, July 11—Essex label chief Dave Miller has acquired the copyright of the rhythm and blues ditty "Paradise Hill" from writers Al Silver and Jack Angel. The deal was completed this week. The tune will be in Miller's Eastwick firm, a BMI affiliate. Tune has been getting action via a Herald label disking by the Embers. Miller is rushing a pop version for release on his Essex label.

R.&B. Beat
(Continued from previous page)

rious auto accident in April.... Shaw Artists are putting together a number of packages for the late summer. One will feature the Griffin Brothers with Chuck Willis starting July 31 in Mobile, Ala. The other will package the Du Droppers with the Joe Morris ork. The latter unit will start out after August 15.... Fats Domino and The Orioles conclude their Texas tour August 18. After that Domino will head toward the West Coast, and the Orioles will return East. The Orioles' latest waxing, "Crying in the Chapel," looks like a real comer.... Lynn Hope is back on tour after a three-week layoff.... A group called the Prisonaires, all inmates of the Tennessee State Penitentiary, in Nashville, are waxing for Sun Records.

DECCA GRABS LITTLE ESTHER: Decca Records is moving ahead in its drive to grab some of the r.&b. traffic. This week the diskery pacted thrush Little Esther, formerly on the Federal label, and warbler Rudy Render. Bobby Shad, new Decca r.&b. head, takes over in his post next week.... Tico Records this week pacted organist Vin Strong, formerly with RCA Victor. Margarita Benitez will be featured with the mambo organist.... Dinah Washington plays the Howard in Washington July 3 and the Royale in Baltimore July 10. Mercury Records will run a "Lean Baby" contest at both theaters in honor of the canary's latest waxing.... Peacock exec Irv

(Continued on next page)

R.&B. Beat
(Continued from previous page)

Marcus hits the road this week for visits with distribs in Maryland, Virginia, North Carolina, Pennsylvania, and Ohio, on his way to Chicago for the NAMM convention.... Dizzy Gillespie, who joined Shaw Artists a few weeks ago, has had a new label created especially for him by Roost Records. The label is Showcase, and the first waxing will be released next week. Tunes, both written by Dizzy, are "Purple Sounds" and "Chris and Diz." Slogan on label reads, "A label dedicated to the jazz experiments of Dizzy Gillespie."

Little Walter plays the Royal Peacock in Atlanta from July 21 to August 3 and then goes on a one-nighter binge thru Florida and along the East Coast.... Willie Mabon opens July 20 at the Celebrity Club, Providence.... Coleman Hawkins and his orch. play Weeke's Cafe in Atlantic City

starting July 24.... Lester Young is set for two weeks at Birdland, New York, commencing July 3.... Sarah Vaughan plays the Three Rivers Inn, Three Rivers, N.Y., July 3.... Ella Fitzgerald will be at the Chicago Theater for two weeks starting July 10.... Arthur Prysock does two weeks at the Midtown Hotel in St. Louis opening July 3.... The Sarah McLawler trio is set for the Howard Theater, Washington, for one week beginning July 3.... Mabel Scott is now summering at the Harlem Club, Atlantic City. She has been booked at the shore resort for a 10-week stand.... The Orioles will be at the Orchid Room, Kansas City, Mo., from July 19 to 25.... T-Bone Walker, Paul Williams and Margie Day play the Celebrity Club, Providence, August 17 to 23, then go out on one-nighters thru the East.

PHILLY FLASHES: Rhythm & blues acts headline the after-dark goings on at the Wildwood seashore resort. The start of the new season finds the Treniers set at the Riptide; the Four Tunes at the Martinique; Daisy Mae and Her Hep Cats at the Bolero Bar; Red Spencer and the Five Red Flames at the Golden Dragon; and Bobby Harris at the Triangle Bar. Meanwhile, the Surf Club, going in for the bigger bands, brings in Lionel Hampton. And at Club Esquire, it's the music of Claude Hopkins for both show and dance. Room also originates the midnight disk jockeying of Ramon Bruce via WCMC.... Jolly Joyce Agency, Philadelphia, has set Romaine Brown and his Romaines at the Riptide Club, Wildwood. Brown was erstwhile pianist with Steve Gibson's Red Caps, and his new combo includes two other ex-Red Caps--Henry Green Tucker on drums and singer Earl Plummer. Bass and guitar round out the unit.

The r.&b. names are also very much in evidence on the after-dark scene in Atlantic City. Weeke's Cocktail Lounge kicked off the season with the Five Keys, Freddie Cole and Milt Buckner.... New policy at Mack's Musical Tavern provided for Oscar Peterson for the kick-off with follow-ups scheduled for Dizzy Gillespie, Art Tatum and Eddie Heywood. New show policy for the Dude Ranch provided a headline spot for The Charioteers. Grace's Little Belmont is set for the season with Johnny Sparrow and his Bows and Arrows. Elsie Campbell and her Calypso Trio are at Burton's Bar. Twin stands at the Fort Pitt house the Picadilly Pipers with Bonnie Davis and the Billy Ford Quintet. At the major cabaret stands, Club Harlem has Jimmy Tyler for show and dance with the "Wild Bill" Davis trio the special lounge attraction. At the Paradise Cafe, it's the music of Tadd Dameron with the Emitt Slay trio in the cocktail lounge.... Stan Pat,

Trenton, N.J., disk jockey who as Pat Pagnotta is a New York theatrical agent, has a four-page write-up in the current issue of Scope magazine.

SHE DUNNE IT: Latest showbusiness success story in Detroit involves local lass Jeanne Dunne, who's dubbed "The Modern Cinderella" in these parts. Jeanne was a soloist in a church choir only one month ago when she was discovered by Al Green, who turned gal over to Maurice King for grooming. After two weeks Green took her to see the owner of the Flame Show Bar, who was so impressed with her voice that he decided to head his next bill with the gal. Deal was reportedly $500 per week, for two weeks, with option. Well, Jeanne is now in her third week at the Flame, reportedly making much more than the original $500 per.

A SEEDY SITUATION?: Leonard Chess is very excited these days about a Browley Guy disking on Checker label entitled "Watermelon Man." Seems the lad, who had done nothing musically before, one day came up to Len with this tune he had written. Len liked the ditty and immediately had it recorded. Len asks, "Remember the men who travelled around from house to house selling watermelons? Well, this tune is very reminiscent of those guys".... Sax Mallard, since his click on Mitzi Mars' Checker waxing of "I'm Glad," is getting big hands nightly for his combo at the Strand Lounge here.... Vivian Carter, r.&b. deejay on WGRY, Gary, Ind. , has started a new r.&b. label, Vee-Jay, in partnership with Jimmy Bracken. First artists signed by the label are Jimmy Reed and the Spaniels.

CHI-TOWN CHATTER: New addition is the midnite show at the Shakespeare Theatre every Saturday. Opening show (11) included Mitzi Mars with Jack Cooley and his band. Management intends to headline show biz's biggest names every week. Cooley is in charge of productions...."Nature Boy" Brown replaces Eddie Boyd at Ralph's Club for a limited engagement.... Al Benson of Parrot Records says he expects big things from the firm's two newest releases, Mabel Scott's "Mr. Fine" and the Chocolateers' "Bartender's Blues".... Riding in a cab this week, this correspondent got to talking with the driver, who by coincidence turned out to be Johnny Jordan, a former member of the Four Vagabonds quartet. Seems sometime ago, a member of the group passed away, causing the boys to disband. A replacement has now been found, however, and the group plans to resume singing under a new monicker, the "Johnny Jordan Quartette." They expect to cut a session soon for a West Coast label.... Edna McGriff making her first appearance in the Midwest, accompanied by Buddy Lucas' band. Gal has just about everything going for her to win a large following in the area.

WEST COASTINGS: It looks like a toss-up between Willie Mae Thornton's "Hound Dog" and Willie Mabon's "I Don't Know" as the hottest record of this or any other season. Only platter we can remember that set up as much of a storm was the old Johnny Moore version of "Drifting Blues".... Joe Bihari looking almost ten years younger just after talking about playing softball with the guys on Sundays.... Aladdin's Eddie Mesner sweltering in New York's heat, taking time out to cut Amos Milburn, Shirley and Lee and Charles Brown. Brother Leo's palace is exactly that—replete with swimming pool, cabannas, etc. Firm's "New Bon Ton Roolay" with Clarence Garlow really starting to step out, despite summer doldrums.... Abe Diamond having problems filling all the orders for Christine Kittrell's "I'll Help You Baby." Seems the Republic firm just ain't shipping 'em fast enough.... Luke Dolphin taking over many of John's duties at the store these days, as John concentrates his efforts on "Keep Cool."

JOHNNY MOORE

July's Record Roundup

Week of July 4

Buy o' the Week
Please Don't Leave Me (Commodore, BMI) b/w The Girl I Love (Commodore, BMI)—Fats Domino—Imperial 5240
Breaking quickly, with solid reports from New York, Dallas, L.A., Durham and Chicago.

Buy o' the Week
Early in the Morning—Roy Milton—Specialty 464
Placed on the St. Louis and L.A. territorials and showed up on juke box chart this week. Flip is "Let Me Give You All My Love."

Territorial Tips
ATLANTA
Turn the Lamp Down Low--Muddy Waters--Chess 1542
ST. LOUIS
Don't Deceive Me--Chuck Willis--Okeh 6985

New R.&B. Releases
THE CLOVERS/Atlantic 1000
•••• Good Lovin'
•••• Here Goes a Fool
RAY CHARLES/Atlantic 999
••• Mess Around
••• Funny
EVA FOSTER & VAN PERRY QUINTET/Atlantic 997
••• You'll Never Know
••• Waxin' for Maxie
THE BLENDERS/MGM 11531
••• Please Take Me Back
••• Isn't It a Shame?
CECIL (COUNT) CARTER/Federal 12135
••• Ginger Bread
•• I Know, I Know
WILLIS (GATOR TAIL) JACKSON/Atlantic 998
••• Shake Dance
••• Walking Home
PAULA WATSON/MGM 11530
••• Chick-Chick-Chick-a-Dee
••• Tennessee Walk
CHRIS WOODS/United 151
••• Brazil
•• Blues for Lew
SONNY THOMPSON/King 4639
••• Low Flame
••• Waiting to Be Loved by You (vo. Lula Reed)

EARL BOSTIC ORCH./King 4644
••• Melancholy Serenade
••• What, No Pearls?
LITTLE WILLIE LITTLEFIELD/Federal 12137
••• The Midnight Hour Was Shining
•• My Best Wishes and Regards
LEM JOHNSON/MGM 11532
••• Never Love Anybody Better Than You Do Yourself
••• Eatin' and Sleepin' Blues
THE FOUR BELLS/Gem 207
••• Please Tell It to Me
••• Long Way to Go
CHARLIE BRANTLEY/King 4640
••• Think About Me, Baby (vo. Whiskey Sheffield)
•• Look at Me (vo. Whiskey Sheffield)
THE ROCKETEERS/Herald 415
• Foolish One
• Gonna Feed My Baby Poison

New Spiritual Releases
MAHALIA JACKSON/Apollo 273
••• I'm Going Down to the River
••• Do You Know Him?
REV. A. JOHNSON/Glory 4025
••• Death in the Morning
••• I Don't Know How to Get Along Without the Lord
SONS OF CALVARY/Glory 4014
••• A Man Taking Names
•• Trust in the Lord
THE MELODY ECHOES/Apollo 274
••• Dip Your Fingers in Some Water
•• When I've Done the Best I Can
MYRTLE JACKSON/Brunswick 84013
•• God Answers Prayers
•• Precious Lord, Hold My Hand

Week of July 11

Buy o' the Week
Shirley's Back (Aladdin, BMI)—Shirley and Lee—Aladdin 3192
Good reports from North Carolina, Nashville, Dallas, Philadelphia and Cleveland. Shaping up as another big one in their cycle of answer songs.

Territorial Tips
NEW ORLEANS
Please Don't Leave Me--Fats Domino--Imperial 5240
CINCINNATI
I'm Crying--Bobby Mitchell--Imperial 5236

Lovie Darling--Cardinals--Atlantic 995
PHILADELPHIA
Your Cheatin' Heart--Bert Keyes--Rama 4
WASHINGTON--BALTIMORE
Paradise Hill--Embers--Herald 410
I Cover the Waterfront--Orioles--Jubilee 5120
LOS ANGELES
Paradise Hill--Embers--Herald 410
Early in the Morning--Roy Milton--Specialty 464
If I Can't Have You--Flamingos--Chance 1133

New R.&B. Releases
JIMMY WITHERSPOON/Modern 909
••• Oh Mother, Dear Mother
••• I'll Be Right on Down
BILLY WRIGHT/Savoy 1100
••• Four Cold, Cold Walls
••• After Awhile
BROWNIE McGHEE/Savoy 899
••• 4 O'Clock in the Morning
••• Sweet Baby Blues
JIMMIE LEE & ARTIS/Modern 907
••• That's Fat Jack
•• That's What Love Can Do
EARL JOHNSON/Savoy 1102
••• Beggin' at Your Mercy
•• Have You Gone Crazy?

New Spiritual Releases
BRO. CECIL L. SHAW/Imperial 5242
••• In Heaven I'll Rest
••• I Know He'll Answer
THE CARAVANS/States 119
••• Why Should I Worry?
••• On My Way Home

Week of July 18

Buy o' the Week
Don't Deceive Me (Rush, BMI)—Chuck Willis—Okeh 6985
Hit three Midwest territorials this week. Good strength also in parts of South. Flip is "I've Been Treated Wrong Too Long" (Rush, BMI).

Buy o' the Week
Here Goes a Fool (Progressive, BMI) b/w Good Lovin' (Barnhill, BMI)--Clovers—Atlantic 1000

Stepping out nicely this week with uniform good and strong reports returned from most checkpoints.

Buy o' the Week

I'll Help You, Baby (Babb, BMI)—Christine Kittrell—Republic 7044
Building steadily. Strong thruout most of the South and Middle West, but has yet to take hold on East and West Coasts. Flip is "L & N Special" (Babb, BMI).

Territorial Tips

ATLANTA
Don't Deceive Me--Chuck Willis--Okeh 6985
DETROIT
Get It--Royals--Federal 12133
CINCINNATI
Good Lovin'--Clovers--Atlantic 1000
PHILADELPHIA
Why, Oh Why--Kings--Jax 314

New R.&B. Releases

BROWLEY GUY/Checker 779
•••• You Look Good to Me
•••• Watermelon Man
BILLY WARD & HIS DOMINOES/Federal 12139
•••• You Can't Keep a Good Man Down
••• Where Now, Little Heart
FATS DOMINO/Imperial 5240
•••• Please Don't Leave Me
••• The Girl I Love
TODD RHODES ORCH./King 4648
•••• Your Mouth Got a Hole in It (vo. Pinocchio)
••• Feathers
VIDO MUSSO SEXTET/RPM 387
••• Vido's Boogie
••• Blue Night
THE SHADOWS/Decca 28765
••• No Use
••• Stay
EDDIE JOHNSON/Chess 1544
••• Tiptoe
••• Twin Rock
LIGHTNING HOPKINS/RPM 388
••• Mistreated Blues
••• Black Cat
JIMMY ROGERS/Chess 1543
••• Left Me With a Broken Heart
••• Act Like You Love Me
LITTLE DONNA HIGHTOWER/Decca 48299
••• Farewell Blues
••• You Had Better Change Your Ways
ARBEE STIDHAM/Checker 778
••• Don't Set Your Cap for Me
••• I Don't Play
PAUL GAYTEN ORCH./Okeh 6982
•• Ooh-Boo
•• Cow Cow Blues
TONY HOLLINS/Decca 48300
•• I'll Get a Break
•• Fishin' Blues

SMILEY LEWIS/Imperial 5241
•• Caldonia's Party
•• Oh Baby
ROSE MITCHELL/Imperial 5243
•• Slipping In
•• I'm Searching
JOHNNY CREACH/Dootone 310
• Neither You Nor I Are to Blame
• Please Be Sure
WILHELMINA GRAY/Seeco 10-011
• Price for Love
• Gotta Have That Man
CARL DAVIS/Seeco 10-010
• Get Your Business Right
• I'm Leaving You Today

New Spiritual Releases

SISTER ROSETTA THARPE & MARIE KNIGHT/Decca 48301
•••• Let's Go On
••• Let Go His Hand
THE SOUTHERN STARS/Chess 1540
••• I Saw the Light
••• Prodigal Son
PROF. HAROLD BOGGS/King 4643
••• After Running the Race
••• Inside the Beautiful Gate

Week of July 25

Buy o' the Week

Crying in the Chapel (Valley, BMI)—Orioles—Jubilee 5122
Already on the Philadelphia territorial chart and rated very strong in Cincinnati, Cleveland, Chicago, Detroit and St. Louis and good in all other areas. A notable exception is Los Angeles where the pop and hillbilly versions have not found acceptance either. Flip is "Don't You Think I Ought to Know?" (Fowler, ASCAP).

Buy o' the Week

You Can't Keep a Good Man Down (Ward-Marks, BMI)—Dominoes—Federal 12139
Good and building in Philadelphia, Pittsburgh, Cincinnati, Nashville, St. Louis and Dallas. Scattered areas such as Buffalo, Chicago, Cleveland and Los Angeles report the record building more slowly than other recent Dominoes releases. Flip is "Where Now, Little Heart" (Ward-Marks, BMI).

Territorial Tips

LOS ANGELES
My Dear, Dearest Darling--"5" Willows--Allen 1000
PHILADELPHIA
Crying in the Chapel--Orioles--Jubilee 5122

New R.&B. Releases

THE ORIOLES/Jubilee 5122
•••• Crying in the Chapel
•••• Don't You Think I Ought to Know?
TAB SMITH/United 153
••• Cherry
••• I've Had the Blues All Day (vo. Johnny Harper)
PAT VALDELER/Mercury 70201
••• Baby, Rock Me
••• Keep Your Hand on Your Heart
JOHNNY MOORE'S THREE BLAZERS/Modern 910
••• Dragnet Blues (vo. Frankie Ervin)
••• Playing Numbers (vo. Frankie Ervin)
LITTLE CAESAR/Big Town 106
••• Big Eyes
•• Can't Stand It All Alone
FRED CLARK/Federal 12136
••• Ground Hog Snooper
••• Walkin' and Wonderin'
HERBIE FIELDS ORCH./Parrot 775
••• Harlem Nocturne
•• Things Ain't What They Used to Be
THE FOUR FELLOWS/Tri-Boro 101
•• Break My Bones
• Stop Crying

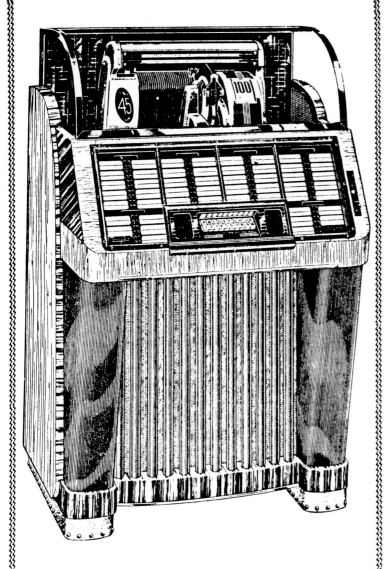

AUGUST 1953

16 Year-Olds Produce Disk Click for Flair

HOLLYWOOD, Aug. 1—Latest phenomenon in these parts is the growing popularity of a quintet of youngsters known as "The Flairs." The group's members, all 16 years of age, attend Jefferson High School here. They have no professional voice training and are still in their third year of high school.

THE FLAIRS

Group was picked up and put on wax by young Joe Bihari, of the well known Bihari recording family. He soon realized the possibilities of the group and signed them to a two-year contract. Their first two sides, "I Had a Love" and "She Wants to Rock," were recently released on the Flair label.

The Flairs will make their first professional appearance at the upcoming Gene Norman jazz concert at the Shrine Auditorium, Hollywood. The lads, Obie Jessie, Cornelius Gunter, Thomas Fox, Beverly Thomson and Richard Berry, write their own material.

Flair's sister label, Modern, is currently hot with Johnny Moore's "Dragnet Blues" with Frankie Ervin on the vocal.

SWING TIME OPENS CHICAGO BRANCH

CHICAGO, Aug. 8—Jack Lauderdale, prexy of Swing Time Records, Coast indie, has opened a branch office here in Chicago. Lauderdale is staying on here to get the new office going in full swing, which he intends to make his main headquarters. Move was made, according to Lauderdale, because he feels that "the center of the rhythm and blues market will shift from the West Coast to Chicago in the very near future."

GALE GRABS LOOT WITH R.&B.; FREED HYPES CLEVE SHOW

NEW YORK, July 25—The Gale Agency's giant rhythm and blues package, featuring Ruth Brown, Joe Louis, the Clovers, Wynonie Harris, Buddy Johnson's orch. and other stars, racked up strong grosses in its first week on the road.

The unit started weakly in Boston on Friday, July 17, and was only fair in Newark, N.J., the following night. However, the Buffalo one-nighter on July 19 pulled over 8,000 spectators; Monday (20) the package grossed $19,500 in Cleveland, and it got $18,700 in Detroit on Tuesday (21). Wednesday (22) the r.&b. unit played Flint, Mich.; Thursday (23), Cincinnati; Friday (24), Evansville, Ind., and tonight (25), St. Louis. Grosses were not available for these cities at presstime, but advance sales were said to be heavy in all four areas.

KING'S NATHAN ENTERS "HOUND DOG" DISPUTE

NEW YORK, July 25—King Records prexy Syd Nathan has injected himself into the copyright controversy over "Hound Dog", which flared anew this week when the Cincinnati record mogul demanded 50 percent of the publisher's share. Publisher's agent and trustee Harry Fox is holding mechanicals in escrow.

A recent r.&b. smash on Don Robey's Peacock label, "Hound Dog" stirred up legal interest when Robey, whose publishing affiliate is Lion Music, sued the Sun Record Company of Memphis, Tennessee, on grounds that the latter's "Bear Cat" with Rufus Thomas, Jr., infringed upon "Hound Dog". Altho the practice of freely cutting "answer" disks has been common in the r.&b. field, the U.S. District Court ruled that Sun's "Bear Cat" was an infringement. BMI denied Sun clearance, and Sun thereupon agreed to pay two cents per record on all disks sold, plus court costs. Lion Music agreed to allow the Sun Record company to continue to manufacture the disk, rather than force ι withdrawal.

Meanwhile, Don Robey is now preparing suits against King Records and a King publishing affiliate, Valjo, for waxing

(Continued on next page)

In Cleveland, the show packed in a Monday night audience of 10,000 at the Cleveland Arena despite 94-degree heat. Promotion of the show was handled there by Lew Platt, of Canton's LCL Productions, and Alan Freed, Cleveland disk jockey. They said gross was nearly $17,000 with a $3 top. Included in the package were Louis, retired heavyweight champion; Leonard Reed, comic; Ruth Brown, vocalist; Buddy Johnson's orchestra with Ella Johnson and Nolan Lewis, the Clovers, Lester Young's band, Wynonie Harris, Dusty Fletcher, Stuffy Bryant and the Edwards Sisters.

Platt was enthused by the results and recalled pre-show predictions were that in view of recent flops by aud-arena shows in Northern Ohio this mid-summer Monday date would be another. Several ads in daily and Sunday newspapers, plus 2,000 window cards, 300 three-sheets and 200 one-sheets were backed by Freed's air plugs via his local radio show.

"Chapel" Hits Seven Positions on Charts

NEW YORK, Aug. 15—This week, for the first time in two-and-a half years, a single song is occupying four positions on the national best-selling popular record chart. Tune is "Crying in the Chapel," published by Valley Music. The last song to hold four positions on the pop chart in one week was "Tennessee Waltz," which, in January 1951, was at its peak. "Chapel," however, also shows up twice on the current country and western best-selling chart and is the No. 1 rhythm and blues seller.

The four versions of "Crying in the Chapel" on the current chart are by June Valli on RCA Victor, Darrell Glenn on Valley, Rex Allen on Decca and the Orioles on Jubilee. The Orioles' record is the top

(Continued on next page)

65

"Chapel" Hits

(Continued from previous page)

rhythm and blues disk as well, and the country and western chart now lists both the Glenn and Allen versions.

Interestingly, both "Chapel" and "Tennessee Waltz" were kicked off via the hillbilly field and emanated from pubbing firms associated with the artist introducing the song. The first recording of "Waltz" was by Pee Wee King on RCA Victor. King was co-writer of the tune with Redd Stewart and also published "Waltz." It should be noted, however, that the latter tune never attained a strong sales position in the rhythm and blues listings.

"Crying in the Chapel" was penned by Darrell Glenn's father, who owns both the Valley label and the Valley publishing firm. Tune is considered to have a better "spread" via the various versions selling pop, hillbilly and rhythm and blues. Additional versions of "Chapel" with Ella Fitzgerald and Rosetta Tharpe on Decca, are selling in what might normally be termed the jazz and spiritual fields.

Some versions also appear to be crossing the lines of demarcation among the many record-selling fields, with the Orioles selling pop and rhythm and blues and the Glenn and Allen versions selling both pop and hillbilly.

How far "Chapel" will go in record sales seems to be anyone's guess right now. In its various versions it has already passed the 1,000,000 mark, even tho none of the records is yet in the "top five" class. "Tennessee Waltz" sold well over 4,000,000 records, with about 2,800,000 attributed to Patti Page's version.

SETTLEMENT NEAR IN "DRAGNET" HASSLE

HOLLYWOOD, Aug. 22—A settlement in the recent hassle with Modern Records over "Dragnet Blues" with Johnny Moore's Three Blazers, and which would withdraw all previous objections to the r.&b. cutting, will be reached soon, according to attorneys for Dragnet Productions and composer Walter Schumann.

Tune is also currently picking up action via renditions by Ray Anthony on Capitol and Buddy Morrow on RCA Victor, in addition to creating some noise in the rhythm and blues field via the original Modern waxing.

Saul Bihari, Modern prexy, stated they would immediately proceed to distribute their platter nationally. Earlier this month composer Walter Schumann assigned the copyright of his theme tune "Dragnet" to Alamo Music, in a move which he said would rid himself of a "headache" that's only "forcing me to make money." Schumann stated that his copyright assignment is a liberal one which also cuts in Jack Webb and his Dragnet Productions, Inc. This is the first time in his experience that Schumann has been literally forced into waxing one of his tunes, he said.

ROYALS' WAX PACES FEDERAL

CINCINNATI, O., July 25—The Royals' recoding of "Get It" on the Federal label this week outsold all other Federal releases, according to King Records execs, with Chicago, Detroit and New Orleans leading the way. An interesting note is that the Dominoes have led all sales on the subsid line since their first record was released about two years ago, and for the first time this week the Royals topped them.

Nathan Enters

(Continued from previous page)

"Hound Dog" with Roy Brown and Little Esther. Valjo, in rebuttal, is claiming 50 percent of the publisher's share of the tune. Basis for the claim, according to King's attorney Jack Pearl, is that one of the writers, Johnny Otis, was under exclusive contract to Valjo when he wrote the tune in collaboration with others. King, therefore, claims both publishers, Valjo and Lion, have a non-exclusive right to license the tune, and both publishers must account to each other on sales.

SHAW INTROS L-A DEPARTMENT

NEW YORK, Aug. 22—One of the most prominent blues and jazz booking agencies, Shaw Artists Corporation, has added a Latin-American department.

The new department, which is under the joint direction of Milt Shaw and Catalino, former L-A orkster, has already pacted close to 20 Latin-American artists, including names like the Joe Loco combo, Tico Records star, and Candido, conga drummer.

In addition to Loco and Candido, the Shaw line-up of L-A names now includes Sabu, Perla Marini (this week inked by Essex Records), the Mambo Aces, Cuban Pete and Nellie, Tanya, Los Monteros, Gladys Serano, the Elmo Garcia ork, the George Lopez ork, the Vincentico Valdez crew and other combos, acts and hoofers. The agency is already booking the above acts, and has set them in clubs as singles or part of regular shows.

The combination of L-A and r.&b. bookings by the Shaw firm seems a logical one. L-A combos and orks have been doing exceptionally well in their own right in resort areas, especially the Borscht Circuit in the summer and Miami in the winter. But among the r.&b. trade, L-A combos and orks have also shown a decided upsurge. Places such as the Band Box and Birdland here, have booked L-A groups again and again with their r.&b. and jazz artists.

Shaw intends to spot their L-A artists in various ways. They will use L-A combos as part of r.&b. units, so that a typical package may consist of a blues shouter, an r.&b. thrush, a jazz ork and a rhumba crew. This would lend more variety to a package than two jazz orks. The agency will also spot its talent as singles for small clubs, such as the booking now being played by Perla Marini and her combo at the Bachelor's Club here.

Notes from the R.&B. Beat

"CHAPEL" HAS DEALERS CRYING FOR MORE: The Orioles' "Crying in the Chapel" continues to build with each passing moment. Jubilee's Jerry Blaine has five presseries working day and night to keep up with demand for the disk.... The Orioles will play a week at the Apollo in New York August 21 to 27.... Billy Ward's Dominoes, now at the Band Box, are negotiating a deal which would team them with Sugar Ray Robinson for an autumn tour. The group, who have sold over five million records in two years for Federal Records, were just invited to perform for President Eisenhower, along with Bing Crosby and Bob Hope, in Denver, Colo., August 19 and 20.... Alan Freed, WJW, Cleveland, plugged the "Big Rhythm and Blues Show" which he emceed at the Cleveland Arena by staging a contest in advance of the event which resulted in 3,424 pieces of mail. There were 822 winners of coupons entitling the bearer to $1 discount on a reserved seat for the show. Freed writes that more than 10,000 paid admissions were racked up for the evening.... Bobby Shad, new Decca r.&b. head, leaves Tuesday on his first recording and promotion trek for tbe firm. He will hit the road for Houston, Tex., visiting jocks along the, way, and cutting some waxings there.

JOE TURNER

Clyde McPhatter, much publicized lead of the Dominoes, who moved over to Atlantic to form his own group, has named them the Drifters. Their long-awaited first session took place this week and Atlantic execs are flipping over the results. First release is skedded for September 1.... Ahmet Ertegun and Jerry Wexler are flying down to New Orleans to cut a session with Joe Turner and Ray Charles. While there the Atlantic duo will sign a new artist, John Cole, who'll be included in the session.... Lawrence Dean Faulkner (he's otherwise known to radio listeners as "Larry Dean"), former program director at WSOK, Nashville, Tenn., and staff announcer at WLOU, Louisville, Ky., has been appointed program director at WCIN, Cincinnati.... Larry Picus, known as "Jack the Bellboy" on station WJIV, Savannah, Ga., has started his own r.&b. label, Family Records. First release will be by Bill Johnson and his Four Steps of Rhythm.... Lew Chudd mighty happy to get a phone call from his New Orleans distrib with an order in four figures for Fats Domino's newest, "Please Don't Leave Me."

ALADDIN RELEASES "ONE SCOTCH": Coast indie Aladdin Records last week released the third "drinking song" waxed by Amos Milburn for the diskery. Aladdin topper Eddie Mesner said disk's advance orders have hit the 50,000 figure. Milburn's latest is "One Scotch, One Bourbon, One Beer." It joins his highly successful "Bad, Bad Whiskey," which sold nearly half a million copies, and "Let Me Go Home, Whiskey," whose sales reached nearly 300,000.... Herman Lubinsky, dean of the be-bop fans and head of Regent and Savoy Records, is filling an order from Japan for 1800 assorted LP's and 1700 assorted EP's on the Savoy label. The disks are Dixieland and r.&b. .... Phil Rose, Brunswick a.&r., will slice several sides with Freddy Mitchell before the saxist leaves soon on his first European tour. Mitchell will start his tour in Italy and appear in several countries before the windup six months hence.

MAMBO MADNESS: Panama Canal Zone organist Vin Strong, formerly with RCA Victor, has signed exclusively with Tico Records. Strong is known thruout Central and South America as "The Mambo King".... Tico prexy George Goldner informs us that, in the interests of promoting Latin music, he has tape recorded 15- and 30-minute Latin shows featuring Tito Puente and Joe Loco bands and is offering them free of charge to any station requesting them.... Goldner also reports congratulations are pouring in his recent acquisition of Lonnie Johnson, formerly with

(Continued on next page)

FREED, DOMINOES SOCKO IN OHIO

CLEVELAND, Aug. 22—Alan (Moon Dog) Freed's "Second Anniversary Dance," featuring the WJW spinner and Billy Ward's Dominoes, plus Rene Hall's ork, drew 3,032 youngsters at the Akron Auditorium on August 14, and 3,087 at the Stambaugh Auditorium in Youngstown, O., on August 15. Total gross for both events was estimated at slightly over $12,000.

One of the most popular r.&b. jocks in the country, Freed, along with his manager Lew Platt, are now considering several r.&b. shows and dances for the fall and winter season in a number of Ohio and Pennsylvania cities. They successfully promoted the Gale Agency's r.&b. show in Cleveland on July 20. Freed is now mixing vacation and business in Las Vegas, where he is meeting with a number of waxery heads concerning promotional angles for r.&b. tunes.

DECCA HYPOES R.&B. VIA TALENT SIGNINGS

NEW YORK, Aug. 8—New artist pactings and a stepped-up release schedule have recently given Decca Records' revitalized rhythm and blues department a shot in the arm. Newly named r.&b. chief Bob Shad has just pacted four new performers, including Savannah Churchill, Lightning Hopkins, the Patterson Singers and jazz trombonist Benny Green. Miss Churchill's first etching for the label, "Shake a Hand" b/w "Shed a Tear," was cut this week and has already been rushed to the jockeys.

Other artists handled by Shad include Sister Rosetta Tharpe, Marie Knight, Little Esther, Louis Jordan, Arthur Prysock and Coleman Hawkins. Diskery will release seven records in the r.&b. category this month, stepping up this schedule to about 10 monthly in September.

SAVOY BALLROOM SOLD AS LANDMARK

NEW YORK, Aug. 1—Another episode in the saga of the famed Savoy Ballroom was authored this week when the City of New York made a payment of more than $500,000 to Moe Gale as partial settlement in the condemnation of the jazz landmark to make way for a new housing project in this city's Harlem area. The Savoy will continue to operate on its present site for at least another three years, however.

Plans for the new housing project include a site for a new Savoy Ballroom, which will be built by the city with state and federal aid to replace the present ballroom, to be demolished in 1956 or 1957. Deal also calls for transplanting several of the Savoy's famous statuettes to the new venue. Gale, naturally, will continue to operate the new spot, when it is opened.

R.&B. Beat

(Continued from the previous page)

King, who's remembered for his fabulous "Tomorrow Night" of several years ago. Johnson's first Rama label release, "Will You Remember," is tagged as the "answer" to the former disk.... Wild Bill Davis' combo will close at the Club Harlem, Atlantic City, in order to fulfill a Labor Day week appearance at Pep's Musical Bar in Philadelphia. The Bill Gaines Organ Trio will make the resort spot replacement, coming in late in the month and staying to the season's end on September 13.... Romaine Brown and the Romaines, holding over for the remainder of the summer season at The Riptide, Wildwood, N.J., are set to usher in the fall season on September 9 at Lee Guber's Rendezvous, Philadelphia.

Recent artist-label switches in the r.&b. field: Joe Morris, formerly on Atlantic Records, is now on Herald; Buddy Lucas, formerly on Jubilee label, now with RCA Victor; Browley Guy, now on Checker label, after cutting sides for United. Fay Adams, formerly Fay Scruggs on Atlantic, is now with Herald Records.... At present there are a lot of powerful records on the charts including Johnny Ace's "The Clock," Ruth Brown's "Wild, Wild Young Men" and "Mend Your Ways," and the Clovers' "Good Lovin'".... Atlantic Records has released its first waxings with Laverne Baker, thrush who used to be with King Records. The diskery has also released some new waxings by Carmen Taylor, Joe Turner and the Diamonds.... Peacock Records' new vocal group, the Four Dukes, has just cut their version of "Crying in the Chapel.... Sun Records, Memphis diskery, has issued its first record by Little Junior's Blue Flames. Sides are "Feelin' Good" and "Fussin' and Fightin'," with Little Junior handling the

vocal.... Bull Moose Jackson has been inked to a new pact by the Gale Agency, his third in a row with the agency.... Lynn Hope will be at the Royal Peacock, Atlanta, from August 21 to 31.... The Charioteers have been pacted to a long term deal by Tuxedo Records, Chris Forde's indie label. Group is booked by GAC.

The Shaw Agency has signed Little Esther, who is now recording for Decca.... Ruth Brown is headed for California, where she will do an eight-day tour of the West Coast with Billy Eckstine. The tour opens on September 11.... Fats Domino begins a three-week California tour on August 30.... The Orioles, Paul Williams' ork, Margie Day and T-Bone Walker are going to the Howard Theater, Washington, for a week on September 18, followed by a stand at the Royal Theater, Baltimore.... The Five Keys and the Woody Herman ork begin a one-nighter tour of 10 dates on October 23.... Joel Cowan, string man for the Four Breezes, sold his r.&b. disk shop, left the musical aggregation, and resumed his old job as arranger for several orks with whom he was originally associated in the Philly area.

AUTO CRASH KILLS BAND MEMBER: An auto accident in Cleveland, Tex., Thursday (13) that involved the car carrying Charlie Ferguson and his all-girl ork resulted in the death of the nineteen-year-old bass fiddle player and seriously injured Ferguson and the other members of the distaff ork. At last word, Ferguson was still on the critical list. The band has been touring the Southwest with the Five Royales. The troupe was on the way to Tyler, Tex., for a one-nighter. The Five Royales, traveling in another car, were not involved in the accident. Carl Lebow, Apollo Records, who manages both groups, left immediately for Texas to assist. The tour, which is booked solidly thru December by Universal, will continue, with the agency going into immediate action to find a substitute ork until the Ferguson aggregation can return to work.... Slim Gaillard will get a chance to sound off with his "vouty" chatter on a new TV seg starting August 31 over WPIX, New York. The show, "The Harlem Talent Search," will feature Gaillard as emsee and will spotlight new acts. It is set for 13 weeks, debuting on Monday night for the first two shows and switching to Sunday nights thereafter.... Clarence Robinson's "Tropicana Revue," which still has two more weeks to run at the Paradise Club, Atlantic City, will open at the Apollo Theater in New York in September. The show will star thrush Ruth Brown when it plays the house. After the Apollo, the package will play the Howard in Washington and then the Royal in Baltimore.

Another big Shaw Artists package that will play the circuit in the fall stars the Orioles, now on top of the r.&b. heap with their waxing of "Crying in The Chapel," along with the Paul Williams ork and thrush

Margie Day. When the unit plays the Royale, it will be joined by T-Bone Walker.... Fay Adams and Joe Morris, who are stirring up a lot of action with "Shake a Hand," their first slicing for Herald Records, will play the Howard Theater, Washington, on October 16 and the Royale, Baltimore, on October 25.... Fats Domino will play three weeks of one-nighters on the West Coast starting September 1 .... Howard Lewis, Texas promoter for r.&b. shows, was in New York this week on vacation .... Charles Brown will do a string of one-nighters thru Texas starting September 30 and continuing to October 22.... Theo (Bless My Bones) Wade, manager of the Spirit of Memphis Quartet, Peacock artists, and host of Memphis station WDIA's "Delta Melodies" show, became the father of a boy last week. WDIA features Nat Williams and Rufus Thomas, of Sun Records, on the "Cool Train" show every Saturday.... The Dominoes just finished their second engagement at the Band Box, New York.... Robert Martin, original vibraharpist with the Lynn Hope unit, returns to the combo after a two-year hitch with the Army at Okinawa in time for a Dixie tour.

CHICAGO CHATTER: Leonard Chess, of Chess and Checker Records, and Gene Goodman of Regent and Harmon Music, have set up a new publishing firm, Arc Music, a BMI firm, in which both will be equal partners. Pubbery will be devoted exclusively to r.&b. tunes. Speaking of Chess, Len came up with one last week that started an avalanche of orders. Seems Al Benson played "Nadine" by the Coronets on his WGES airer and station's phones were promptly jammed. "We're airfreighting the orders and filling them only in rotation as they are received," Chess claimed. The group, incidentally, hails from Cleveland, where they were discovered by WJW deejay Alan (Moon Dog) Freed. Sax Mallard's combo backs the group on their disk.

Art Sheridan, Chance Records, has purchased the master of "Baby, It's You" by the Spaniels, originally released on Vee-Jay. Art claims it's his biggest seller at the moment.... Incidentally, Sheridan Records Distributing Corporation is moving to new quarters next door. The new address is 1153-55 East 47th Street and provides double the space of the old headquarters.... Amos Milburn's Chi fans will have to travel some to catch him at a one-nighter at Decatur's Danceland, August 14, then on to the Gary Armory for his next date. Amos reportedly is giving serious thought to disbanding his aggregation and going out as a single.... Eartha Kitt spent a day signing copies of her "C'est Si Bon" at Al Benson's Record Shop in close to 100 degree heat, then later did a broadcast with Al.... Jack Lauderdale, of Swing Time, visiting our city and singing the praises of Marvin Phillips' "Sweetheart Darling".... Eddie "Lockjaw" Davis setting arrangements for his

appearance at the Bee Hive Lounge. The former Basie sideman is remembered for his work on "Paradise Squat" which hit the charts some time ago.... Club 34 currently features Cool Breeze and his Cool Breezes, United Records artists.

DETROIT ARROWS: Gale Agency's r.&b. show headed by Joe Louis, Ruth Brown, the Clovers, Lester Young and his combo, Wynonie Harris, Dusty Fletcher and Buddy Johnson orchestra packed 'em in at the 14,000 capacity Detroit Olympia this week.... Hear tell that Bristoe Bryant, deejay at WJLB, Detroit, has an uncanny knack of picking the hits on his "Hub Cap Caravan" show.... United's Leonard Allen pacted popular jump singer Helen Thompson, now appearing at the Flame Show Bar.... T-Bone Walker, blues shouting guitarist, opens at the Flame next week.... Local promoter Frank Brown doing solid business with r.&b. packages booked at the Graystone ballroom here. Latest show featured Billie Holiday, Charlie Ventura, Tiny Bradshaw and Roy Milton, and the joint really rocked. The Original Royals, local lads whose "Get It" on Federal is causing lots of noise here, will appear at the Graystone next week in a show headlined by Dinah Washington.

WEST COASTINGS: A stellar event in the rhythm and blues field took place at the Shrine Auditorium, Saturday August 15. Top headliners in Gene Norman's "Fourth Annual Rhythm and Blues Jubilee" included Johnny Ace and his orchestra, Willie Mae Thornton, the Flairs, the Robins, Linda Hopkins, Camille Howard, Roy Milton and his band, Helen Humes, Jimmy Witherspoon, Chuck Higgins and his orchestra, Gil Bernal, Maxwell Davis, Marvin Phillips, Slappy White and deejay-emcee Dick "Uncle Huggie Boy" Hugg.... Caught Jules Bihari at Modern preparing a big shipment of Johnny Moore's smasheroo "Dragnet Blues".... Joe Bihari was last reported on his way to Las Vegas to meet with Cleveland deejay Alan Freed. From there Joe will head for Chicago to cut new sides with B.B. King for the RPM label, then it's on to Detroit for sessions with Elmore James, Johnny Jones and John Lee Hooker.... Joe's 16 year-old group the Flairs had their platter picked by r.&b. spinner Hunter Hancock as his "Record of the Week".... Harry (the Hipster) Gibson last week was signed by Aladdin Records to record a series of "hep talk" sides based on Grimm's fairy tales. First disk, just released, carries Gibson's versions of Goldie Locks backed with Cinderella. Gibson, currently appearing at the Say When Club, San Francisco, was inked by Aladdin prexy Eddie Mesner to a one-year pact with a four-year option.

Hot with local distribs is Sonny Knight's "But Officer" on Aladdin, with the Crows' Rama slicing of "Gee" beginning to show.... Sid Talmadge of Record Merchandising Co. really rolling these days with

Herald's "Paradise Hill" with the Embers and Excello's "Banana Split" with Kid King's Combo.... Pete Doraine's Allen line doing exceptionally well in this area with a socko first release, "My Dear, Dearest Darling" by the Five Willows.... Bob Geddins, a.&r. for 4-Star Records, was down from Oakland on business. Announced that their new studio has just been completed in Oakland.... Specialty Records has just signed a new group, the Metronomes. The label also claims that Jimmy Liggins has just recorded the first "3-D" platter for the rhythm and blues field.... Ralph Bass of Federal Records tells us the Monday nite amateur shows which he started at the Club Alabam have already brought out some terrific hidden talent.... Eastman Records, local independent label, resumes operations by entering the country and western field with a new disk due for release within the next two weeks.

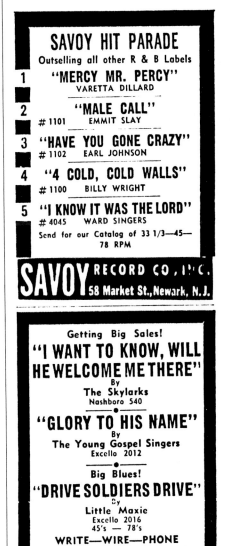

August's Record Roundup

Week of August 1

Buy o' the Week
Get It (Lois, BMI)—Royals—Federal 12133
Broke out this past week in all territories checked nationally and placed on the national best-seller chart. Flip is "No, It Ain't" (Lois, BMI).

Buy o' the Week
Dragnet Blues (Modern, BMI)—Johnny Moore—Modern 910
Overwhelmingly favorable initial reaction, with good and strong reports from Cleveland, Cincinnati, Pittsburgh, Chicago, Nashville, Durham and St. Louis. First excitement on the West Coast has cooled somewhat. Flip is "Playing Numbers" (American, BMI).

Buy o' the Week
Too Much Lovin' (Bess, BMI) b/w Laundromat Blues (Bess, BMI)—"5" Royales—Apollo 448
Only out a week, disk has already zoomed onto the New York territorial chart and has received enthusiastic reception in various Southern territories.

Territorial Tips
NEW ORLEANS
Rent Man Blues--Mercy Dee--Specialty 466
NEW YORK
Too Much Lovin'--"5" Royales--Apollo 448

New R.&B. Releases
MERCY DEE/Specialty 466
•••• Rent Man Blues
••• Fall Guy
THE CRICKETS/Jay-Dee 777
•••• When I Met You
••• Dreams and Wishes
FLOYD DIXON/Aladdin 3196
••• Married Woman
••• Lovin'
WOO WOO MOORE/Mercury 70204
••• Something's Wrong
••• Five Long Letters
JOHN GREER AND HIS RHYTHM ROCKERS/Victor 20-5370
••• Beginning to Miss You
••• Rhythm in the Breeze

ROOSEVELT SYKES/United 152
••• Come Back Baby
•• Tell Me True
THE TRENIERS/Okeh 6984
••• This Is It
•• I'd Do Nothing But Grieve (vo. Cliff Trenier)
MR. SAD HEAD/Victor 20-5388
••• Black Diamond
•• Make Haste
JUNIOR WELLS/States 122
•• Cut That Out
•• Eagle Rock

New Spiritual Releases
ORIGINAL FIVE BLIND BOYS/Peacock 1714
••• I Know the Lord Will Make a Way
••• Somewhere Listening for My Name

Week of August 8

Buy o' the Week
That's My Desire (Mills, ASCAP) b/w Hurry Home, Baby (Joni, BMI)—Flamingos—Chance 1140
With fine showing of the group's "If I Can't Have You" still fresh in memory, the Flamingos' latest is coming up just as fast. Good reports from New York, Philadelphia, Pittsburgh, Cleveland, Detroit, Nashville, St. Louis and L.A. With the exception of the West Coast, majority of territories checked preferred "Desire."

Buy o' the Week
Rent Man Blues (Venice, BMI)—Mercy Dee—Specialty 466
After success of "One Room Country Shack," this disk must have been eagerly awaited in a number of territories. Initial reaction strong in New Orleans, Dallas, Nashville, Cleveland and St. Louis. Flip is "Fall Guy" (Venice, BMI).

Territorial Tips
CHARLOTTE
Rot Gut--Wynonie Harris--King 4592

New R.&B. Releases
THE "5" ROYALES/Apollo 448
•••• Too Much Lovin'
•••• Laundromat Blues
BIG MAYBELLE/Okeh 6998
•••• Send for Me
•••• Jinny Mule

BIG JAY McNEELY/Federal 12141
••• Nervous, Man, Nervous
••• Rock Candy
MARGIE DAY/Dot 1172
••• String Bean
••• Don't Talk to Me About Men

Week of August 15

Buy o' the Week
Dreams and Wishes (Beacon, BMI) b/w When I Met You (Beacon, BMI)—Crickets—Jay Dee 777
Good action in Philadelphia, Durham, Tennessee, Cleveland, Dallas and Cincinnati. All reports show growing activity. Side preference varies by area.

Buy o' the Week
Cherry (Pamlee, BMI)—Tab Smith—United 153
Big in St. Louis. Good in Cincinnati, Cleveland, Chicago, Detroit and L.A. Flip is "I've Had the Blues All Day" (Pamlee, BMI)

Territorial Tips
DETROIT
Baby It's You--Spaniels--Chance 1141

New R.&B. Releases
LITTLE JUNIOR'S BLUE FLAMES/Sun 187
•••• Feelin' Good
••• Fussin' and Fightin' Blues
THE FLAMINGOS/Chance 1140
•••• That's My Desire
•••• Hurry Home Baby
CARMEN TAYLOR/Atlantic 1002
•••• Ding Dong
••• Lovin' Daddy
JOE TURNER/Atlantic 1001
••• Crawdad Hole
••• Honey Hush
GRIFFIN BROTHERS/Dot 1171
••• Move It On Over
••• Bouncing Home
BLAZER BOY/Imperial 5244
••• Waiting for My Baby
• Surprise Blues
HERB FISHER/Imperial 5246
•• Cryin' in My Sleep
• You Don't Live But Once
J.D. EDWARDS/Imperial 5245
•• Hobo
• Crying

THE PRISONAIRES/Sun 186
•• Baby, Please
•• Just Walkin' in the Rain
THE FOUR VAGABONDS/Lloyds 102
• P.S. I Love You
• Lazy Country Side

Week of August 22

Buy o' the Week
**Shake a Hand—Faye Adams—
Herald 416**
Record has literally zoomed in the last
week picking up enough strength to
make the national chart. A definite
"must." Flip is "I've Gotta Leave You."

Buy o' the Week
Baby It's You—Spaniels—Chance 1141
Moving up very fast. Already a top seller
in Detroit, record is gaining popularity in
St. Louis, Dallas, L.A. and Cleveland.
Flip is "Bounce."

Buy o' the Week
**Off and On—Tiny Bradshaw—
King 4647**
Strong in Philadelphia. Good in St.
Louis, Durham, Dallas, L.A., Chicago and
Buffalo. Flip is "Free for All."

Territorial Tips
**LOS ANGELES
That's My Desire--Flamingos--
Chance 1140**

New R.&B. Releases
ELMORE JAMES/Flair 1014
••• Can't Stop Lovin'
••• Make a Little Love
MEMPHIS SLIM/United 156
••• The Come Back
••• Five O'Clock Blues
LIGHTNING HOPKINS/Mercury 70191
••• My Mama Told Me
••• What's the Matter Now?
THE DIAMONDS/Atlantic 1003
•••• Two Loves Have I
••• I'll Live Again
RUDY GREEN/Chance 1139
••• Love Is a Pain
•• No Need of Your Crying
JOAN SHAW/Gem 209
••• Oh How I Hate to Say Goodbye
•• Baby, Come On
THE CHARMS/Rockin' 516
•• Loving Baby
•• Heaven Only Knows
THE MARVELEERS/Derby 829
•• For the Longest Time
•• One-Sided Love Affair
ART SHELTON'S ORCH./Atlas 1031
•• Dynaflow
• You Thrill Me So (vo. Lester Gardner)

Week of August 29

Buy o' the Week
**One Scotch, One Bourbon, One Beer
Amos Milburn—Aladdin 3197**
Record has taken off in Philadelphia,
Detroit and Central Tennessee. Chicago,
Cincinnati and St. Louis also came thru
with good reports. Flip is "What Can I
Do?"

Buy o' the Week
**The Come Back (Pamlee, BMI)—
Memphis Slim—United 156**
Stepping out in Detroit and L.A. Good
action also starting in New York, Cincin-
nati, Chicago and St. Louis. Flip is "Five
O'Clock Blues" (Pamlee, BMI).

Buy o' the Week
**Feelin' Good (Delta, BMI)—Little
Junior's Blue Flames—Sun 187**
Very strong in some Texas areas and also
in Chicago and St. Louis. Two Southern
reports say good action. Flip is "Fussin'
and Fightin'" (Delta, BMI).

New R.&B. Releases
LLOYD PRICE/Specialty 471
•••• I Wish Your Picture Was You
••• Frog Legs
JOHNNY MOORE'S THREE BLAZERS/
Modern 911
••• In the Home (vo. Mari Jones)
••• Old Worry (vo. Mari Jones)
EDWARD GATES WHITE/States 124
••• Mother-in-Law
••• Rockabye Baby
CLIFF BUTLER/States 123
••• People Will Talk
••• When You Love
JIMMY LIGGINS/Specialty 470
••• Drunk
•• I'll Never Let You Go
LAVERNE BAKER/Atlantic 1004
••• How Can You Treat a Man Like This
••• Soul on Fire
PATTY ANNE/Aladdin 3198
•• Beginning to Miss You
•• Sorrowful Heart
FRANK MOTLEY/D-C 6004
•• That Ain't Right
• Dual Trumpets Bounce
THE ROYAL HAWK/Flair 1013
•• I Wonder Why
• Royal Hawk
GENE MOORE/Specialty 472
• She's Gone
• That's Bad
NELDA DUPUY/United 157
• Riding With the Blues
• Stop Feeling Sorry for Yourself

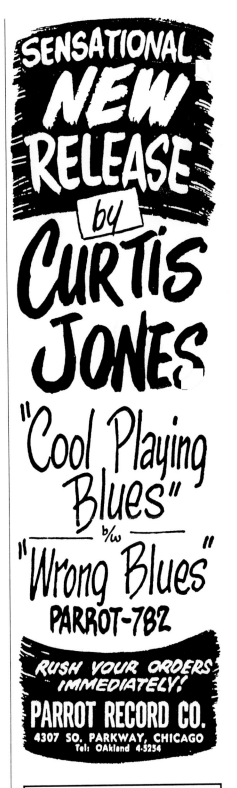

First Record for Decca !

BIG, BIGGER, BIGGEST

SAVANNAH CHURCHILL SINGS

"SHAKE A HAND"

b/w

"SHED A TEAR"
Decca 28836 and 9-28836

DECCA RECORDS

Pop-Country-Blues Disk Categories Merge Closer; Old Distinctions Fade

NEW YORK, Sept. 7—Those arbitrary lines in the disk business that set off pop from c.&w., and the latter from r. &b. disks, have grown especially hazy during the past few weeks. Five records, hits in one of three fields, have jumped over the demarcation lines recently to become hits in others.

The five platters are Darrell Glenn's "Crying in the Chapel" on Valley, which has made it in the c.&w. and pop field; the Rex Allen version of the same tune on Decca, which made it first in c.&w., and next in pop; the Orioles' version of the tune on Jubilee, which made it solidly in r.&b. and in pop; Rusty Draper's "Gambler's Guitar" on Mercury, which has broken out in the hillbilly field after becoming a big pop hit; and "A Dear John Letter" by Jean Shepard and Ferlin Husky on Capitol, which is now breaking thru into the pop markets.

While it's not rare to have a record sell in more than one market, it is unusual to have five platters do it within a month's time. Occasionally the jump is due to the general appeal of the tune, sometimes to the strength of the artist, and occasionally to the all-around production of the disk itself. "Crying in the Chapel" is the perfect illustration, at this moment, of the wide appeal of a tune in all fields.

An artist who can sell his cuttings in more than one market is most unusual today. Rusty Draper's break-thru from the pop to the country field with "Gambler's Guitar" is a trick turned by few pop singers over the past years. Patti Page did it with "Tennessee Waltz" and Bing Crosby and a few others used to do it now and then. The loyalty of c.&w. fans to their favorites seems to exclude easy entry in the market for pop warblers.

Altho country artists occasionally become strong in the pop field, as did Hank Williams and Pee Wee King's orch., they do not turn then to the pop field. Here is one market that shies away from artists who switch to pop records. One of the best examples of this is Jimmy Wakely, who after a number of hits in the pop field had a hard time with his former Western fans.

Rhythm and blues names, too, often break into the pop field with their records, and if enough of their platters do it, they become standard pop artists, such as Billy

(Continued on next page)

JUBILEE TO DISTRIBUTE NATIONAL DISKS

NEW YORK, Sept. 19—Jerry Blaine, owner of Jubilee Records, and Al Green, president of National, this week concluded a deal whereby the National Records catalog will be marketed by Blaine thru his Jubilee distributors. The catalog includes over 600 sides, many of which have been previously unreleased.

Blaine, who plans to use the National label, will concentrate on EP's and LP's as well as turn out some previously unreleased sides as singles. The initial shipment, which is set for October 15, will include 16 EP's and six LP's.

A sampling of the artists with masters in the National catalog includes Billy Eckstine, Eileen Barton, the Ames Brothers, Joe Turner, Tommy Edwards, Pete Johnson, the Ravens and Charlie Ventura.

Hy Siegel Back in Biz; Forms Timely Records

NEW YORK, Sept. 5—Herman (Hy) Siegel, one of the original founders of the Apollo label, is re-entering the disk business with a new rhythm and blues label, Timely. Siegel's diskery is a subsidiary of the SKM Corporation, which is also the parent company of Simek Music, publishing affiliate of the label.

Timely has already inked two vocal groups, the Ambassadors and the Gay Tunes. First sides by the groups are currently being released thru independent distributors in major markets. The diskery will also issue spiritual records by a group called the Colemanaires. Plans call for using only new talent on the label.

Faye Adams Disk Released by Atlantic

NEW YORK, Sept. 5—A new Faye Adams slicing was announced this week by Atlantic Records. Miss Adams, who is currently one of the hottest properties in the rhythm and blues field with her "Shake a Hand" on the Herald label, was signed by Atlantic Records with Joe Morris and his Blues Cavalcade. When both Miss Adams, who was Faye Scruggs at the time, and Joe Morris moved over to Herald, Atlantic had several unreleased etchings in the can.

Joe Morris authored "Shake a Hand" and provided the orchestral backing on the platter. Disk is stirring up loads of action around New York, New Jersey and Philadelphia. Points south are beginning to report the disk and indications are that the tune will be breaking nationwide before long.

Bobby Shad at Decca also has covered the tune with Savannah Churchill with a slightly different treatment. While the Adams etching has a shade of the religious kick, the Churchill version reportedly leans more to the R&B with a pop possibility.

Faye Adams is currently under the management of Phil Moore, who also handles Columbia Records' Helene Dixon.

Decca Expands Artist Roster

NEW YORK, Sept. 5—Decca Records' bid for a growing share of the rhythm and blues business was strengthened this week by two new signings. Bob Shad, recently named head of the department, inked songstress Margie Day, formerly of the Dot label, and tenor saxist Lucky Thompson.

At the same time, Milt Gabler, Decca a.&r. chief, signed jazz pianist Eddie Heywood to a term pact. The artist was last with the label in 1947.

Notes from the R.&B. Beat

"SHAKE A HAND" BOOSTS MORRIS' CAREER: "Shake a Hand," Faye Adams' and Joe Morris' first cutting for the Herald label, is now in the top spot on both the best-selling and the most played in juke box charts. The record has only been out about five weeks. Morris' recent career indicates the power of a hit record in restoring an artist to top demand in night clubs. Morris, who had had a number of strong records on Atlantic a few years ago, had a rough time breaking thru with any disk during the last year. Before "Shake a Hand" came out, Morris was booked for two dates during September. Since the record broke open, Morris has been booked right thru September and now has only three open dates for October.

THE ORIOLES

GROUPS INVADE R.&B. FIELD: The charts this week point out again the current strength of vocal groups in the r.&b. field, with seven quartets and quintets in the top 10, either on the best-seller or the juke box chart, or both. Groups include the Orioles, the Clovers, the Five Royales, the Royals, the Spaniels, the Dominoes and the Coronets. Another point of interest concerning the charts this week is that only one fem singer is represented. This latter situation will probably change shortly tho, since Ruth Brown, Willie Mae Thornton and Varetta Dillard are out with new releases.

Billy Ward's Dominoes mark their third anniversary as a vocal unit when they headline the September 18 bill at the Apollo Theater, New York. The group plays the Band Box in Gotham for two weeks starting September 29.... Margie Day, now with Decca Records, cut her first wax this week. Sides will be out shortly.... Billy Eckstine, Ruth Brown and Leslie U. Crane will go out on a Southern trek next February.... The Deep River Boys will make their seventh London Palladium appearance in the theater's fall show which begins mid-October. The team, Harry Douglass, Vernon Gardner, Edward Ware and pianist Cam Williams, has signed for nine weeks and will double in a late-night cabaret appearance at the Colony Restaurant.

A STATUS SYMBOL?: Rama label's George Goldner, with tongue-in-cheek and fire in his eyes, asks: "Is it a measure of success when your records start being bootlegged?" George is currently off on a three-week tour of the country.... Tunesmith Rudy Toombs around town saying thanks to all for making Amos Milburn's "One Scotch, One Bourbon, One Beer" the biggie that it is. Rudy heading back to Coast this week.... Bobby Robinson, little guy who operates Bobby's Record Shop and Red Robin label has been put to bed for a month under doctor's orders and told to keep away from work until after first of the year. Bobby doesn't have to fret, tho, 'cause his old friend and standby Joel Turnero will be looking after things until he makes his return.

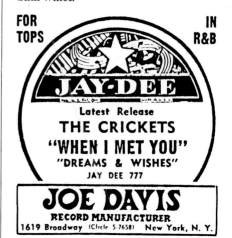

JOEL TURNERO

Clyde McPhatter and the Drifters signed with the Gale Agency this week.... Freddie Mitchell and his ork and thrush Laverne Baker are now in Europe on a one-nighter tour. The pair arrived in Europe in August for a three-month run thru Germany and Italy.... The Clovers played the Apollo Theater in New York this week with the Lucky Millinder orch. .... Miriam Abramson, of Atlantic Records, is back in New York after visiting her husband, Lt. Herb Abramson, in Germany.... Fats Domino is on a one-nighter tour of the West Coast.... The Ward Singers with Clara Ward appeared at the National Baptist Convention, U.S.A., in Miami this

(Continued on next page)

Categories Merge
(Continued from previous page)

Eckstine, Nat Cole and Sarah Vaughan. These artists have retained their following and can appear on both pop and r.&b. charts with a big hit. Occasionally pop artists spread over into the r.&b. field, as Johnnie Ray did with "Cry" two years ago.

ROBISON BUYS ABBOTT

HOLLYWOOD, Aug. 29—General manager Fabor Robison, of Abbott Records, has purchased all outside interests in the company, making him sole owner and operator of the label. Indie country and western firm has in eight months grown from five distribs to a nation-wide network of 31, with disks currently being pressed in Los Angeles, Memphis and Philadelphia.

Abbott this week signed hillbilly star Rudy Grayzell, who bows on wax with "The Heart That Once Was Mine" and "I'm Looking at the Moon." Label scored its initial success via "Mexican Joe" and has maintained the pace via its current clicks, "Caribbean" and "The Marriage of Mexican Joe."

PIERCE ANKLES 4-STAR

HOLLYWOOD, Sept. 19—Don Pierce has resigned his position with 4-Star Records after a six-year association. Pierce was an assistant to Bill McCall, prexy of 4-Star Records, and their BMI affiliate, 4-Star Sales Company. He gave no reasons for leaving 4-Star, altho he did disclose that he was dickering with several music publishers and recording companies and expected to announce his plans shortly.

The 4-Star firm recently attracted nation-wide attention via their click "Don't Let the Stars Get in Your Eyes" waxing by Slim Willet.

R.&B. Beat

(Continued from previous page)

week.... Louis Jordan and his combo will play two weeks in Las Vegas, Nev., starting September 16. The group will then hit the road for engagements in Los Angeles, Seattle, New York and Montreal.... Danny Kessler, new RCA Victor r.&b. chief, was in New Orleans last week cutting disks for the label.

A new package consisting of the Clovers, the Roscoe Gordon ork, Little Esther and Chuck Willis will be sent out by Shaw Artists Corp. for a 15-day swing thru Southern territory starting October 1. Trek will be handled by promoter Eli Weinberg.... Howard Lewis, Texas promoter, and Eli Weinberg, Southern promoter, have been in New York this week buying talent for one-nighter tours.... Charles Brown will team up with Johnny Moore's Three Blazers for a Texas one-nighter trip September 30 to October 20.... Ruth Brown heads South on a new concert tour starting November 4. She will open at the Apollo, New York, on September 25 and then plays the Howard in Washington.... The Orioles do a week at the Orchid Room, Kansas City, Mo., November 2 thru 9 and then play a string of one-nighters thru the South down as far as Miami. The tour will end in Washington.

Edna Gallmon Cooke, Republic label's great spirituals singer, is reported recouperating at her home in Philadelphia after undergoing serious surgery in Thomasville, Ga.... Republic has just signed a new vocal group, the Orchirds, now featured with Sonny Thompson and his orchestra.... A new voice was added to the Spirit of Memphis Quartet recently when Theo Wade, manager of the group, was presented with a brand new baby boy.... Memphis station WDIA's "Cool Train" is unique in that it features Nat Williams, first Negro jock in the area, and Rufus "Bear Cat" Thomas, Sun Records artist. Two join together for three hours each Saturday as conductor and engineer of this popular streamliner.... Herman Lubinsky, Savoy Records topper, spending weekends, on his cabin cruiser, just fishing.... Jack Walker, New York deejay and Atlantic flack, will be heard on one of Atlantic's soon-to-be-released waxings.... Rainbow Records pacted a new group this week, the Rainbows.... N.B. Mayhams (Norris the Troubadour) has been visiting deejays in up-state New York, plugging his new Co-Ed record "Mint Julep."

DISTRIB DOINGS: The extra push that salesman Hy Weiss of Cosnat Distributors puts to the Five Crowns' record of "You Could Be My Love" on Old Town has accounted for big New York play.... Alpha Distributors' Johnny Halonka tells us his

big sellers are "I Love You So" by the Crows on Rama, with requests for the flip "Gee" coming in stronger and stronger; "Why, Oh, Why" by the Kings on Jax; and the Prisonaires' "Just Walkin' in the Rain" on Sun. Also showing definite hit signs is Glory's "Heaven Only Knows" with the Charms.

PHILLY FLASHES: The new season finds a strong array of r.&b. talent lined up at the Philadelphia music rooms. Pep's Musical Bar offered Willie Mabon on Monday (21) as the kick-off attraction; Ida James and Fats Wright are back in town at Spider Kelly's, while Club Chateau will bring in Doc Bagby and his Organ Trio; Cecil Young will get the spotlight at Club Bill and Lou, while Buddy Lucas will make his first local stand at the Powelton Cafe.... Jimmy Tyler, finishing a season at the Club Harlem, Atlantic City, heads for the road with Clarence Robinson's "Tropicana" revue.... Fabulous Preston returns with his organ stylings on Labor Day at Ted Johnson's Cotton Club, Lawnside, N.J. .... In Philadelphia, Joe Loco comes back to the Blue Note on Labor Day ... Clara Ward Singers, Ruth Brown, Buddy Johnson, Dorothy Dandridge, Arthur Prysock, the Ravens and possibly King Cole were named for the Pittsburgh Courier annual swing concert, which will be held for the first time at Philadelphia's Academy of Music on September 25.... Earl Hines and Wynonie Harris are set by proprietor Lennie Sloane to usher in the fall season next month at his newly renovated Emerson's Grille in south Philadelphia. Also skedded are Eddie Heywood on September 14; Bull Moose Jackson on September 21, and Joe Morris for the September 28 week.

IT RUNS IN THE FAMILY: It seems Marshall Chess, 10 year-old son of Leonard

(Continued on next page)

Rhythm and Blues Tattler

GIVE TO THE RUNYON CANCER FUND

R.&B. Beat
(Continued from previous page)

Chess of Chess Records is getting an early start in the disk biz. Marshall's now traveling thruout the South with his busy dad. Meanwhile Len is taking orders like mad for Willie Mabon's latest, "You'se a Fool" and "Monday Woman," along with Little Walter's "Quarter to Twelve" and "Blues with a Feeling" .... Roscoe Gordon and Ray Charles are prepping themselves for a road tour beginning in Decatur, Illinois and winding up on September 26 at the Belmont Ballroom, Toledo, Ohio.... Another tour set to go teams Hot Lips Page, Chuck Willis and Anita Echols for one-nighters thru Kentucky, Ohio and Indiana.... The Five Flamingos will headline an all-star swing bill at the Park City Bowl on Labor Day. Also on the bill will be Sonny Stitt and his band. Big event of the night will be a swing battle between the Flamingos and the Coronets, group who sliced "Nadine" for Chess.... "Slap-Happy Daze"

AL BENSON

is the current floorshow at the Club DeLisa, starring the Three Chocolateers... Al Benson vacationing from the air, due to return following Labor Day. His Parrot label is going strong meantime with Mabel Scott's rendition of "Mr. Fine," which is starting to break into the Hot Charts.... Red Saunders and his ork are now at the New Club DeLisa; Arnett Cobb and his crew set to follow Earl Bostic at the Capitol Lounge. Rudi Richardson is at the Clover Club. The Pershing Hotel Lounge is featuring the Fritz Jones combo. A new spot, the Toast of the Town, has booked T-Bone Walker for an upcoming show, and has set dates for the following top r.&b. artists over the rest of the year: Wynonie Harris, B.B. King, Eddie Boyd, and Ivory Joe Hunter. Lefty Bates and his ork plus baritone man Leo Parker are at the Nob Hill, and Horace Henderson and his band are set for a limited engagement at the Strand Lounge.... Sonny Stitt's combo is packing 'em in at the Beehive, while Coleman Hawkins, who preceded Sonny at the "Hive", is now playing the Toast of the Town Club.

Leonard Allen of United now back behind his desk after an extensive Southern junket, during which he signed two femme vocalists, Helen Thompson and Terry Timmons.... The Five Blazes now in their 20th week at the Club Bagdad and continue to pack 'em in.... Charley Bennett

and his Co-Ben diskery bust into the r.&b. biz with two brand new releases and two more on the way. Charley, by the way, cut one of the forthcoming hunks of wax himself.... McKie Fitzhugh tells us he's opened a second record shop, this one called "McKie's Bop Shop No. 2." Seems that McKie's business is always booming.... Art Sheridan, of Sheridan Distributing Company here, has gone into partnership with Dave Freed, formerly with Ohio Record Sales, in the formation of a new firm, Lance Distribution, Inc., located on Prospect Street in Cleveland. Sheridan is president of the firm, and Freed vice-president. Dave is the brother of Al "Moon Dog" Freed, top deejay and discoverer of the Coronets.... Sam Evans' brand new deejay show airs from South Center Department Store over WWCA, Mondays thru Saturdays, 1:30 to 3:30 p.m. The seg features latest releases, guest interviews, etc., and the public's invited to attend festivities.

PEACOCK'S ROBEY ON COAST: Don Robey, Peacock prexy, flew in from Houston to cut new sessions with Johnny Ace and Willie Mae Thornton which will be released soon on the Duke and Peacock labels. After these new etchings, the Ace-Thornton duo will leave for a series of one-nighters and theater engagements in the Midwest and East. Robey also announced that Johnny Otis has been inked as an artist and will cut some new sessions for the Houston firm.... Percy Mayfield is taking a vacation before leaving on his Eastern jaunt September 10.... Specialty's Art Rupe says that "Drunk" by Jimmy Liggins is causing quite a commotion in Baltimore and the East as well as here in L.A. Rupe also reports that Alex Bradford's spiritual etching "I Don't Care What the World May Do" b/w "Too Close to Heaven" is taking off big and has even invaded the rhythm and blues field.

HEARD IN HOLLYWOOD: Joe Bihari, of Modern Records, back from a three-week tour thru the Midwest, during which he signed singer Connie Mac Booker.... Ralph Bass, a.&r. for Federal Records, states that all advance predictions on the Lamplighters are proving out. He reports that their first release "Turn Me Loose" is taking hold with some very big sales reported.... Robin Bruin is the new disk jockey over at KWKW with a 2:30 to 5 early-morning show.... Crystalette label execs Carl Burns and Mike Coleman announce they have re-entered the r.&b. field with the signing of vocalist Linda Hopkins. Thrush's first offering on the label is "Tears of Joy" and "Three Time Loser".... It's reported that Randy's Record Shop in Gallatin, Tenn., has put Johnny Moore's disking of "Dragnet Blues" in its package of big sellers, which is usually a sure sign of a hit.... We hear the Sweethearts of Rhythm will be touring the West Coast the last of October. This is the first Western tour the group has made in quite a spell.

September's Record Roundup

RATING SYSTEM
•••• Excellent ••• Very Good
•• Good • Fair

Week of September 5

Buy o' the Week

Jinny Mule b/w Send for Me—Big Maybelle—Okeh 6998

Showing well in Detroit, Tennessee, St. Louis and Cincinnati. Philadelphia and Durham say "good." Most action on "Jinny."

Buy o' the Week

I Had a Love b/w She Wants to Rock—Flairs—Flair 1012

Going strong in Los Angeles, St. Louis and Cincinnati. Also good in Philadelphia and Chicago. Action in most areas on "I Had a Love."

Buy o' the Week

The Very Thought of You b/w Memories—Earl Bostic—King 4653

Already off to a fast start in parts of the South. Good strength also reported from St. Louis, Pittsburgh and Philadelphia.

Territorial Tips

LOS ANGELES
Baby, It's You--Spaniels--Chance 1141

New R.&B. Releases

THE SPANIELS/Chance 1141
•••• Baby, It's You
••• Bounce
THE CORONETS/Chess 1549
•••• Nadine
••• I'm All Alone
SAVANNAH CHURCHILL/Decca 28836
•••• Shake a Hand
••• Shed a Tear
THE 4 DUKES/Duke 116
••• I Done Done It
••• Crying in the Chapel
THE LAMPLIGHTERS/Federal 12149
••• Turn Me Loose
••• Part of Me
LITTLE ESTHER/Federal 12142
••• Cherry Wine
••• Love Oh Love
MELVIN SMITH/Victor 20-5406
••• It Went Down Easy
•• Why Do These Things Have to Be?
LULA REED/King 4649
••• Don't Make Me Love You
••• Going Back to Mexico
THE ORCHIDS/King 4661
••• Oh Why?
••• All Night Long

Week of September 12

Buy o' the Week

Nadine—Coronets—Chess 1549

Big in Chicago and strong in Philadelphia, Cleveland, L.A. and Durham. Flip is "I'm All Alone."

Buy o' the Week

Somebody Work on My Baby's Mind b/w Whatever You're Doin'—Du Droppers—RCA Victor 20-5425

Very strong in Durham and St. Louis. Good reports from Philadelphia, Buffalo and Central Tennessee. Most action on "Somebody."

Territorial Tips

ST. LOUIS
Nadine--Coronets--Chess 1549

New R.&B. Releases

VARETTA DILLARD/Savoy 1107
•••• I Love You
••• I Love You Just the Same
THE FLAMES/7-11 2107
••• Baby, Pretty Baby
••• Together
EARL BOSTIC/King 4653
••• Memories
••• The Very Thought of You
CHUCK WILLIS/Okeh 7004
••• Why My Day Is Over
••• My Baby's Coming Home
HENRY HAYES ORCH./Savoy 1105
••• Last Nite (vo. Elmore Nixon)
••• If You'll Be My Love (vo. Elmore Nixon)
T-BONE WALKER/Imperial 5247
••• Everytime
•• Tell Me What's the Reason
THE ROBINS/Victor 20-5434
••• Let's Go to the Dance
••• How Would You Know?
ROY BROWN/King 4654
••• Laughing but Crying
••• Crazy, Crazy Women
MORRIS PEJOE/Checker 781
••• It'll Plumb Get It
••• Can't Get Along
JIMMY REED/Chance 1142
••• Roll and Rhumba
•• High and Lonesome
JAMMIN' JIM/Savoy 1106
••• Shake Boogie
••• Jivin' Woman
BUSTER SMITH ORCH./Meteor 5010
••• Crying in the Chapel

•• Leapin' in Chicago
THE "5" WILLOWS/Allen 1002
••• All Night Long
•• Dolores
RENE HALL ORCH./Victor 20-5407
••• Don't Take Me for a Fool (vo. Courtland Carter)
•• Two Guitar Boogie
BILLY VALENTINE TRIO/Decca 28801
••• You May Be Trash to Someone, but Baby You're a Queen to Me
•• Don't Cry, Baby (vo. Floyd Smith)
LIGHTENING HOPKINS/Decca 28841
••• Policy Game
••• The War Is Over
THE IMPERIALS/Savoy 1104
••• My Darling
•• You Should Have Told Me
SONNY BOY WILLIAMSON/Trumpet 144
••• I Cross My Heart
••• West Memphis Blues
PRESTON LOVE ORCH./Federal 12145
••• Suicide Blues (vo. Frankie Ervin)
• My Love Is Draggin' (vo. Frankie Ervin)
LIL' SON JACKSON/Imperial 5248
•• Movin' to the Country
• Confession

Week of September 19

Buy o' the Week

Quarter to Twelve b/w Blues with a Feeling—Little Walter—Checker 780

Showing strength in Cleveland, Dallas, St. Louis and Detroit. Good reports from Chicago. Most action on "Twelve."

Buy o' the Week

Drunk—Jimmy Liggins—Specialty 470

Good reports from L.A., Dallas, Durham, New York and Philadelphia. Shapes up as Jimmy's first big one in a long time. Flip is "I'll Never Let You Go."

Buy o' the Week

I Love You So—Gee—Crows—Rama 5

Stepping out in L.A. Reports from Dallas and St. Louis are strong. Nashville and Philadelphia say good. Most areas favor "Love."

Territorial Tips

ATLANTA
Feelin' Good--Little Junior's Blue Flames--Sun 187
(Continued on next page)

Record Roundup
(Continued from previous page)

CHARLOTTE
One Scotch, One Bourbon, One Beer--
Amos Milburn--Aladdin 3197

CINCINNATI
Baby, It's You--Spaniels--Chance 1141

New R.&B. Releases
RUTH BROWN/Atlantic 1005
•••• The Tears Keep Tumbling Down
••• I Would If I Could
FATS DOMINO/Imperial 5251
•••• You Said You Love Me
•••• Rose Mary
JOE MORRIS ORCH./Herald 417
•••• I Had a Notion (vo. Al Savage)
••• Just Your Way Baby (vo. Al Savage)
CLYDE McPHATTER/Atlantic 1006
•••• Money Honey
•••• The Way I Feel
THE THRILLERS/The Thriller 170
••• The Drunkard
••• Mattie, Leave Me Alone
BOBBY MITCHELL & THE TOPPERS/
Imperial 5250
••• 4--11 = 44
••• One Friday Morning
JOE MORRIS & FAYE ADAMS/
Atlantic 1007
••• Sweet Talk
••• Watch Out I Told You
JIMMY NELSON/RPM 389
••• Big Mouth
••• Second Hand Fool
THE BLENDERS/Jay-Dee 780
••• You'll Never Be Mine Again
••• Don't Play Around with Love
JOHNNY ACE/Flair 1015
••• Midnight Hours Journey
••• Trouble and Me (vo. Earl Forest)
LAWRENCE STONE/Modern 913
••• I'll Surrender Anytime
••• Please Remember Me
DAVE BARTHOLOMEW/Imperial 5249
••• No More Black Nights
•• Air Tight
THE ORCHIRDS/King 4663
••• I've Been a Fool From the Start
•• Beginning to Miss You
JIMMIE HUFF/RPM 390
•• Don't You Know
•• Big City Bound
THE GAY TUNES/Timely 1002
• Wh-y-y Leave Me This Wa-ay-ay
• Thrill of Romance

Week of September 26

Buy o' the Week
TV Is the Thing b/w Fat Daddy—Dinah Washington—Mercury 70214
Strong reports from Philadelphia, Cincinnati, Chicago, Cleveland and St. Louis. Air play trouble is reported but record is selling nevertheless. Most action on "TV."

Buy o' the Week
Please Hurry Home (Modern, BMI)—B.B. King—RPM 391
This record has taken hold very fast. Strong in St. Louis, L.A. and Nashville, with Philadelphia and Pittsburgh adding good reports. Flip is "Neighborhood Affair" (Modern, BMI).

Buy o' the Week
I Wish Your Picture Was You (Venice, BMI) b/w Frog Legs (Venice, BMI)—Lloyd Price—Specialty 471
Doing well in Philadelphia, Cincinnati, Cleveland and Dallas. Showed greatly increased strength this week. Most action on "Wish."

Buy o' the Week
Perfect Woman—Four Blazes—United 158
Showing strength in St. Louis, L.A., Nashville, Cleveland and Cincinnati. Strong in Chicago. Flip is "Ella Louise."

Territorial Tips
NEW ORLEANS
Blues with a Feeling--Little Walter--
Checker 780
CHICAGO
Baby, It's You--Spaniels--Chance 1141
LOS ANGELES
Feelin' Good--Little Junior's Blue
Flames--Sun 187
NEW ORLEANS
Feelin' Good--Little Junior's Blue
Flames--Sun 187

New R.&B. Releases
B.B. KING/RPM 391
•••• Please Hurry Home
••• Neighborhood Affair
RAY CHARLES/Atlantic 1008
••• Heartbreaker
••• Feelin' Sad
BULL MOOSE JACKSON ORCH./King
4655
••• Hodge-Podge
••• If You'll Let Me
WILLIE MAE THORNTON/Peacock
1621
••• They Call Me Big Mama
••• Cotton Picking Blues

ACE HARRIS/Brunswick 84020
••• Please Don't Put Me Down
••• At Your Beck and Call
JACK DUPREE/King 4651
••• Ain't No Meat on de Bone
••• Please Tell Me Baby
JOE LIGGINS/Specialty 474
••• The Big Dipper
••• Everyone's Down on Me
RUFUS THOMAS, JR./Sun 188
••• Tiger Man
•• Save That Money
THE SWALLOWS/King 4656
••• Trust Me
••• Pleading Blues
THE FIVE KEYS/Aladdin 3204
••• I'm So High
••• Teardrops in Your Eyes
JIMMY DeBERRY/Sun 185
••• Take a Little Chance
••• Time Has Made a Change
PERCY MAYFIELD/Specialty 473
••• How Deep Is the Well?
••• The Bachelor Blues
SMILEY LEWIS/Imperial 5252
••• Little Fernandez
••• It's Music
EDDIE TOWNES/Modern 914
••• On the Bottom
••• Trials and Tribulations
JACKSON BROS. ORCH./Victor 20-5446
••• There's No Other Way (vo. Billy Henderson)
•• Flat Foot Boogie
EFFIE SMITH/Aladdin 3202
••• Dial That Telephone
•• Don't Cha Love Me?
VICKIE NELSON/Brunswick 84021
•• I Belong to You
•• Toys
MAXWELL DAVIS ORCH./Aladdin 3201
•• No Other Love
•• Strange Sensation
LEE RICHARDSON/Lloyds 104
• Don't Take Your Love From Me
• I Had to Live and Learn

New Spiritual Releases
SISTER WYNONA CARR/Specialty 855
•••• The Ball Game
••• I Know By Faith
THE ZION TRAVELERS/Score 2147
•••• Tell Them That You Saw Me
••• Lord, I'll Go
CHRISTIAN TRAVELERS/Peacock 1715
•••• Make More Room for Jesus in Your
Life
••• Well Done
THE FOUR INTERNS/Federal 12146
••• Stepped in the Water
••• Holy Father
BRO. CLEOPHUS ROBINSON/
Peacock 1719
••• When I Can Read My Title Clear
••• In the Sweet By and By
MYRTLE JACKSON/Brunswick 84019
• He Lifted Me
• The Lord Will Make a Way Somehow

OCTOBER 1953

GOSPEL JUBILEE PULLS CAPACITY AT CARNEGIE HALL FESTIVAL

NEW YORK, Oct. 10—Over 2,500 paying customers witnessed Joe Bostic's Fourth Annual Negro Gospel and Religious Music Festival, starring Mahalia Jackson, at Carnegie Hall Sunday (4). The event pulled a capacity crowd, in spite of a World Series game taking place across the river at Ebbets Field that same afternoon.

Headlining the list of outstanding performers and groups participating in the event was Mahalia Jackson, who virtually dominated the show. Appearing after the Gospel Harmonettes, who had already set the staid hall reeling, Miss Jackson brought the spectators out of their seats and into the aisles with her magnetic voice and manner. Several nurses were on hand to revive those who passed out from sheer enthusiasm.

Beginning with her rendition of "I Believe," which was performed in an impressively simple and moving manner, Miss Jackson showed her voice for the powerful organ that it is. Then, performing in a more traditional spiritual vein, Miss Jackson really brought the house down. Turning up the volume and picking up the tempo, she was at her peak in "God Spoke to Me," "In the Upper Room" and "Just Over the Hill," most of which she has recorded for Apollo Records.

Miss Jackson's stature in this field was proven again from the way she stood out over an otherwise impressive array of talent. Besides the Gospel Harmonettes, groups that stirred the crowd included the Daniels Singers, the Dixie Humming Birds and the Davis Sisters. The Los Angeles radio singer, J. Earle Hines, also scored a hit with the audience with his comic showmanship.

This annual event remains one of the most exciting spectacles to hit Carnegie hall, and portions of it are a good bet for TV.

Romance Blooms Via Aladdin Disk Pair

NEW YORK, Oct. 3—Shirley and Lee, boy-girl disk team on Aladdin label, are currently carrying on one of the most enchanting romances in the record world. In fact, it could be the only romance of its kind ever carried on records. But certainly it shows imagination and ingenuity on the part of the Mesner brothers, who head the label, and it points out that there are more ways to sell r.&b. records than is always realized.

The love affair began, or perhaps one should say it looked like it ended, when Aladdin brought out a Shirley and Lee disk last year titled "I'm Gone." To a pounding blues beat, Shirley explained why she had left Lee. The platter hit the national r.&b. charts and stayed up there for many weeks.

(Continued on next page)

Fats Domino Inked for 9 Years by Imperial

HOLLYWOOD, Sept. 26—Fats Domino, rhythm and blues recording star, has renewed his contract with Imperial Records for a nine-year term to run thru 1962.

With three releases in "Please Don't Leave Me," "Rose Mary" and "Poor, Poor Me" currently on the market, Domino has sold over two million records in his four-years association with Imperial Records, according to prexy Lew Chudd.

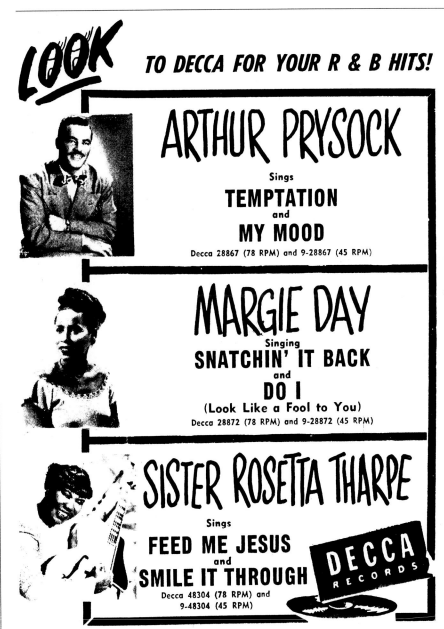

LOOK *TO DECCA FOR YOUR R & B HITS!*

ARTHUR PRYSOCK
Sings
TEMPTATION
and
MY MOOD
Decca 28867 (78 RPM) and 9-28867 (45 RPM)

MARGIE DAY
Singing
SNATCHIN' IT BACK
and
DO I
(Look Like a Fool to You)
Decca 28872 (78 RPM) and 9-28872 (45 RPM)

SISTER ROSETTA THARPE
Sings
FEED ME JESUS
and
SMILE IT THROUGH
Decca 48304 (78 RPM) and
9-48304 (45 RPM)

DECCA RECORDS

Romance Blooms
(Continued from previous page)

As a follow-up, or what seemed at the time merely an answer record, Shirley and Lee's next release this past March was a plea by Lee entitled "Shirley, Come Back to Me." This record, too, jumped into the charts, and established the pair as hot disk artists.

Lee pleaded so well that about three months later a new Aladdin disk was released, this one titled "Shirley's Back." And on it Shirley expounded her reasons for returning to her boy friend, and Lee chimed in with heartfelt thanks. By now Aladdin had established the pair, both as personalities in their own right, and as two people in love who had gone thru all the throes of pain and happiness that beset any love affair.

And this month the diskery issued the fourth in the Shirley and Lee saga. As should happen with two people in love, it tells of "The Proposal." Lee asks Shirley for her hand, and Shirley is in seventh heaven. However, with due propriety, she informs Lee that he must ask her parents.

As any hip a.&r. man can see, the prospect is now bright for a string of additional Shirley and Lee records. This observer suspects that December's release could be called "The Marriage" and the August or September release could be called "Our Little One." They could have many children, each one necessitating a new record, or they could have a spat and separate, with all of their domestic tiffs recorded permanently on wax. Under any circumstances, Aladdin is not tipping its hand this far in advance.

Apollo Sues King Over "Do It" Answer

NEW YORK, Oct. 10—Bess Music, Apollo Records' publishing affiliate, filed suit this week in federal court against King Records and its affiliated publishing concerns, Jay & Cee and Lois Music, over an answer to the hit r.&b. platter by the Five Royales entitled "Baby, Don't Do It."

Action charges that the defendants infringed on the Five Royales' tune via their answer ditty, "Baby, I'm Doing It," recorded on King by Annisteen Allen. Latter, it is claimed, is a direct copy of "Baby, Don't Do It," which was written by Lowman Pauling in 1952. The suit asks for an injunction and damages plus impounding of alleged infringing master until the court action is settled.

DR. KINSEY'S BOOK SPARKING DISK ACTION

NEW YORK, Oct. 10—It seems the eminent Dr. Kinsey is on his way to immortality, or perhaps notoriety, in waxing circles. For the third consecutive week, a new record has been issued which concerns the co-author of the literary thesis "Sexual Behavior of the Human Female." The titles of the tunes indicate the popularity of the good doctor's work—"Kinsey's Book," a country disk with Charlie Aldrich on Intro; "Hey, Dr. Kinsey," a rhythm and blues record featuring Big Duke on Flair, and the forthcoming "What's Her Whimsy, Dr. Kinsey?" with Stomp Gordon on Mercury, also in the r.&b. field.

A listen to the lyrics of the first two tunes indicate that the writers of "Kinsey's Book" and "Hey, Dr. Kinsey" have burned the midnight oil to glean the factual info from the Kinsey opus. The Flair disk, for instance, contains more percentage quotations than a stock market report. Both the Flair and the Intro records are catching action in their fields and were picked as "Records to Watch" by the leading trade journals.

PHIL ROSE EXITS CORAL-BRUNSWICK

NEW YORK, Sept. 26—Phil Rose has quit his job as a.&r. exec in charge of rhythm and blues at Coral-Brunswick to take over as professional manager of Challenge Music, a pubbery formed earlier this year. He will continue personal management activities. Rose now manages songstress Bette McLaurin and the Sarah McLawler Trio.

BREACH OF CONTRACT CLAIMED BY "HOUND DOG" TEAM

HOLLYWOOD, Oct. 17—Cleffers Jerry Leiber and Mike Stoller filed suit through their guardians in Superior Court here last week against Peacock Records, Houston waxery; prexy Don Robey of the label; and the firm's publishing subsidiary, Lion Publishing Company, claiming breach of contract arising out of their agreement in writing the song "Hound Dog."

The songscribe team has asked the court for an attachment, and have also served an attachment against Irving Shorten, of Allied Record Sales Company, Peacock distributor in Los Angeles area. They allege their agreement with Peacock called for the payment of one cent per side of the record, and are suing for an amount in excess of $4,750. The plaintiffs are also asking for an accounting, claiming Robey reported sales of only 182,258 platters. It is plaintiffs' allegation that the record sold well in excess of 200,000.

Pierce Buys Piece of Star-Day; Forms Hollywood Plattery

HOLLYWOOD, Oct. 3—Don Pierce, formerly with 4-Star Records here, has acquired a one-third interest in Star-Day Records, hillbilly diskery located in Houston. Pierce will handle sales, production and national distribution of the indie label and will headquarter here. Pierce has also formed a publishing affiliate, Star-Rite Publishing Company, via a BMI license.

Also disclosed by Pierce was the formation of Hollywood Records, indie rhythm and blues label. He will lease masters from r.&b. dealer John Dolphin, who has a 50 per cent share of the plattery and whose sole business activity will be limited to recording and signing talent. Pierce will likewise set national distribution and handle sales and promotion for Hollywood Records.

4-Star Named in 10G Suit

HOLLYWOOD, Oct. 10—In an action filed here in Superior Court Friday (2), Richard A. Nelson charged breach of contract against 4-Star Records, indie waxery. Suit, which involves approximately $10,000, alleges that 4-Star neglected to fully assume the liabilities of the corporation as provided for when Bill McCall took over the reins of the firm in November, 1946.

A former owner of 4-Star, Nelson had a judgment obtained against him by L.D. Dicker, assignee for the now defunct Jack Gutshall Distributing Company in 1950, with Nelson instigating suit against the plattery to ostensibly clear the judgment.

MAGID EXITS SAVOY TO HEAD OWN LABEL

NEW YORK, Oct. 24—Artist and repertoire exec Lee Magid left Savoy Records this week to start a new r.&b. waxery, tagged Central Records. The new firm is a partnership deal with Larry Newton, head of Derby Records. Magid and Newton will each have a 50 per cent interest in the new firm.

First Central label releases will be ready in November. Magid will headquarter at Derby's offices at 520 West 50th Street here. Magid had been with Savoy Records for the past four years. His replacement has not yet been named by Savoy.

ATLANTIC INKS RIDGLEY, LONGHAIR

NEW YORK, October 3—Jerry Wexler of Atlantic Records this week announced the signing of two New Orleans blues artists to the label's already imposing talent roster. They are Tommy Ridgley and Prof. Longhair (Roy Byrd). The latter is a pianist as well as blues shouter.

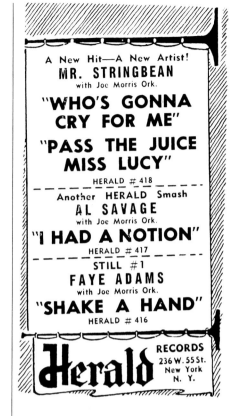
BIHARI SUFFERS 5G FIRE LOSS

HOLLYWOOD, Sept. 26—The Cadet Record Pressing Company, owned by Jules Bihari here, suffered $5,000 damages in a flash fire Thursday (24). Loss was limited to the plant's boiler room, which the fire department condemned, and a stock of platters, labels, packing and supplies which were water soaked. Origin of the fire was determined as due to an electrical short, which subsequently spread the blaze to three adjoining stores.

Bihari indicated that all pressings had been transferred to another plant and that shipments would continue to flow normally. The Cadet plant will be closed for one week to make minor repairs.

R.&B. Labels Sign Vocal Groups

NEW YORK, Sept. 26—A pair of new vocal quartets were added by two indie labels this week.

Joe Davis adds to his already impressive stable of vocal groups with the addition of the Sparrows. Davis currently has two top-flight groups in the Crickets and the Blenders. Davis is currently high on the Crickets and their disking of "I'm Not the One You Love" on his Jay-Dee label. At the same time, Davis announced the signing of Otis Blackwell and nine year-old Irene Treadwell, who will wax a couple of Christmas items shortly.

Over at Savoy Records of Newark, N.J., prexy Herman Lubinsky and a.&r. exec Lee Magid have what they claim is the first really different sounding group to vie for top honors, the Wanderers. Their new etching is a jumper titled "Hey, Mae Ethel."

Notes from the R.&B. Beat

"LITTLE JAZZ" ON THE MEND: Everyone is glad to see Charlie "Little Jazz" Ferguson back in he saddle again, now fully recovered from a near fatal auto wreck of a few months ago. Charlie, whose dynamic tenor saxing is featured on records such as "Red Top," "Cool Goofin'," "Baby Don't Do It" and the current big one by Willie Mabon, "You'se a Fool," moves into New York's Hunts Point Palace with the Velvets.... Peacock's sales manager Irv Marcus really did a bang-up job during his short stay in this city. He not only spark plugged Johnny Ace's "The Clock," but also was so elaborate in describing the forthcoming 4 Dukes waxing which he and

IRVING MARCUS

sidekick Joel Turnero cut while in town, that all the disk dealers are anxiously awaiting its release. Duke Records has just released Roscoe Gordon's "Ain't No Use" and Bobby Bland's "Army Blues" plus two spirituals. They are also releasing the long-awaited sides by sax star Billy Graham and his gang. Long a standout with Dizzy Gillespie-Joe Carroll duo before setting out on his own, Graham and his swingsational little combo are going into their sixth month at "Snookie's" nitery. One of the Graham ditties recorded by Marcus features the voice of young tunesmith Joel Turnero.

The national r.&b. charts this week, both the best seller and juke box list, are notable in that they do not contain a single answer disk. Ever since Willie Mabon's "I Don't Know" of last winter, there has invariably been one or two answer records among the top 10. One of the reasons for the lack of answers now might be due to the fact that there is no big hit of the stature of "I Don't Know" or that material like "Crying in the Chapel" or "Shake a Hand" is tough to re-do, but under any circumstances at this moment no answer record is moving up on the charts.... Fats Domino will make his first appearance in New York when he plays the Audubon Ballroom on October 11.... Promoter Teddy Powell will present Amos Milburn, Ruth Brown, Fats Domino, Margie Day and the Paul Williams ork at Laurel Gardens in Newark, N.J., on October 18 for a one-night stand.

The Joe Morris ork and thrush Faye Adams join up with the Orioles and Mr. Stringbean for one of the strong fall packages from the Shaw Artists Corporation starting November 13 in Little Rock, Ark. Package is booked to Christmas week, and will play one-nighters thru the South, Texas, Florida and the East, in that order.... Charles Brown, Johnny Moore's Three Blazers and thrush Mari

MARI JONES

Jones will trek thru Texas for promoter Howard Lewis during October.... Ruth Brown and Paul Williams' ork are set for a Southern tour from November 4 thru November 27.... Shaw Artists pacted the Spaniels this week. Group recently came thru with a hit waxing, "Baby It's You," on Chance label.... Lynn Hope has been going into percentage on his recent appearances thru the Midwest. Hope has added a youngster to his act, Little Nat Henderson, who is 11 years old. The lad sings, dances and does acrobatics and wears a turban, just like his boss.

COURIER JAZZ SHOW HITS PHILLY: "Operation Music," the Pittsburgh Courier's jazz concert to honor the winners of its annual music poll, took place in Philadelphia this week, Friday (25) at the Academy of Music. The talent line-up was fabulous, featuring such stars as the Ward Singers, Ruth Brown, the Dominoes, Arthur Prysock, Dinah Washington, Joe Louis, Dolores Parker, Milt Buckner, Debbie Andrews, Billie Holiday, the Ray-O-Vacs, Earl Hines, Buddy Johnson and many, many more. Among honors received was the Bessie Smith Award won

(Continued on next page)

ABBOTT BOWS FABOR SUBSIDIARY

HOLLYWOOD, Oct. 24—Abbott Records, company recently purchased by Fabor Robison here, will intro its new subsidiary Fabor label shortly via two new country and western artists. Latter are singers Ginny Wright and Tom Beardon, signed by Robison on a recent talent scouting expedition.

According to Robison, the new label will primarily be concerned with releases in the country field. Robison also disclosed his Abbott diskery will enter the rhythm and blues field shortly via a spiritual release by the Willy Caston Gospel Singers, who were also recently added to the firm's talent roster.

R.&B. Beat
(Continued from previous page)

by Ruth Brown for winning the newspaper's recent music poll as top blues singer. Proceeds from the show will go to The Courier Charities Fund and the National Association for the Advancement of Colored People's Legal Defense Fund.

Chuck Willis will do a string of one-nighter dates with the Milt Buckner crew starting November 4.... Joe Turner, whose Atlantic waxing of "Honey Hush" hit the national charts last week after grabbing attention in New Orleans, is set for a string of one-nighters thru the Texas area with his ork, starting October 10 until November 22. After that the vocalist goes into the Louisiana-Mississippi territory, where he will work until January.... Amos Milburn will play club dates as a single during November, while Paul Williams is out on a Southern tour. Milburn will join up with Charles Brown and the Choker Campbell orch. in December, and the package will do one-nighters during December and January in the South. Campbell and his orch. have been signed by Atlantic Records.... Bert Fleishman, F & F Distributors, Charlotte, N.C., now in the manufacturing bizness as he releases his first on the Magnet label. Tune, "Screamin' and Dyin'" is a big hit locally and could spread over into a national hit.

Johnny Ace and Willie Mae Thornton have been pacted to appear at the Apollo Theater, New York, for their initial Eastern appearance. Ace, who is with the Duke label, has come up with three hits in a row,

CHANCE 1145, a recent release by the Flamingos, is taking off all over the country and showing real strength in the South. The pairing of "Teardrops" and "Carried Away" get a great reading by the boys and it should soar high on the lists. SABRE 102, featuring a new group, the Five Echoes, has already been selling great on "Lonely Mood" side and now sales are showing the other side, "Baby, Come Back to Me," to be gaining fast. Good pairing.

JOB 1016, with J. B. Lenore doing "I'll Die Trying," backed with "I Want My Baby," is moving better than our already high expectations. She does a terrific job on both sides. Get on this one.

A new singing find from Baton Rouge is featured on a new release by CHECKER 783. The new sensation is Sugar Boy and he does wonders on two good sides, "I Don't Know What I'll Do," backed with "Overboard." You can't miss on this disking. Good for spins as well as jukes. CHECKER 782, by the Bluejays, is getting good response from across the country. The two sides, "White Cliffs of Dover" and "Hey, Pappa," are plenty good and worth buying.

Muddy Waters does a splendid job on his new release on Chess 1550. He does "Mad Love" and "Blow, Wind, Blow." Very effective lyrics and music. This one can't miss.

Tab Smith, UNITED 162, blows a terrific alto sax on "All My Life" and then switches to the tenor sax for a jump tune which he wrote himself titled "Seven Up." This guy is great. The tiny singer of great talent, Helen Thompson, gives her sultry blues voice a good turn on her latest record out on STATES 126. She pairs "All by Myself" and "Going Down to Big Mary's" for a very effective bit of pleasant listening.

Eddie Chamblee gives his tenor sax a workout on United 160, in which he does "Walkin' Home" and "Lonesome Road." This is a two-sided hit if I ever saw one. Don't miss it.

Your dealer has these "picks" in stock now. Call or see him today. (Adv.)

"My Song," "Cross My Heart" and "The Clock".... Duke Records has signed Joseph (Mr. Google Eyes) August, blues singer who hails from New Orleans.... The Royals,

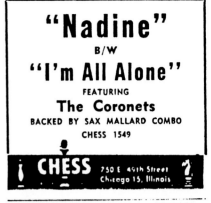

on the Federal label, go into the Trocavera Club in Columbus, O., next week.... Ray Charles is set for a two-weeker in New Orleans starting October 23.... Gladys Hill, new thrush on the Peacock label, is now out on a one-nighter package with B.B. King and Bill Harvey. Singer will appear at the Texas State Fair in Dallas on October 19.... The Shaw Artists giant package with Fats Domino, Paul Williams ork, Amos Milburn and thrush Margie Day packed the Newark Mosque last week on a one-nighter date.... A noticeable item about the charts this week is the fact that Atlantic Records has

(Continued on next page)

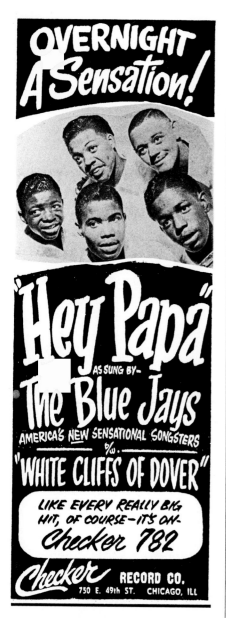

R.&B. Beat
(Continued from preceding page)

come up with three best-sellers at one time—"Good Lovin'" with the Clovers, "Honey Hush" with Joe Turner, and "Money Honey" with Clyde McPhatter and the Drifters. The tune "Shake a Hand," by the way, is also a hit in the country field via the Red Foley cutting on Decca.

Ruth Brown had to cancel out of a number of one-nighter dates in the East as well as a week's engagement in Cleveland because of illness. Thrush is now resting.... The Orioles, by the way, as a result of their two smash records, "Crying in the Chapel" and "In the Mission of St. Augustine," are booked up solidly thru New Year's. The same is true of the Joe Morris ork, due to his still solid waxing of "Shake a Hand".... Chuck Willis, The Five Keys and the Milt Buckner combo will play a week of one-nighters in the East starting November 24.... Charles Brown and Johnny Moore's Three Blazers are skedded for the Howard Theater, Washington, on November 4, and for the Apollo Theater, New York, for another week immediately after.... Savannah Churchill will play a week at the Farm Dell, Cleveland, opening October 22.... Eddie Heywood will start October 23 for 10 days at the Orchid Room, Kansas City, Mo.

Marie Adams and Johnny Otis, both of the Peacock stable, are now out on a one-nighter trek.... Raymond Taylor's ork and the Tempo Toppers quartet will play two dance dates in Oklahoma City on October 30 and 31.... Clarence (Gatemouth) Brown is now playing one-nighters thru the South.... The Charms' cutting of "Heaven Only Knows" and "Loving Baby," originally released on the Rockin' label, has now been issued on the De Luxe label. Both Rockin' and De Luxe are subsidiary labels of King Records.... Charlie Parker starts October 19 at the Blue Note in Philadelphia for a week.... Frank (Floorshow) Culley will be at the Loop Lounge in Cleveland on October 19.... Savoy Records has pacted Babs Gonzales.... The Ink Spots with Bill Kenny will play the Seville in Montreal opening October 22 for one week.... Zilla Mays, Southern blues singer, has been pacted by Mercury Records. Her first slicing will be released in a few weeks.

GOTHAM GLEANINGS: Derby Records is entering the EP field. First releases will be issued within 10 days, and future releases will be issued at the rate of two per month.... Joe Davis will send out over 250 three-minute film strips to TV stations to exploit his cutting on the Jay-Dee label of "Dear Santa, Bring My Daddy to Me." Films are complete, containing the music and drawings to illustrate the tune.... Danny Kessler, RCA Victor r.&b. chief, is back in New York after a month's recording on the road. He cut disks with the Robins and the Jackson Brothers, and added Sonny Terry, blues singer Square Walton and New Orleans tenorman Sam Butera to the label.... The Dominoes, skedded to go into the Band Box with the Sugar Ray Robinson unit, have cancelled out, and the Ravens will replace them for the New York date. The Dominoes, however, are set to go out with the Robinson package when it hits the road for one-nighters.... Dizzy

Gillespie, The Orioles, Wild Bill Davis' trio and a top mambo ork will play a one-nighter at the Rockland Palace, New York, on New Year's Eve.

THE UPTOWN SCENE: The Apollo this week really "has the blues" with Wynonie Harris, Varetta Dillard, the Three Chocolateers and the Frank Humphries band all under the same roof.... Clyde McPhatter brought his Drifters Quartet into the Apollo for their first theater showing and the ovation was tremendous.... Ticket agents said to be doing a brisk biz for the show over at the Hunts Point Palace which stars Atlantic Records' Ruth Brown, Clyde McPhatter and his Drifters, who record for the same label, the Cavaliers, vocal stylists for Atlas Records, and the heated mambo rhythms of Eduardo's band.... Warren ("Baby Don't You Cry") Evans, Decca's baritone vocal star of a few seasons ago, now entertaining at the famed Smalls Paradise in Harlem.... Austin Powell and his Cats and Fiddle back in the nabe after long stays in Atlantic City, Trenton, Philadelphia and the Ohio areas. Austin and the gang just cut a batch of disks for the 7-11 label, and reports he's pleased with the way things turned out... The Three Hi-

Hatters, who include Maithe Marshall, Leonard Puzey (just back from a stint with Uncle Sam) and Louis Hayward move into the Baby Grand club.... Betty McLaurin, Derby record artist, is the new headliner at Detroit's Flame Show Bar.

CHICAGO CHATTER: Johnny Vincent, Specialty Records, visiting Chicago on a deejay tour plugging the label's latest, "Drunk." He heads for Detroit and Cincinnati.... Leonard Chess has just released a new disking by a group called the Blue Jays, who hail from Washington, D.C. The group was discovered by Maxie Silverman of Quality Music Shop, who is also responsible for discovering the Clovers.... Ahmet Ertegun and Jerry Wexler, Atlantic Records execs, in town to record Joe Turner.... Dave Clark is now handling public relations chores for United Records. A showbiz columnist for the Associated Negro Press, Clark formerly worked out of Detroit, but is now covering the Chicago area.... Art Sheridan came up with a new release which looks very promising. On the Sabre label, it's called "Lonely Mood" b/w "Baby Come Back to Me", sung by the Five Echoes, a new group from right here in Chi. Art's "Golden Teardrops" may be replaced with some gold by the Flamingos, if the record continues to go the way it started.

Joe Turner, currently hot with "Honey Hush" on Atlantic, is entertaining nitely at Cadillac Bob's.... Joe Brown of J.O.B. Records announces he has once again taken over national distribution for his label.... Eddie Chamblee and His United Records Orchestra open at the Bagdad October 26.... Tab Smith, another United Records band, is booked for an appearance at the Capitol Lounge sometime in November.... Arthur Prysock and Mabel Scott headline the show at the Regal Theater.... Al Hibbler will appear at the Toast of the Town for three weeks beginning October 13.... Lester Young is skedded to open at the Bee Hive for four weeks starting October 23.... Chance Records has signed the Moonglows to a recording contract. The four-man group, which hails from Cleveland, is managed by Al (Moon Dog) Freed.... United Records just signed two bands and a vocalist to recording contracts. T.J. Fowler and his band, and Horace Henderson and his outfit were the pactees. Jean Cunningham, the newly signed vocalist, is currently appearing at the Strand Lounge.... Paul Bascomb and his All-Stars heading the bill at the Club Relax, Chicago.... Terry Timmons, United Records artist, featured at the Windy City's Bagdad....Red Saunders currently backing the show with his band at the Club DeLisa.

HEARD IN HOLLYWOOD: Fats Domino completed a successful LA engagement and departed for one-nighters in Las Vegas, Denver and points east. Topping the bill at the 5-4 Ballroom this past week was Little Willie Littlefield, who packed them in. His success here was spearheaded by his recent Federal waxing of "Miss K.C.'s Fine" and "Rock-A-Bye Baby" which had just been delivered to deejays and distribs in the area.... Jimmy Wilson's "Blues at Sundown" and "A Woman Is to Blame" on Big Town are getting a lot of comments hereabouts. It's the first release for the chanter since his big hit "Tin Pan Alley".... Big Town also this week signed blues chanter Fats Gaines and the Reverend Landers.... The Bihari brothers recently released "All That Oil in Texas" by the Oscar McLollie crew on Modern. Tune was originally recorded as an r.&b. number, but almost instantly jumped into the pop field. Indications are it could break out big.

The Kinsey Book, out only a little over a month already, is being well covered by the record industry. First a western version called "Kinsey's Book" was released, then r.&b. distribs were hit with "Hey, Dr. Kinsey" by Big Duke on the Flair label. Now Mercury has released "What's Your Whimsey, Dr. Kinsey" with Stomp Gordon... The sensational Flairs, teen agers from Jefferson High, stole the show when they jammed the 5-4 Ballroom recently with record crowds.... Deejay Dick "Uncle Huggie Boy" Hugg was most pleased platter spinner in the biz over a turnout he got at a recent party held during his broadcast at Autumn's Record Shop. He had invited 27 recording artists to the party and all of them showed up, which Huggie Boy admits is a real record.

MAXIE'S BACK: Leo and Eddie Mesner of Aladdin happy now that arranger Maxwell Davis is back from the East to handle their recording sessions. They're excited about their new one with the Ebonaires singing "Baby You're the One" and "Three O'Clock in the Morning".... Jim Warren and Jack Andrews of

Central Record Sales here report some up-and-comers in Lawrence Stone's "Please Remember Me" on Modern and "Run, Gal, Run" on Million Dollar with Christine Chatman and Peppy Prince's orchestra.... Jake Porter and his trumpet are causing a lot of commotion here with "El Toro" and "Beanville", both out on the Combo label which Jake also happens to own.... Another top R.&B. show for the West Coast was staged at the Richmond, Calif., Auditorium recently when promoter Bob Phillips put on "The World Series of the Blues." Show starred Roy Milton, Little Willie Littlefield, Tiny Bradshaw, Sonny Thompson, Lula Reed, Camille Howard, Freddie Clark and many more. This is the first show of this kind which has been put on in the Oakland Bay area.

October's Record Roundup

Week of October 3

Buy o' the Week
The Tears Keep Tumbling Down—Ruth Brown—Atlantic 1005
Picked up strongly this week as record got better distribution in Philadelphia, Cincinnati and St. Louis. Flip is "I Would If I Could."

Buy o' the Week
You Said You Love Me b/w Rose Mary—Fats Domino—Imperial 5251
Strong reports from Philadelphia, St. Louis, Durham, Cleveland and Tennessee. Most action on "You Said."

New R.&B. Releases
DINAH WASHINGTON/Mercury 70214
•••• TV Is the Thing
•••• Fat Daddy
THE ORIOLES/Jubilee 5127
•••• In the Mission of St. Augustine
••• Write and Tell Me Why
WILLIE MABON/Chess 1548
•••• You're a Fool
••• Monday Woman
THE CRICKETS/Jay-Dee 781
••• I'm Not the One You Love
••• Fine as Wine
JIMMY RICKS & THE RAVENS/Mercury 70213
••• Rough Ridin'
••• Who'll Be the Fool
THE FOUR TUNES/Jubilee 5128
••• Marie
••• I Gambled on Love
THE CHARIOTEERS/Tuxedo 891
••• I'm a Stranger
•• Thanks for Yesterday
AL SMITH'S PROGRESSIVE JAZZ/Meteor 5013
•• Beale Street Stomp
•• Slidin' Home

Week of October 10

Buy o' the Week
Mission of St. Augustine (Republic, BMI) b/w Write and Tell Me Why (Valley, BMI)—Orioles—Jubilee 5127
Already on the Philadelphia chart and very good reports received from St. Louis, one L.A. store., Cleveland and Durham. Except for L.A., it's "Mission."

Buy o' the Week
The Proposal (Aladdin, BMI)—Shirley and Lee—Aladdin 3205
Disk is strong in Durham, good in Philadelphia, Buffalo, L.A. and Cleveland. Flip is "Two Happy People" (Aladdin, BMI).

Buy o' the Week
Money Honey b/w The Way I Feel—Clyde McPhatter—Atlantic 1006
Yet to be received in many areas, but already strong in Dallas, Cleveland and Durham. Good in L.A. and Pittsburgh.

Territorial Tips
ATLANTA
Blues With a Feeling--Little Walter--Checker 780
LOS ANGELES
Rose Mary--Fats Domino--Imperial 5251
NEW ORLEANS
Rose Mary--Fats Domino--Imperial 5251
PHILADELPHIA
In the Mission of St. Augustine--Orioles --Jubilee 5127

New R.&B. Releases
JOHN LEE HOOKER/Modern 916
•••• Too Much Boogie
••• Need Somebody
CHRISTINE KITTRELL/Republic 7055
••• Every Day in the Week
••• Evil-Eyed Woman
OSCAR McLOLLIE/Modern 915
••• All That Oil in Texas
•• Be Cool, My Heart (vo. Berdell Forrest)
THE HUNTERS/Flair 1017
••• Down at Hayden's
••• Rabbit on the Log
RICHARD BERRY/Flair 1016
••• I'm Still in Love with You
•• One Little Prayer
CAMILLE HOWARD/Federal 12147
••• You're Lower Than a Mole
••• Losing Your Mind
LITTLE TOMMY BROWN/King 4658
••• 'Fore Day Train
••• How Much Do You Think I Can Stand?
SAM BUTERA/Victor 20-5469
••• Easy Rocking
•• Chicken Scratch
SONNY THOMPSON/King 4657
••• My Heart Needs Someone (vo. Rufus Junior)

•• Let's Move
JACK COOLEY/States 125
••• Could But I Ain't
••• Rain on My Window
THE LOVE NOTES/Imperial 5254
••• Get on My Train
•• Surrender Your Heart
TOMMY DEAN/States 120
••• Scammon Boogie
•• How Can I Let You Go?
ROSCOE THORNE/Atlas 1033
•• Dolores
•• Peddler of Dreams
CESTA AYRES/Imperial 5255
•• Love Is So Low Down
•• You Got a Time
OTIS HINTON/Timely 1003
•• Emmaline'
•• Walkin' Down Hill
BOOGIE BILL WEBB/Imperial 5257
• I Ain't For It
• Bad Dog
JESSE ALLEN & AUDREY WALKER/Imperial 5256
•• Gonna Tell My Mama
•• Gotta Call That Number
KING PERRY ORCH./RPM 392
•• Welcome Home, Baby
• Card Playin' Blues
RAILROAD EARL/Nucraft 115
• Foldin' Money
• Pretty Baby

New Spiritual Releases
THE SILVER STARS/Checker 766
••• 12 Years Old
••• Take to the Lord
BRO. CECIL L. SHAW/Imperial 5253
••• I Got Jesus in My Heart
••• Heaven Bells Have Called Mother Home
THE PRISONAIRES/Sun 189
••• My God Is Real
••• Softly and Tenderly
THE COLEMANAIRES/Timely 101
••• Old Ship of Zion (Pts. 1 & 2) (vo. Cynthia Coleman)
BILL LANDFORD QUARTET/Victor 20-5459
••• I Dreamed of a City Called Heaven
•• You Ain't Got Faith

Week of October 17

Buy o' the Week
Marie (Berlin, ASCAP)—Four Tunes—Jubilee 5128

Picking up action in Philadelphia, Pittsburgh and St. Louis. Durham, Cleveland and Detroit reports were good. In some markets it's beginning to move pop. Flip is "I Gambled with Love." Still to be delivered in some sectors.

Buy o' the Week

I Had a Notion (Herald, BMI)—Joe Morris—Herald 417
Building in Philadelphia, Cleveland and St. Louis. Pittsburgh, Cincinnati and Durham reported good action. Flip is "Just Your Way."

Territorial Tips

DETROIT
Mattie, Leave Me Alone--Thrillers--Big Town 109
NEW YORK
TV Is the Thing--Dinah Washington Mercury 70214

New R.&B. Releases

LYNN HOPE ORCH./Aladdin 3208
••• Swing Train
••• Rose Room
THE RAVENS/Mercury 70240
••• Without a Song (vo. Jimmy Ricks)
••• Walkin' My Blues Away (vo. Jimmy Ricks)
CHARLES BROWN/Aladdin 3209
••• Cryin' and Driftin' Blues
••• P.S. I Love You
LUCKY THOMPSON/Decca 28871
••• Flamingo
•• The Scene Is Clean
EDDIE KIRKLAND/King 4659
••• Time for My Lovin' to Be Done
••• No Shoes
ROSCO GORDON ORCH./Duke 114
••• Ain't No Use
•• Rosco's Mambo
LITTLE HUDSON/J.O.B. 1015
•• Rough Treatment
•• I'm Looking for a Woman

New Spiritual Releases

THE FLYING CLOUDS OF DETROIT/Nashboro 537
••• John Saw a Mighty Number
••• When Jesus Comes
THE CARAVANS/States 128
••• I Know the Lord Will Make a Way (vo. Albertina Walker)
••• What a Friend We Have in Jesus (vo. Nellie G. Daniels)

Week of October 24

New R.&B. Releases

THE "5" ROYALES/Apollo 449
•••• All Righty
•••• I Want to Thank You
BIG DUKE ORCH./Flair 1018
•••• Hey, Dr. Kinsey
••• Hello Baby
SAVANNAH CHURCHILL/Decca 28899
•••• Peace of Mind
••• Stay Out of My Dreams
OTIS BLACKWELL/Jay-Dee 784
•••• Daddy Rollin' Stone
••• Tears, Tears, Tears
THE ROYALS/Federal 12150
••• I Feel That-a-Way
••• Hello, Miss Fine
MARGIE DAY/Decca 28872
••• Snatchin' It Back
••• Do I?
TINY BRADSHAW/King 4664
••• South of the Orient
••• Later
THE WANDERERS/Savoy 1109
••• Hey, Mae Ethel
••• We Could Find Happiness
BOBBY BLUE BLAND/Duke 115
••• No Blow, No Show
••• Army Blues
THE BLUE JAYS/Checker 782
••• White Clifs of Dover
••• Hey Pappa

Week of October 31

Buy o' the Week

All Righty—"5" Royales—Apollo 449
Disk is losing little time in establishing itself nationally. Territories in which the record was reported strong were Philadelphia, Buffalo, Cincinnati, Durham and St. Louis. Flip is "I Want to Thank You."

Buy o' the Week

Rose Room—Lynn Hope—Aladdin 3208
Moving steadily in several territories since time of release, disk has started to shape up in many important r.&b. markets. Good to strong reports received from Philadelphia, Pittsburgh, Cincin-

nati, Cleveland, Chicago and St. Louis. Reported only fair thus far in South and L.A.

New R.&B. Releases

THE FLAMINGOS/Chance 1145
•••• Carried Away
••• Golden Teardrops
TAB SMITH/United 162
•• All My Life
•• Seven Up
JOAN SHAW/Gem 212
••• You Make Me Cry Myself to Sleep
••• Do What You Want With Me
LITTLE CAESAR/RPM 393
••• Chains of Love Have Disappeared
••• Tried to Reason With You, Baby
LOUIS JORDAN/Decca 28883
••• I Want You to Be My Baby
••• You Know It Too
MUDDY WATERS/Chess 1550
••• Blow, Wind, Blow
••• Mad Love
TERRY TIMMONS/United 161
••• Never Let Me Go
•• My Last Cry
MILT TRENIER & HIS SOLID SIX/Victor 20-5487
••• You're Killin' Me
••• Flip Our Wigs
THE ROBINS/Victor 20-5489
••• Ten Days in Jail
•• Empty Bottles
FRANKIE ERVIN ORCH./RPM 394
••• False Love
•• If You Don't Love Me
J.B. LENORE/J.O.B. 1016
••• I Want My Baby
••• I'll Die Tryin'
HELEN THOMPSON/States 126
••• All By Myself
•• Going Down to Big Mary's
JOE MITCHELL/Monarch 703
••• Jail Bird
•• Please, Eloise
EDDIE CHAMBLEE/United 160
••• Walkin' Home
•• Lonesome Road
JIMMY WILSON/Big Town 107
••• Blues at Sundown
••• A Woman Is to Blame
IVORY JOE HUNTER/MGM 11599
••• I Must Be Talking to Myself
•• My Best Wishes
CLARENCE GREEN/Monarch 701
•• Bad Shape Blues
•• How Can a Pretty Girl Be So Mean?
FATS GAINES ORCH./Big Town 108
•• Home Work Blues (vo. Rose Johnson)
•• He's a Real Fine Man (vo. Rose Johnson)
CLIFF (KING) SOLOMON/Okeh 7010
•• But Officer (vo. Gigi Gryce)
•• Lil' Daddee (vo. Ernestine Anderson)
KID KING'S COMBO/Excello 2018
•• The Brass Rail
•• Gimmick

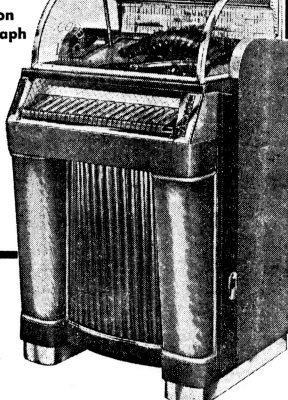

BOOTLEGGING RETURNS TO WEST COAST

HOLLYWOOD, Oct. 31—Record bootlegging, a situation that caused much furor thruout the record industry during the years of the platter ban, reared its head again this week, with bogus copies of the Prestige recording of "Moody's Mood for Love" by King Pleasure literally flooding this city.

Large quantities of the bootleg disk are appearing on the market and are attracting immediate sales. The tune, a standard in the rhythm and blues field, has been in strong demand for several weeks.

The bootleg disk shows a black label which is totally nondescript, bearing no label identification whatsoever other than the imprint of the song title itself. The platter's only other means of identification is a stamper number.

Some years ago, law enforcement agencies here passed an ordinance making it a misdemeanor for the offenders if found guilty of disk piracy. To date, there are no federal statutes on the books prohibiting the bootlegging of records, although the U.S. Internal Revenue Bureau, Division of Excise Tax Enforcement, is concerned because of the excise tax existing on phonograph records.

Aladdin Signs Louis Jordan

HOLLYWOOD, Oct. 31—Orkster Louis Jordan, after an association of almost 10 years with Decca Records, leaves the waxery at the expiration of his present

LOUIS JORDAN

pact January 1. Jordan has signed a recording contract with local indie Aladdin Records calling for guarantee over and above the standard recording royalty. Paper is for one year, with an automatic renewal clause.

Aladdin a.&r. chief of Eddie Mesner signed Jordan in New York this week, where the maestro is currently appearing at the Cafe Society. Label plans additional talent pactings in the future and will restrict itself to the rhythm and blues and folk fields.

Jordan's hit waxings for Decca included "Choo Choo Ch' Boogie," "Ain't Nobody Here But Us Chickens," "Stone Cold Dead in the Market Place," "Caldonia" and "Beware."

LEBOW NEW DE LUXE A.&R. CHIEF

NEW YORK, Nov. 14—Carl Lebow, previously with Apollo Records, has been named a.&r. head of the De Luxe label, King Records subsidiary. The pacting of Lebow, the former recording and sales director at Apollo, marks the re-activation of the De Luxe line.

Lebow's King contract, described as a "highly profitable" one, includes an interest in Franlin Music, new BMI firm affiliated with De Luxe, and permits him to continue his active participation in artist management. Lebow currently handles the Five Royales and Charlie Ferguson.

In addition to r.&b. waxings, Lebow's contract will cover pop, and possibly c.&w., as well, for De Luxe. He will headquarter in King's New York offices.

VICTOR MAPPING PLANS FOR NEW R.&B. LABEL

NEW YORK, Oct. 31—A special new label for rhythm and blues releases is now in the planning stages at RCA Victor. Diskery execs at this point are still undecided as to when such a label will be issued, but it is known that the legal department is checking registrations for several possible label names.

It is thought that Danny Kessler,

(Continued on next page)

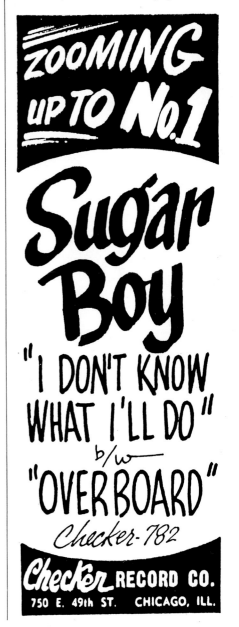

Victor Mapping
(Continued from preceding page)

current rhythm and blues repertoire chief, will most likely handle both sales and repertoire for the r.&b. label—as he now does for the same material on the Victor label. Jimmy Hilliard will also handle both sales and repertoire activities for the label "X" division.

Should the new rhythm and blues label and the new previously announced 35-cent label come into being, RCA Victor would be distributing seven different labels. These would be RCA Victor, HMV, Camden, label "X," Bluebird, the 35-cent line and the r.&b. line.

Profits Down, Gate Levels Off for Touring Packages; High Costs Cited

NEW YORK, Oct. 31—The one-nighter package business is apparently suffering this season from a number of factors, including high prices for talent, rising promotion costs, and the lack of strong new names, according to veteran observers.

A pair of key packages which have hit the trail again this year, Norman Granz's "Jazz at the Philharmonic" and the Gale Agency's "Biggest Show of '53," have, in spite of good grosses, been running behind last year's figures. And the new Associated Booking Corporation's unit with Sugar Ray Robinson, the Dominoes and Count Basie's ork, hasn't broken any records in Philadelphia, Richmond, Baltimore or other Eastern cities, after a fair opening in Yonkers.

In the case of the JATP unit and the "Biggest Show of '53," the slump in business is linked to the high talent-promotion cost rather than the lack of pulling power of the shows. There has been an attendance decline, to be sure, which has been partially offset by Granz this year raising admission prices. But the cost of the shows is now at such a level that they preclude the fabulous profits of other years, especially since attendance has leveled off instead of increasing.

Tradesters claim that the so-so drawing power to date of the Robinson-Dominoes-Basie unit is due to the fact that Ray Robinson is unknown as a performer, and that the Dominoes and Basie have been on many other tours before. In any event, the latter unit is not picking up gold on the one-nighter trail, tho it is believed that Midwest grosses will improve the picture somewhat.

WDIA Sponsors "Good Will" Revue

MEMPHIS, Tenn., Nov. 7—Radio station WDIA's "Fifth Annual Goodwill Revue for Handicapped Negro Children" will present one of the strongest spiritual and rhythm and blues talent line-ups ever, it was learned this week.

A crowd of up to 6,000 is expected to fill the Ellis Auditorium on December 4 to see the all-star blues and spiritual show featuring B.B. King, Lloyd Price, Muddy Waters, Eddie Boyd, Little Walter, Helen Thompson, the Soul Stirrers and WDIA personalities Professor Alex Bradford, the Caravans, Rufus Thomas, Moohah, the Spirit of Memphis Quartet, the Southern Wonders and Al Jackson's band.

All of the artists are giving their time in order to raise money for the charity. And their diskeries—Specialty, Chess, United, and Starmaker—are defraying their expenses to and from Memphis.

ALL-NEGRO STAFF FOR WNJR

Newark, N.J., Nov. 14—Radio outlet WNJR here is announcing plans to operate with an all-Negro staff which will work out of offices on Union Ave. in Union, N.J. Deejays slated for positions at the station are George Hudson, Ramon Bruce, Hal Jackson, Hal Wade, Charlie Green and Babs Gonzales.

A two-hour daily "Moon Dog" show, taped in Cleveland by spinner Alan Freed, will be one feature of the daily schedule.

Notes from the R.&B. Beat

NEW ADAMS DISK POSES "PROBLEM" FOR HERALD EXECS: The new Faye Adams release on Herald has execs Jack Angel and Al Silver in a quandry. Orders have been flooding in but reaction has been split about evenly between "Happiness to My Soul" and "I'll Be True." It's hard to say at his point which side will step out.... Dinah Washington and Faye Adams are the only two thrushes represented on the charts over the past month.... James Moody and his ork open at Birdland in New York on November 12 for a week.... Dinah Washington starts at Gotham's Cafe Society on November 23 for a week stand.... The new Ink Spots, featuring Charlie Fuqua, are booked solidly for one year, according to Universal Attractions. Dates include some Hawaiian and Japanese stands and a number of West Coast engagements. The group waxes for King Records.

FAYE ADAMS

After eight weeks in the top position on the national best-selling and most-played r.&b. charts, the Herald waxing of "Shake a Hand" with Faye Adams and the Joe Morris orch. has been displaced by "Money Honey," Clyde McPhatter's debut slicing for Atlantic Records. McPhatter, former lead singer with Billy Ward's Dominoes, is backed on the Atlantic disk by his new group, The Drifters.... Johnny Otis and his ork made their first waxings for Peacock Records last week. Peacock added another name to its talent stable this week with the signing of Robert Ketchum, San Antonio blues singer. The warbler's first sides are "She's Gone From Me" and "Stockade".... Fred Dunn, the boogie-woogie pianist, is recording again after a long illness from a throat operation. He cuts his sides for Jiffy Records, new r.&b. label out of West Monroe, La. .... The Okeh label, Epic's r.&b. line, recently pacted singers Herb Cooper and Sammy Cotton. Talent was signed by Marv Holtzman, a.&r. exec for the Epic pops and the Okeh label.

Atlantic Records demonstrated unusual speed in getting out a new disk this week when the rhythm and blues label recorded alto sax star Budd Johnson doing an instrumental version of "Off Shore." The session was held yesterday (6), and the results were mastered and mothered the same day, with the disk skedded to go

DU DROPPERS

on the presses today (Saturday). First shipments are set for Monday morning.... In a special recording session held Thursday night (5) here, RCA Victor's pop a.&r. chief Joe Carlton coupled the label's pop thrush Sunny Gale with the diskery's top rhythm and blues group, the Du Droppers. This marks the first time the diskery has attempted such a coupling, tho it has paired two top pop artists in disk sessions.... New RCA Victor signings include Danny (Run Joe) Taylor and the Heavenly Echoes.

MOON DOG HARVESTS OHIO CROWDS: Cleveland deejay Alan (Moon Dog) Freed's Harvest Moon Ball in Akron, O., Friday (13) attracted 2,480 customers at $2 each. The dance featured Freed, Clyde McPhatter and the Drifters, and the Bull Moose Jackson orch. The same package did strong business the previous week in Steubenville and Youngstown, 0. .... Lee Magid, who left Savoy Records a few weeks ago to start a new r.&b. label, Central, has signed his first talent to the label. They include Emmett Hobson, blues shouter, Georgia Lane, a new thrush from Cleveland, and the Rag-Muffins, a new vocal group.... Otis Blackwell, of Jay-Dee Records, visited deejays in Washington this week, and appeared on the Hal Jackson show at the Northeast Ballroom there.... Amos Milburn, now out on a series of one-nighter dates thru the South, is working as a

(Continued on next page)

Lewis Airs R.&B. on Four Stations

SHREVEPORT, La., Oct. 31—Stan Lewis, owner of Stan's Record Shop here, is one of the most active men in the business. In addition to his extensive record selling activities, Lewis conducts four shows on the airwaves, all of which he programs and two of which he sponsors entirely by himself.

Both of the programs completely sponsored by Lewis are heard via 50,000-watt stations. KTHS in Little Rock, airing from 10:30 to 11:15 p.m., and KWKH in Shreveport, on the air from 10:30 to 11:30 p.m. The two 5,000-watters are co-sponsored. They are KCIG, Shreveport, for three hours nightly, and KENT, Shreveport, for one and a half hours nightly.

Lewis reports two of his hottest numbers currently are LaVern Baker's "Soul on Fire," which smouldered for about two months before breaking wide open, and Ray Charles' "Heartbreaker." Both tunes are on the Atlantic label.

R.&B. Beat

(Continued from preceding page)

single.

The Griffin Bros. ork and thrush Claudia Swan play one-nighters thru West Virginia territory starting the end of November.... Ruth Brown plays a week at Gleason's, Cleveland nitery, beginning December 14 .... The Clovers take a two-week vacation in December and then start a Texas trek with Fats Domino starting December 21.... Lynn Hope and his ork, and Little Nat are now at Gleason's in Cleveland.... King Records signed Danny "Run Joe" Taylor (he penned "Good Lovin") to a recording contract after diging him on a couple of Jesse Powell sides. King execs are wasting no time in getting the young man into the studio for a session.... Joe Glaser signed the Ebonaires after watching them knock the Apollo audience cold.... Savoy chief Herman Lubinsky excited about his new Babs Gonzales release "Get Out of That Bed and Get Me Some Bread." Herman cut top Savoy thrush Varetta Dillard this week and the next release should be a humdinger.

NEW CHANTER MAKES IMPRESSION: When the Johnny Ace-Willie Mae Thornton "big show" rolled into the Apollo Theater here recently, one of the big guns of the affair was a terrific little blues belter by the name of Junior Parker, currently being groomed by Duke mahoff Don D. Robey for big things.... Irving Marcus, where are you? Your friends are calling in almost every day with inquiries as to your whereabouts. Last heard from Irv a couple of weeks ago and on the doctor's orders, he has to slow down a bit. Doc told him sleep might help.... Great to see Morris Lane and his big horn back in these parts after dates in Chicago and the midwest.... Pete Doraine over at Allen Records has a promising novelty in "I'm Gonna Chunk You Down" by Jimmy

Newsome. Doraine is trying to follow up the Five Willows' "My Dear, Dearest Darling" which scored on charts all over the country.... Johnny Otis in Houston last week for four days. He and his J.O. All Stars backed Little Richard, Joe "Papoose" Fritz and Luvenia Lewis on tunes cut by each. After the Bayou City, Otis and his band did four days at Kansas City's Orchid Room.

REIG TO HANDLE SAVOY A.&R.: Teddy Reig is set to handle a.&r. work for Savoy Records. Reig has been freelancing for the past few years.... David J. Mattis, who started Duke Records last year, has a new label now, Starmaker Records. Talent with the label includes Danny Day and

Moohah, with records cut by these artists already being shipped out to the jocks and to stores. The label is affiliated with radio station WDIA in Memphis.... Charles Brown is now at the Apollo Theater in New York.... Lynn Hope and his ork played a one-nighter at the Paradise Ballroom in Cleveland on November 21....The Five Keys play a string of one-nighters thru the East this week.... Fresh from a long list of successful engagements here and abroad comes Hadda Brooks to Harlem's Apollo Theater with a stellar array of headline attractions, including Teddy Hale, Rose Hardway and the groovy little band of Gene Ammons and his tenor horn.... Harlem's Baby Grand Club this week headlines Big Maybelle and the new sounds of the Wanderers vocal quartette.

PHILLY FLASHES: Two Philly hot spots this week become the originating point for disk jockey shows. With the opening of Tab Smith plus the Dorothy Ashby swing trio, Pep's Musical Bar will also originate the nightly record sessions of Jocko Henderson and his "Swing Train" via WDAS. And with the return of Joe Loco to the Blue Note, Tommy Roberts initiates a nightly spinning session of modern jazz platters via WCAM, Camden, N.J. Also on the Philadelphia scene, Snub Mosely comes back to town after an absence of several years at the Chateau Club. Fats Domino is next in at the Showboat; Jackie Davis and his organ trio take over at Club

Bill & Lou, the Horton Trio is new at the Glenn Hotel's Carver Bar, and Club 51 becomes the newest musical room in town, kicking off with Kenneth Billings at the organ and Beulah Frazier for the unit offering.... Garfield Henry's Silvertones polishing off their vocals for their TV bow on the Ed Sullivan show this Sunday (15).

CHI-TOWN LOWDOWN: Nellie Lutcher is now appearing at the Crown Propeller Lounge where Rudy Green and Muddy Waters appear on alternate nights. The club recently changed its policy and now plans to feature only name attractions. McKie Fitzhugh has been put in charge of talent for the Propeller. Skedded to follow the current show is Valaida Snow. Miss Snow has been signed by Chess Records and her first release is set for around Christmas.... Phil Chess of Chess Records tells us that Muddy Waters' 'Mad Love' has just passd the 5,000 mark. "In fact, any new release, if made on Friday, sells a minimum of 1,500 over the weekend," he states. "The Maxwell Street record dealers never order less than 100 of any new Muddy Waters disk".... The Flamingos, just signed by Associated Booking Corp., are currently touring with Duke Ellington.... Eddie Boyd drawing good crowds at Ralph's Club on West Madison Street.

Tab Smith and his United Recording Band are currently appearing at the Capitol Lounge.... Charlie (Yard Bird) Parker and his All-Stars are holding forth at the Bee Hive Lounge.... T-Bone Walker is set to follow Arthur Prysock into the Toast of the Town.... Eddie Chamblee closed last week at the Bagdad.... Sugar Ray Robinson, Billy Ward and his Dominoes, and Count Basie play the Thanksgiving Music Festival sponsored by the Artists Society of America at the Dusable High School Auditorium, November 28.... Red Saunders still holding the stage with his Okeh Records band at the Club DeLisa.... Earl Bostic and his band are currently appearing at the Capitol Lounge.... Johnny Hodges moves into the same spot for the coming holidays.... Paul Bascomb, Parrot Records, moved into the Strand Lounge on November 18 for a return engagement.... It is reported that Horace Henderson will soon make a personal appearance engagement at the Bagdad.... Gene Ammons, back from an appearance at the Apollo in New York, making arrangements to perform locally.

L.A. CONFIDENTIAL: Jim Warren of Central Record Sales here says Floyd Dixon's 'Hole in the Wall' is taking off real crazy like here in L.A. Specialty owner Art Rupe verifies this and adds that it's also clicking thruout the country.... Jimmy Wilson of 'Tin Pan Alley' fame appeared at Billy Berg's 5-4 Ballroom with thrush Linda Hayes. Both artists put on a great

show which included tunes from their latest diskings.... Lawrence Stone came up from San Diego to see the Bihari brothers at Modern Records and slice several new numbers. Speaking of the Biharis, they have another fine seasonal etching in "God Gave Us Christmas" on the Modern label. This beautiful offering is ably done by Oscar McLollie and his Honey Jumpers. Leon Rene wrote the tune and his professional manager, Parker Prescott, came in from New York for conferences and to help arrange the recording sessions. Another all-time Christmas favorite, "Silent Night"

and "I'll Be Home for Christmas" have been dressed up by the Pilgrim Travelers and released on the Specialty label.

PEACOCK RECORDS INTO NEW HQ

HOUSTON, Tex., Oct. 31—Peacock and Duke Records last week moved into its ultra-modern and swanky new air-conditioned headquarters. Prexy-owner Don D. Robey said "this is the most epochal step in Peacock history."

The new site will contain the business offices, recording studios and pressing plant and handle every phase of disk production from cutting the session to label printing. New address is 2809 Erastus Street, Houston 26, Texas.

BAND BOX UNDERGOES CHANGES

NEW YORK, Oct. 31—The Band Box, spot operated by Bill Levine, which has been using Negro names and tab shows headed by Negro attractions, will undergo some major changes soon. Club will close for a minor face lifting, change its name, and will reopen with a Latin policy.

Chief reason for move was club's failure to compete successfully with the Birdland, using a similar bill of fare. The room will shutter about November 3 and will reopen about 10 days later.

November's Record Roundup

Week of November 7

Buy o' the Week

Mad Love—Muddy Waters—Chess 1550
Gathering strength in Pittsburgh, Central Tennessee, Cleveland and St. Louis. Good in Durham and Chicago. Flip is "Blow, Wind, Blow."

Buy o' the Week

Later b/w South of the Orient—Tiny Bradshaw—King 4664
Moving well in Buffalo, Philadelphia, Pittsburgh, Cincinnati and St. Louis. Action on both sides in some areas, but most reports favored "Later."

Territorial Tips

NEW ORLEANS
Ain't No Use--Rosco Gordon--Duke 114

New R.&B. Releases

BILLY WARD & HIS DOMINOES/King 1280
•••• Rags to Riches
•••• Don't Thank Me
THE CLOVERS/Atlantic 1010
•••• The Feeling Is So Good
••• Comin' On
THE CHECKERS/King 4675
•••• White Cliffs of Dover
••• Without a Song
SONNY KNIGHT/Aladdin 3207
••• Dear Wonderful God
••• Baby, Come Back
GLADYS HILL/Peacock 1618
••• Don't Touch My Bowl
••• Prison Bound
THE EBONAIRES & MAXWELL DAVIS ORCH./Aladdin 3211
••• Baby, You're the One
••• Three O'Clock in the Morning
STOMP GORDON/Mercury 70246
••• What's Her Whimsey, Dr. Kinsey
••• Juicy Lucy
LITTLE ESTHER/Decca 48305
••• Stop Cryin'
••• Please Don't Send Me
LIGHTNIN' HOPKINS/TNT 8002
••• Lightnin' Jump
•• Late in the Evening
SONNY TERRY/Victor 20-5492
••• Hoopin' and Jumpin'
••• Hooray, Hooray
EARL HINES ORCH./King 4667
•• When I Dream of You (vo. Johnny Hartman)

•• In the Attic (vo. Johnny Hartman)
SQUARE WALTON/Victor 20-5493
•• Gimmee Your Bankroll
•• Pepper Head Woman
PINEY BROWN/Jubilee 5130
•• Ooh, You Bring Out the Wolf in Me
• Don't Pass Me By
JIMMY SWAN/Peacock 1622
•• Hey Now, Baby, Hey
•• Laughing, Laughing Blues

New Spiritual Releases

DIXIE HUMMING BIRDS/Peacock 1722
•••• Let's Go Out to the Programs
••• I'll Keep On Living After I Die

Week of November 14

Buy o' the Week

Take Me Back—Linda Hayes—Hollywood 1003
Broke this past week in the New Orleans and Washington areas, where it made the territorial charts. Good and strong reports also from St. Louis, Chicago and Nashville. Flip is "Yours for the Asking."

Buy o' the Week

Rags to Riches—(Saunders, ASCAP)—Dominoes—King 1280
Strong in L.A., St. Louis, Cincinnati and Philadelphia, with good reports also from Cleveland, Durham and one Chicago source. Flip is "Don't Thank Me" (Ward-Marks, BMI).

Territorial Tips

NEW ORLEANS
Mad Love--Muddy Waters--Chess 1550

New R.&B. Releases

THE DU DROPPERS/Victor 20-5504
•••• Don't Pass Me By
••• Get Lost
BUDDY JOHNSON ORCH./Mercury 70251
••• I'm Just Your Fool (vo. Ella Johnson)
••• A-12
THE LAMPLIGHTERS/Federal 12152
••• Be Bop Wino
••• Give Me
T-BONE WALKER/Imperial 5261
••• I'm About to Lose My Mind
••• I Miss You, Baby
ROY BROWN ORCH./King 4669
••• Caldonia's Wedding Day
••• A Fool in Love

BILLY WARD & HIS DOMINOES/King 1281
••• Christmas in Heaven
••• Ringing in a Brand New Year
LITTLE CAESAR/Big Town 110
••• What Kind of Fool Is He?
••• Wonder Why I'm Leaving?
WYNONIE HARRIS/King 4668
••• Please, Louise
••• Nearer My Love to Thee
LIL' SON JACKSON/Imperial 5259
••• Little Girl
••• Dirty Work
KING PLEASURE/Prestige 860
•• Sometimes I'm Happy
•• This Is Always
ZILLA MAYS/Mercury 70253
••• (If You Were) On the Other Side
•• Thank You
DANNY SMALL ORCH./DeLuxe 6007
••• Free Sugar (tenor--Don Wilkerson)
•• Don Juan (tenor--Don Wilkerson)
THE FLAIRS/Flair 1019
••• Tell Me You Love Me
•• You Should Care for Me
MEMPHIS MINNIE/J.O.B. 1101
••• Kissing in the Dark
• World of Trouble

New Spiritual Releases

SISTER ROSETTA THARPE/Decca 28754
••• I'll Meet You Over Yonder
••• All Alone With Christ the Lord
CHRISTLAND SINGERS/Peacock 1720
••• Someday, Somewhere
••• I Am Too Close

Week of November 21

Buy o' the Week

I Want You to Be My Baby b/w You Know It Too—Louis Jordan—Decca 28883
Record has been out several weeks and has been holding up well. Good reports from St. Louis, Durham, Pittsburgh, Chicago, Cincinnati, Dallas and Detroit.

Territorial Tips
CHICAGO
The Proposal--Shirley & Lee--Aladdin 3205
PHILADELPHIA
Rags to Riches--Dominoes--King 1280
Baby Doll--Marvin & Johnny--Specialty 479

New R.&B. Releases
B.B. KING/RPM 395
•••• Blind Love
••• Why Did You Leave Me?
EDDIE BOYD/Chess 1552
•••• Tortured Soul
••• That's When I Miss You So
SUGAR BOY/Checker 783
•••• Overboard
••• I Don't Know What I'll Do
BUDD JOHNSON ORCH./Atlantic 1013
••• Off Shore
••• Don't Take Your Love From Me
FLOYD DIXON/Specialty 477
••• Hole in the Wall
••• Old Memories
JIMMY NELSON/RPM 397
••• Mean Poor Girl
••• Cry Hard Luck
THE SWALLOWS/King 4676
••• It Feels So Good
••• I'll Be Waiting
THE PLATTERS/Federal 12153
••• Give Thanks
•• Hey Now
STICKS McGHEE/King 4672
••• Dealin' From the Bottom
••• Jungle Juice
JO JO ADAMS/Parrot 788
••• Rebecca
••• Call My Baby
JOHNNY MOORE/Hollywood 1001
••• In the Clay (vo. Charles Brown)
•• Strange Love (vo. Charles Brown)
JIMMY WITHERSPOON/Federal 12156
••• Move Me, Baby
•• Sad Life
RUDY GREEN/Chance 1146
•• The Letter
•• It's You I Love
NORMAN DUNLAP & MAXWELL DAVIS TRIO/Aladdin 3213
•• It's Easy to Remember
• Dream and a Prayer
DANNY DAY/Starmaker 502
• You Scare Me
• Wishing

New Spiritual Releases
THE FOUR INTERNS/Federal 12154
••• You'd Better Mind
••• I Just Rose to Tell You
EDNA GALLMON COOKE/Republic 7063
••• Higher Ground
••• Evening Sun
THE GOLDEN CLOUDS/DeLuxe 6015
••• Upon the Cross of Calvary
•• Work Until My Day Is Done

Week of November 28

Territorial Tips
DETROIT
Gee--Crows--Rama 5

New R.&B. Releases
FAYE ADAMS & JOE MORRIS ORCH./Herald 419
•••• Happiness to My Soul
•••• I'll Be True
FATS DOMINO/Imperial 5262
•••• Something's Wrong
•••• Don't Leave Me This Way
SUNNY GALE & THE DU DROPPERS/Victor 20-5543
•••• Mama's Gone, Goodbye
••• The Note in the Bottle
VARETTA DILLARD/Savoy 1118
•••• I Ain't Gonna Tell
•••• (That's the Way) My Mind Is Working
MARVIN & JOHNNY/Specialty 479
•••• Baby Doll
••• I'm Not a Fool
OSCAR McLOLLIE/Modern 920
••• Lolly Pop
•• God Gave Us Christmas
JOE HOUSTON ORCH./Modern 917
••• Blowin' Crazy
••• Goin' Crazy
THE SHADOWS/Decca 48307
••• Don't Be Bashful
••• Tell Her
THE SPANIELS/Vee-Jay 103
••• House Cleaning
••• The Bells Ring Out
LAWRENCE STONE/Modern 919
••• New Love
•• Too Much Lovin'
TAMPA RED/Victor 20-5523
••• So Crazy About You, Baby
••• So Much Trouble
JOHN BULLARD/De Luxe 6019
••• Spoiled Hambone Blues
•• Western Union Blues
MOOHAH/Starmaker 501
••• All Shook Out
•• Candy
BOBBY PRINCE ORCH./Victor 20-5520
••• Movin' Down the Line
•• Have a Little Pity

New Spiritual Releases
MAHALIA JACKSON/Apollo 278
•••• I Wonder If I Will Rest
••• Come to Jesus
THE FAMOUS WARD SINGERS/Savoy 4047
•••• Who Shall Be Able to Stand
••• I Want to Be More Like Jesus
THE PILGRIM TRAVELERS/Specialty 854
•••• Go Ahead
••• I've Got a New Home
WINGS OVER JORDAN/King 4677
••• I Cried and I Cried
••• I've Been 'Buked
REVEREND A. JOHNSON/DeLuxe 6010
••• Run Children Run
•• The Lord Will Make a Way Somehow

WMRY Official Denies Chess Negotiation

NEW ORLEANS, December 12—Mort Silverman, general manager of station WMRY, New Orleans, this week put the lid on rumors to the effect that Leonard Chess, of Chess Records, and record shop owner Stan Lewis are involved in negotiations to buy the station.

A letter received by this office from Mr. Silverman read, in part: "I recall meeting a Leonard Chess who made considerable utilization of our recording facilities and the services of some of our personnel. I understand that promises of reimbursement were made but not fulfilled. Mr. Chess did not speak to me in any way regarding the possible purchasing of these facilities. Furthermore he did not talk with anyone else of authority or make any negotiations toward the purchase of these facilities as this station is not for sale and can only be sold by consent of the Board of Directors, which has not met in a number of months."

While in town, Chess signed and cut a session with a new artist, Sugar Boy, whose first sides have just been released.

Fulson, Glenn Ink Aladdin Pacts

HOLLYWOOD, Dec. 5—Prexy Eddie Mesner, of indie r.&b. firm Aladdin Records, this week announced the signings of Lowell Fulson and Lloyd Glenn to standard recording pacts.

First wax has already been cut and is set for immediate release. Fulson and Glenn formerly waxed for Swing Time Records. Mesner departs for New York December 18 for recording sessions with the recently pacted Louis Jordan.

KING TO HANDLE McCALL LINES

CINCINNATI, Nov. 28—Bill McCall's 4-Star, Gilt-Edge and Big Town labels will be distributed by King Records, it was announced this week. The move constitutes the second major switch in distribution policy within a year for the Cincinnati diskery. Deal was consummated by McCall, along with King prexy Syd Nathan and veepee Jack Kelley.

The three lines will be carried in all King branches except St. Louis, Kansas City, Oklahoma City, Dallas, Houston, San Francisco and Los Angeles. Earlier this year, Nathan switched long-standing King policy by handing out to independent distribs the King, Federal and De Luxe lines in Boston, Seattle, Minneapolis, Newark, N.J., and Ogden, Utah.

MERCURY ADDS R.&B. NAMES

CHICAGO, Dec. 19—W.D. (Dee) Kilpatrick, director of Mercury Records' country and western and rhythm and blues a.&r. departments, this week announced the signing of several artists.

In the r.&b. field, Mercury signed Zilla Mays, Atlanta thrush, whose first sides are "On the Other Side" and "Thank You, Thank You." Also signed was Mel Walker, who was being released previously on the Mercury label until his releases were involved in a legal action. He is now back with the label. He cut "Unlucky Man" and "My Baby." Kilpatrick is leaving for the West Coast just before the first of the year to cut the Ravens and Sue Thompson, among others.

Little Junior Parker Signs with Duke

HOUSTON, Tex., Dec. 12—Duke and Peacock Records prexy Don Robey this week announced he has signed vocalist "Little Junior" Parker to a waxing pact.

Parker, who also plays the drums and harmonica, held his first session for Duke on December 3, backed by Bill Johnson and his Blue Flames. Johnson also backed Parker on his hit releases "Feelin' Good" and "Love My Baby" on the Sun label.

Since September 1, Parker and the Blue Flames have been touring as part of the Willie Mae Thornton-Johnny Ace package, but beginning January 2 they are scheduled to make a tour of the country as a separate unit.

Robey also announced the signing of vocalist and guitarist Lester Williams to a two-year deal. Williams is best known for his original tune, "Wintertime Blues," which is reported to have sold 30,000 copies when released a few years ago.

CASH BOX *Picks These*

King AND **Federal RECORDS**

"TEXAS POLKA"
"NO HEART AT ALL"
Bonnie Lou
King 1279

"BIMBO"
"BOY YOU GOT YOURSELF A GIRL"
Ruby Wright
King 1293

"CHRISTMAS IN HEAVEN"
"RINGING IN A BRAND NEW YEAR"
Billy Ward & His Dominoes
King 1281

AVAILABLE ON 45 RPM

DISTRIBUTED BY **King** RECORDS

AVAILABLE IN CANADA ON **Quality** KING RECORDS

CROWN NEWEST BIHARI LABEL

HOLLYWOOD, Nov. 28—Prexy Jules Bihari of Cadet Record Pressing Company here, and previously associated with the Modern and RPM record firms, this week bowed his entry in the rhythm and blues field via a label tagged Crown Records.

Bihari disclosed the signing of four artists to term papers with the firm. Under contract are Vido Musso, Joe Houston, Willard McDaniel and Lorenzo Holden. Initial releases of the new label have already been cut, with Bihari currently setting nationwide distribution.

RAMA'S "GEE" A SWITCHEROO

NEW YORK, Dec. 5—One of the most unusual reactions ever accorded a tune is that which is happening to the Crows and their Rama disk of "Gee."

The record's initial buying surge starting a few months ago was in Philadelphia, followed by Baltimore and then New York-Newark, N.J. area. Action at that time was on the flip side, "I Love You So." The disk stayed localized until Los Angeles charts showed it breaking out, but it was the "Gee" side which sparked the new action. Further reports of the disk's progress were coming from places such as San Francisco and the Oakland area.

When the West Coast showed the "Gee" side, Rama label prexy George Goldner was elated to learn that jocks in the East were flipping the disk and the demand switched over. Now "Gee" is showing very strong signs in Dallas, Texas and Detroit, where it's already broken into the charts.

Goldner has just waxed another version of "Gee" with Joe Loco's mambo stylings for release on Tico, Goldner's affiliate label. The tune is now experiencing a startling upsurge in Philadelphia via the mambo tempo and, if it follows the pattern set by the r.&b. version, should spread over the country.

NEW INDIE BOWS IN DETROIT

DETROIT, Dec. 5—A new record label headquartering here, tagged Great Lakes Records, tees off its first release December 8, pairing Don Sebastian, a new pop artist, and a new r.&b. quartet, the Imperials, on the disk, according to prexy Kenneth C. Campbell, Jr. Plans are to present a complete line of pop, r.&b. and jazz disks, with distribution handled thru United Distributors of Chicago.

Besides the aforementioned artists, the firm has pacted Debbie Andrews, Jimmy Hamilton's Ellington Big Eight, Sonny Johnson's Octet, Sax Kari's orch., Gloria Irving, Della Reese, Kenny Burrell, Cha Cha Hogan and the Mello-Larks. Heading the departments are Tony Vance, pops and jazz, and Kari, r.&b. Ray Gahan, formerly with Columbia, will handle publicity and promotion.

ANDREWS MASTER BOUGHT BY MARX

HOLLYWOOD, Dec. 5—Trend Records chief Albert Marx this week purchased a much sought-after Ernie Andrews master of "Don't Lead Me On" and "Make Me a Present of You" from the defunct Vogue Records plattery. Andrews subsequently inked a one-year recording deal with Trend. Tunes were assigned to the Howie Richmond pubbery in New York.

Notes from the R.&B. Beat

DOMINO A HOT PROPERTY: Fats Domino, who plays the Showboat in Philadelphia starting January 25, has turned into one of Shaw Artist Corporation's hottest properties. He has been booked for 15 straight one-nighter dates in the East from January 31 to February 15 and is set for a week at the Celebrity Club, Providence, after he finishes the trek. Domino's hit platters have helped his drawing power no end; the warbler's latest sock waxing on Imperial, "Something's Wrong," hit the national best-selling r.&b. chart this week.... Herald's Jack Braverman tells us that young Al Savage, heard on "I Had a Notion," is breaking up the show wherever the Joe Morris-Faye Adams-Al Savage package appears. In Texas the teeners were tearing the clothes off his back. A rush order of 5,000 pictures of the handsome singer was planed down for distribution to his fans.

Little Richard, Peacock Records, has formed a new outfit called the Upsetters and will play Macon, Ga. for the Christmas holidays.... The Willie Mae Thornton-Johnny Ace package with Junior Parker started its Southern tour Monday in Hattiesburg, Miss. This is the first trip South for the artists since July. On Thanksgiving B.B. King joined the thrush and Ace in Houston for a giant holiday show.... A Thanksgiving night attraction in Meridian, Miss., featured the Tempo Toppers, backed by Raymond Taylor's Deuces of Rhythm.... Peacock Records' spiritual groups are set for a busy fall season. The Sensational Nightingales are starting a one-nighter trek that will take them thru Arkansas, Louisiana, Kentucky and Indiana; the Bells of Joy and Sister Jessie Mae Renfro are now doing one-nighters in Tennessee; and the Southern Wonders are prepping a tour thru Ohio and Kentucky... Carl Lebow, who with Ike Berman manages the "5" Royales, back from a two-week tour of the South. Lebow announced the signing of two new artists to the De Luxe label: Country Homes, described as a romantic country blues singer from South Carolina, and Martha Moore, whom Lebow called "the most different singer in the world." Lebow handles a.&r. duties at the reactivated King Records subsid.... Fred Mendelsohn has returned to Regent Records and will be in charge of the a.&r. department for classical, pop and kiddie records. Regent is a subsidiary label of Herman Lubinsky's Savoy Records. Savoy has just pacted Big Bertha, a blues singer. Savoy topper Herman Lubinsky just returned from a two-week trip thru the South, stirring up business for the firm.... Chris Forde of Tuxedo Records informs us he has signed Lloyd Trotman, of "Castle Rock" fame and former sideman to Johnny Hodges, to his label. Releases are due in January. The Charioteers, now with Tuxedo, are now set on a string of night club dates thru the Midwest and Canada due to their new slicing, "Thanks for Yesterday"

LITTLE RICHARD

THE UPTOWN SCENE: Bobby Robinson, head of Red Robin label, this week announced a quartet of new releases. One intros Robinson's newest group, the Velvets, on a smooth ballad titled "I." Other artists in the release include newcomer Sadie Birch, Allen Bunn and Tiny Grimes. Over the past several months, the Red Robin firm has become known for its introduction of such national artists as the Du Droppers, the Vocaleers and Jack Dupree.... Faye Adams, Al Savage and the Joe Morris orch. are set for the Apollo, New York, the week of January 8.... The Orioles follow them at the theater starting January 15.... Over at Harlem's Dawn Casino they're headlining Eunice Davis, the Five Crowns and Big Joe Medlin, along with Hot Lips Page and his band.... Into

BOBBY ROBINSON

(Continued on next page)

R.&B. Beat

(Continued from preceding page)

the Baby Grand goes Coral Records' singing Dell-Tones for a two-week stay.... Capitol recording songstress Georgia Carr has signed up with WOV, New York, to broadcast nightly with Jack Walker on the station's three-hour, across-the-board "Life Begins at Midnight" stanza. She arrived in New York last Friday from Los Angeles where she made frequent TV appearances. This marks Miss Carr's debut as a deejay.... Larry Fuller (he's the conductor of "Harlem's Gospel Train," which is aired daily over station WLIB here) says that with each hearing of the Dixie Hummingbirds' "Let's Go Out to the Programs" he finds himself loving it more and more.... The Amsterdam News Annual Benefit Show, which will be held at the Apollo Theater here Friday (11), has lined up an imposing roster of performers. Josh White, Lucky Millinder, Willie Bryant, Nipsey Russell, Johnny Hartman, Harold Jackson, Mildred Davee, Sam Pruitt, Ethlyn Butler, Leeta Harris, Roy Armstrong's ork, Buddy Bowser and Sara Lou Harris, and the Miller Sisters are already set, with scores of guest artists expected to appear. Moe Gale, of the Gale Agency, is lending his services for the 17th annual Amsterdam News Midnight show.

A sudden shift has taken place in the popularity of vocalists in the r.&b. field. A few months ago a majority of the places on the national r.&b. charts—best sellers and juke box—were held down by vocal groups. This week's chart, however, shows that the singers, both male and female, are coming back into favor. On the best-selling chart, only Clyde McPhatter and the Drifters, the Dominoes and the Four Tunes are in the first 10, and on the juke chart, only the McPhatter group and the Four Tunes are up there. The top male vocalist is Joe Turner, with thrush Faye Adams close behind with two platters on the best-selling

list. Other vocalists in the money are Amos Milburn, Dinah Washington, Big Maybelle, Lloyd Price, Muddy Waters, Little Walter and Al Savage who shares honors on the Herald "I Had a Notion" platter with the Joe Morris orch.... Marv Holtzman, a.&r. head of Okeh Records, has pacted warbler Roy Hamilton for the label. Hamilton hails from Jersey City, N.J. .... A new r.&b. label started during the last few weeks is Bruce Records, which is headed by Monte Bruce, New York.... King Records has re-activated its De Luxe label, and has transferred several masters from the Rockin' label to De Luxe.

Joe Davis, of Jay-Dee Records, spent three days in Chicago this week visiting deejays and working out distribution for the label.... The tune "Oh, My Papa (O, Mein Papa)," which is grabbing a lot of action in the pop field, has been cut as an r.&b. instrumental by Don Hill on the RCA Victor label. Danny Kessler handled the a.&r. work on the session, and the disk will be out on the market next week.... Joe Morris' ork and the Orioles hit percentage on their one-

nighter in Atlanta on Wednesday (18) for promoter B.B. Beamon.... Gatemouth Brown and the Al Grey ork are now touring Florida.... Julian (Daddy Jule) Silver, formerly with WPNX, Columbus, Ga., is now doing an hour-and-a-half rhythm and blues show and a two-hour pop show at WMIE, Miami.... Station WNJR, Newark, N.J., is now airing 18 hours per day of r.&b. and jazz platters. The station recently switched to the r.&b. policy after new ownership took gver. Deejays Hal Jackson, Charlie Green, Ramon Bruce and Hal Wade are spinning the disks and Alan (Moon Dog) Freed is aired via tape recording each day.

Jerry Wexler and Ahmet Ertegun, Atlantic toppers, returned this week from New Orleans after waxing a lot of talent in the First City of Jazz. New signings by the label include Professor Longhair (Roy Byrd), who was with the label in 1948; Mr. Blues (George Jackson), from suburban New Orleans, and the Jackson Gospel Singers.... Fats Domino and the Clovers play one-nighters in California after their current Texas tour is over in January.... Ginger Smock, hot fiddle player now on the Federal label, has been signed by Shaw Artists. The violinist may be sent out with a group.... Teddy Reig's first waxing date for Savoy features Varetta Dillard singing "I Ain't Gonna Tell" and "My Mind is Working".... Edna McGriff is now set for a location date in Bermuda, Christmas week.... Amos Milburn and the Paul Williams ork start a southern tour in Columbus Ga., January 6.... Music publisher Dave Dreyer, of Raleigh, Bristol and Biltmore Music, has become one of the hottest r.&b. pubbers in the business. His current tunes number more than a dozen, including "Good Lovin'," "Blues With a Feeling," "Going Down to Big Mary's House," "Every Day in the Week," "Jinny Mule," "Playboy," "Pepper Head Woman," and more. His latest tunes, "Love Needs a Helping Hand" and "The Man I Crave," are sung by Sadie Birch on Red Robin Records.

PHILLY FLASHES: The Jolly Joyce Theatrical Agency, Philadelphia and New York, has taken over the management of Daisy Mae and the Hep Cats, opening the unit December 21 for two weeks at the V.F.W. Club, Hanover, Pa. The office also handles Eastern bookings for the Three Loose Nuts and a Bolt, headed by Eddie Cole, brother of Nat (King) Cole, starting with a two-weeker beginning December 21 at Dumond's Sho Bar, Philadelphia. The Joyce Agency reports bookings for the remainder of the month brings the Five Vibra Notes on December 21 to the Mucho Club, Pennsgrove, N.J.; the Top Notes at Mattero's Tea-Bar, Chester, Pa., for four weeks starting December 21; Romaine

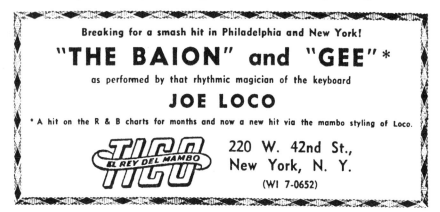

Brown and The Romaines returning December 23 at the Rendezvous, Philadelphia, and back in Philadelphia on January 11 for another two weeks at Sciolla's Theater Cafe, and the Four Tunes opening December 28 for a two-weeker at the Brown Derby Club, Toronto. Also on the Philadelphia rhythm and blues scene, Oscar Pettiford returns to the town at the Blue Note; Big Nick Nicholas takes over this week at Club Bill & Lou, and the organology of Kenneth Billings marks the new management by Eddie Cox of the 51 Club, formerly known as The Last Word Cafe.

MAXWELL LAUNCHES PRIZE RECORDS: Bob Maxwell, WWJ-TV, Detroit disk jockey, formed his own record firm, the Prize Record Company. Dave Usher is managing the artists and repertoire for the new label, which already has acquired 14 year-old kid-singer and composer Willie John and a vocal group, Three Lads and a Lass. First Prize release features John singing "Mommy What Happened to Our Christmas Tree" and "Jingle Bells." John, who has appeared in Detroit theaters, and Usher will go out on a Midwestern deejay trip next week.... Day, Dawn and Dusk, booked by Bob Corash, are pulling good crowds into the Wolhurst, one of Denver's top-drawer clubs. Billy Ward's Dominoes signed up for the same club on New Year's Eve.... Beulah Bryant, Jay-Dee artist, is pulling crowds into the Ozark Club, Great Falls, Mont., where she was booked by Denver agent Dave Strause.

WINDY CITY BLUES: Len Chess reports a mishap in the lives of two of Chess' biggest artists this week. Seems that Willie Mabon and Little Walter were on their way by car to the "Good Will Revue" show conducted in Memphis by station WDIA there. Just about 20 miles outside Cairo, Illinois, they were involved in an accident which left them unable to continue the trip to Memphis. They returned to Chicago the following Monday, with Willie's "I Gotta Go" and Walter's "You're So Fine" both wearing out juke box needles in this town.... Mitzi Mars, Checker Records thrush, informs us she's now appearing at Joe's Los Angeles club here.... Shaw Artists here say they are about to sign Bobby Prince to an exclusive contract. Prince is the lad who cut some sides for Chance sometime ago.... Charlie and Ella Mae's brand new Supper Club currently stars Dr. Jo-Jo Adams, whose Parrot disk of "Call My Baby" looks very promising.... Danny Overbea is currently featured at Martin's Corner, while saxophonist Sonny Stitt is jamming at the Bee Hive, Elmore James and Eddie Boyd are alternating at Silvio's Lounge, and Johnny Hodges makes a return to the Capitol Lounge.

Rhythm and Blues Tattler

A new group featured on SABRE 103, the Five Blue Notes, do a fine job on "Ooh, Baby," backed with "My Gal Is Gone." Good reports on this from New York and Los Angeles. Keep your eye on this. Another disk that has plenty of potential is a Christmas tune by the Moonglows on CHANCE 1150. The boys come out with "Just a Lonely Christmas," backed with "Hey, Santa Claus." This one is just too good to pass up for the holiday sales crowds. Get it now.

A new release on Specialty 482 by Guitar Slim is already showing promising results in Chicago. This boy is really great. Hear this coupling of "The Things That I Used to Do" and "Well, I Done Got Over."

UNITED RECORDS has just released a sequel to "After Hour Joint." This time it's "Raid on the After Hour Joint" and it's by Jimmy Coe and his outfit on STATES 129. The hot biscuit is flipped by "He's Alright With Me," with Helen Fox, the band's vocalist, doing a fine job on the lyrics. Don't miss this one. Another new release is "Lonesome Baby" and "I Can't Believe," by that Cleveland group, The Hornets, on STATES 127. Good harmony on this waxing. Will sell great.

The Staple Singers, a spiritual group consisting of an entire family, the father, a son and two daughters, come up on a new release, "It Rained Children" and "Won't You Sit Down," on United 165.

A new release by CHESS records, number 1555, is all set to hit the country by storm; a snowstorm, that is. Valaida Snow is featured on the disk and she does a great job of vocal interpretation on "I Ain't Gonna Tell" and "If You Don't Mean It." This is bound to sell like hot cakes, so if you're smart and take my advice you'll order heavy right now.

Len Chess, head of the diskery, informs me he is tickled pink over the prospects ahead for Christmas. He says he will release absolutely two of the best Christmas numbers ever put out and they'll create a sensation. One by Willie Mabon and one by Little Walter. Watch for them.

Get these "picks" at your dealer.

(Adv.)

WEST COASTINGS: Saul Bihari was going around the Modern Records plant passing out cigars after his wife had presented him with his brand new 7-lb. boy. Brother Joe also came by to tell us they had just signed a new group, the Five Hearts, who etched "The Fine One" b/w "Please,

Please, Baby" for the Flair label. Another new group called the Whips cut two new ones for the Modern subsid titled "Pleadin' Heart" and "She Done Me Wrong." Joe leaves for Houston in a few days to cut new sessions with Connie Mac Booker, pianist formerly featured with B.B. King and his

(Continued on next page)

R.&B. Beat
(Continued from preceding page)

orchestra.... The Billy Shaw office here is mapping big plans for Linda Hayes, whose recording of "Take Me Back" on the Hollywood label is continuing to build nicely. Miss Hayes will cut four more sides for Hollywood at Decca's studios, with the possibility that two of these will be issued on Decca. Monroe Tucker will continue to arrange and conduct the band for Miss Hayes' sessions.

Johnny Otis had the crowds at Billy Berg's 5-4 Ballroom rockin' with his newest on the Peacock label, "Rock Me Baby" for two solid week-ends. Otis also presented

his "Jazz-O-Rama" show at the Carlton Theater with Marie Adams and the Ravens before leaving for engagements in Portland, Seattle and the Northwest.... Joe Houston poured out hot licks for the crowd at the Burbank Armory, then moved over to the Odd Fellows Hall in Lincoln Heights for another session of dance-type rhythms.... Chuck Higgins and his crew completed a successful stint at Ventura's Green Mill Ballroom, then took

JOHNNY OTIS

over the Elks Hall here on Sunday night.... The Robins are presenting their big Sugar Hill Revue at the Club Oasis every night.... Eddie Mesner of Aladdin label announced that their songstress, Patty Anne, will open Christmas day at the Regal Theater in Chicago with Duke Ellington.

HUGGY BOY STAGING TALENT SHOWS: Dick "Uncle Huggy Boy" Hugg is now staging a talent show every Wednesday night at the Red Feather here. Effie Smith also now appears on the stage of the Red Feather. "Huggie Boy" now broadcasts his r.&b. deejay stint nightly from the window of Dolphin's of Hollywood.... George Goldner, head of Rama-Tico Records, New York, is spending the holidays in southern California.... Ben Waller Enterprises moved into new offices at 8910 Melrose Blvd., West Hollywood, and presented a Yuletide housewarming party that was attended by many in the trade.... Larry Mead, of Vita Records, hospitalized this past week in Pasadena.... Joe Bihari off for Houston sessions with Connie MacBooker.... Percy Mayfield provided the dance rhythms for the holiday crowds at the 5-4 Ballroom, along with the Ravens group.

December's Record Roundup

RATING SYSTEM
•••• Excellent   ••• Very Good
•• Good   • Fair

Week of December 5

Buy o' the Week
Comin' On (Progressive, BMI) b/w The Feeling Is So Good (Marvin, ASCAP)— Clovers—Atlantic 1010
Showed strength last week in Philadelphia (where it placed on the territorial chart), upstate New York, Cleveland, Nashville, St. Louis and Dallas. Pittsburgh and Detroit also rated the disk good. This past week "Comin' On" placed on the national juke box chart. Action reported on both sides.

Buy o' the Week
I'll Be True (Angel, BMI) b/w Happiness to My Soul (Ajax, ASCAP)— Faye Adams—Herald 419
Placed for the second week on the Washington-Baltimore territorial chart and was also reported strong in Philadelphia, Buffalo, Pittsburgh, Chicago and St. Louis. Good reports were received from the Southeastern U.S., Nashville and New York. Both sides are selling, with a slight edge on "I'll Be True."

Buy o' the Week
Baby Doll (Venice, BMI)—Marvin and Johnny—Specialty 479
Broke on the national juke box chart this past week. Strong in Los Angeles, Philadelphia and New York. Disk also got good ratings in the Detroit, Nashville and St. Louis. Flip is "I'm Not a Fool" (Venice, BMI).

Territorial Tips
WASHINGTON--BALTIMORE
My Girl Awaits Me--Castelles-- Grand 101

New R.&B. Releases
WILLIE NIX/Sabre 104
••• Just Can't Stay
•• All By Yourself
THE HARP-TONES/Bruce 101
••• A Sunday Kind of Love
••• I'll Never Tell
WILLIE MAE THORNTON/Peacock 1626
••• I Ain't No Fool Either
••• The Big Change
LITTLE JUNIOR'S BLUE FLAMES/ Sun 192
••• Mystery Train

••• Love My Baby
MAXWELL DAVIS ORCH./Aladdin 3216
••• The Joe Louis Story Theme
••• Hey, Boy
WILLIE JOHN/Prize 6900
•• Mommy What Happened to Our Christmas Tree?
• Jingle Bells

New Spiritual Releases
SISTER ROSETTA THARPE & MARIE KNIGHT/Decca 48309
•••• Shadrack
••• Nobody's Fault
ROBERTA MARTIN SINGERS/Apollo 279
••• Marching to Zion
••• I'm Too Close
THE JEWELL GOSPEL SINGERS/ Aladdin 2039
••• Rest, Rest, Rest
••• At the Cross

Week of December 12

Buy o' the Week
Don't Leave Me This Way (Commodore, BMI)—Fats Domino— Imperial 5262
Breaking quickly, with very strong reports from Los Angeles, Milwaukee, Buffalo and Durham. Good reports also from Cleveland, Detroit and Nashville. Flip is "Something's Wrong" (Commodore, BMI).

Buy o' the Week
Blind Love b/w Why Did You Leave Me?—B.B. King—RPM 395
Strong action reported in upstate New York, Nashville, Milwaukee, St. Louis, Dallas and Los Angeles. Also rated good in Cleveland, Chicago, Philadelphia and the Carolinas. While most action was on "Blind Love," New York, Nashville and Dallas preferred the flip.

New R.&B. Releases
AMOS MILBURN/Aladdin 3218
•••• Good, Good Whiskey
••• Let's Have a Party
CHUCK WILLIS/Okeh 7015
•••• You're Still My Baby
••• What's Your Name?
ELMORE JAMES/Flair 1022
••• Strange Kinda' Feeling

••• Please Find My Baby
WILLIE BAKER/De Luxe 6023
••• Goin' Back Home Today
••• Before She Leaves Town
MERCY DEE/Specialty 481
••• Get to Gettin'
••• Dark Muddy Bottom
THE MAGIC-TONES/King 4681
••• Cool, Cool Baby
••• How Can You Treat Me This Way?
CLARENCE (BONTON) GARLOW/ Flair 1021
••• Route "90"
••• Crawfishin'
ROBERT KETCHUM/Peacock 1623
••• Stockade
••• She's Gone From Me
THE FIVE KEYS/Aladdin 3214
••• Oh Babe
••• My Saddest Hour
EDDIE BURNS/De Luxe 6024
••• Hello Miss Jessie Lee
••• Dealing With the Devil
BERNIE HARDISON/Excello 2020
••• Love Me Baby
•• Yeah! It's True
NORMAN ALEXANDER/Hollywood 1004
••• Dim Lights
•• My Baby Left Me
GEORGIA LANE/Central 1001
••• Oo-Wee, Mr. Jeff
EMMETT HOBSON
••• Looka Here, Mattie Bee
JESSE POWELL ORCH./Federal 12159
••• Love to Spare (vo. Dan Taylor)
•• Rear Bumper
CLARENCE (GATEMOUTH) BROWN/ Peacock 1619
••• Gate Walks to Board
••• Please Tell Me Baby
THE TRENIERS/Okeh 7012
••• You Know, Yea! Tiger
•• Bug Dance
THE PRISONAIRES/Sun 191
••• I Know
••• A Prisoner's Prayer
BIG JOHN GREER/Victor 20-5531
••• Drinkin' Fool
••• Getting Mighty Lonesome for You
LOWELL FULSON/Aladdin 3217
••• Don't Leave Me Baby
•• Chuck With the Boys
THE MOONGLOWS/Chance 1150
•• Hey Santa Claus
•• Just a Lonely Christmas
EDDIE KIRKLAND/King 4680
•• I Mistreated a Woman
• Please Don't Think I'm Nosy

(Continued on next page)

Record Roundup
(Continued from preceding page)

COUNTRY SLIM/Hollywood 1005
•• What Wrong Have I Done?
MISS COUNTRY SLIM
• My Girlish Days
GUITAR SLIM/Specialty 482
•• Well, I Done Got Over It
• The Things That I Used to Do
WELLINGTON BLAKELY/Vee-Jay 104
• Sailor Joe
• A Gypsy With a Broken Heart

New Spiritual Releases
MAHALIA JACKSON/Lloyds 105
•••• No Matter How You Pray
•••• My Cathedral
THE PILGRIM TRAVELERS/
Specialty 856
••• Silent Night
••• I'll Be Home for Christmas

Week of December 19

Buy o' the Week
**Good, Good Whiskey (D&M, BMI)—
Amos Milburn—Aladdin 3218**
Already reported strong in New York,
Buffalo, Pittsburgh, Durham and St.
Louis. Good reports from Philadelphia,
Cleveland, Detroit and Nashville. Flip is
"Let's Have a Party" (Mesner, BMI).

Buy o' the Week
**Saving My Love for You (Lion, BMI)—
Johnny Ace—Duke 118**
Strong in New York, Philadelphia,
Buffalo, Nashville, St. Louis and Dallas.
Flip is "Yes, Baby" (Lion, BMI).

Buy o' the Week
**Off Shore (Hanover, ASCAP) b/w Don't
You Do It (Lois, BMI)—Earl Bostic—
King 4683**
Disking has been out several weeks, and
is now reported strong in New York,
Philadelphia, St. Louis, Dallas and Los
Angeles. Good reports from upstate New
York, Cleveland, Pittsburgh and
Nashville. Action reported on both sides,
with the edge on "Off Shore."

Territorial Tips
DETROIT
Christmas in Heaven--Dominoes--
King 1281
LOS ANGELES
Gee--Crows--Rama 5

New R.&B. Releases
JOHNNY ACE/Duke 118
•••• Saving My Love for You
JOHNNY ACE & WILLIE MAE
THORNTON
•••• Yes, Baby
JOE TURNER/Atlantic 1016
•••• TV Mama
••• Oke-She-Moke-She-Pop
CARMEN TAYLOR/Atlantic 1015
•••• Mama Me and Johnny Free
••• Big Mamou Daddy
JIMMY COE/States 129
•••• Raid on the After Hour Joint
••• He's Alright with Me (vo. Helen Fox)
VALAIDA SNOW/Chess 1555
•••• I Ain't Gonna Tell
••• If You Don't Mean It
LITTLE WALTER/Checker 786
••• You're So Fine
••• Lights Out
TINY BRADSHAW ORCH./King 4687
••• Powder Puff
••• Ping Pong
TAMPA RED/Victor 20-5544
••• Taxi, Taxi 6963
••• Right and Ready
THE ROYALS/Federal 12160
••• That's It
••• Someone Like You
THE HORNETS/States 127
••• Lonesome Baby
••• I Can't Believe
WILLIE MABON/Chess 1554
••• I Got to Go
••• Cruisin'
MR. GOOGLE EYES AUGUST &
JOHNNY OTIS ORCH./Duke 117
••• Oh What a Fool
••• Play the Game
CHOKER CAMPBELL ORCH./Atlantic
1014
••• How Could You Do This? (vo. Harold
Young)
••• Last Call for Whiskey (vo. Harold
Young)
WILLIE LOVE/Trumpet 173
••• Vanity Dresser Boogie
••• 74 Blues
SONNY BOY WILLIAMSON/Trumpet
212
••• Cat Hop
•• Too Close Together
BERTICE READING/Victor 20-5567
••• I'm Alone
••• Tears of Joy
THE DIAMONDS/Atlantic 1017
••• Romance in the Dark
••• Cherry
BERT KEYES/Rama 13
••• At Home
•• I Was Such a Fool
ERNIE ANDREWS/Trend 68
•• Don't Lead Me On
•• Make Me a Present of You

New Spiritual Releases
THE STAPLE SINGERS/United 165
••• It Rained Children
••• Won't You Sit Down?

Week of December 26

Buy o' the Week
**You're So Fine (Arc, BMI)—Little
Walter—Checker 786**
Strong in Chicago, Cleveland, Milwau-
kee, St. Louis, Nashville and New York.
Disk also appears on Detroit's territorial
chart this week. Flip is "Lights Out"
(Arc, BMI).

Buy o' the Week
**The Things That I Used to Do (Venice,
BMI)—Guitar Slim—Specialty 482**
In areas where disk has been delivered, it
has lost no time in getting action. Strong
in New York, Cleveland, Chicago,
Nashville, Milwaukee and Dallas. Also
reported good in Detroit and L.A. Flip is
"Well, I Done Got Over It" (Venice, BMI).

Buy o' the Week
**You're Still My Baby (Berkshire,
BMI)—Chuck Willis—Okeh 7015**
Going strong in Dallas, St. Louis,
Milwaukee, Nashville, Cleveland,
Durham and New York. Flip is "What's
Your Name?" (Berkshire, BMI).

Territorial Tips
DETROIT
15-40 Special--Joe Weaver--
De Luxe 6006

New R.&B. Releases
CHARLIE (LITTLE JAZZ) FERGUSON/
Apollo 817
••• 2:30 Break
••• So Much of a Little Bit
MEMPHIS SLIM/United 166
••• Call Before You Go Home
••• This Is My Lucky Day
DOZIER BOYS/United 163
••• Early Morning Blues
••• Cold, Cold Rain
DANNY (RUN JOE) TAYLOR/
Victor 20-5558
••• You Look Bad
•• Gator Tail
SAM BUTERA/Victor 20-5545
•• Wailin' Walk
•• Shine the Buckle

New Spiritual Releases
THE LARKS/Apollo 1189
••• Honey in the Rock
••• Shadrach

INDEX

Boldface indicates listing in "Record Roundup" section. Parentheses ( ) indicate advertisement listing and/or artist photograph.